# JUDGMENT COMETH

# JUDGMENT COMETH

## (And That Right Soon)

By

SCOTT PRATT

ISBN: 1944083014
ISBN 13: 9781944083014

*"Foolish men imagine that because judgment for an evil thing is delayed, there is no justice; but only accident here below. Judgement for an evil thing is many times delayed for some day or two, some century or two, but it is sure as life, it is sure as death.*
**Thomas Carlyle**

*This book, along with every book I've written and every book I'll write, is dedicated to my darling Kristy, to her unconquerable spirit and to her inspirational courage. I loved her before I was born and I'll love her after I'm long gone.*

# PROLOGUE

# TWENTY YEARS AGO

Graduation day should have been special, but it had quickly turned into a day that made twelve-year-old David Craig wish he'd never been born. His father was looming over him, sweating and cursing and moaning occasionally, as David engaged in the unspeakable conduct that was being demanded of him.

"You have your mother to thank for this," the major said. "If she had stayed, you wouldn't be down here."

David's mother, a timid, plain woman named Ann, had loaded most of her clothing and her toiletries into a suitcase and had disappeared on a Monday just two months earlier. David figured she must have gotten on a bus. His father had not called the police, had not reported her missing, because his father knew why she'd left. David knew why she'd left, and David's brother, Michael, knew why she'd left. She was gone because the boys couldn't protect her from the monster her husband had become.

There was a room in the basement, one that David's father had built himself and that neither of the boys was allowed to enter, that became the place where Ann Craig lost her dignity, and, David believed, probably her sanity.

David had dared one time to descend the stairs into the basement while his mother and father were down there. He'd heard his mother's muffled cries of pain through the door, had heard her begging David's father to stop doing whatever it was he was doing, but both David and Michael felt powerless to stop what was going on in their own home. Their father was an officer, a major in the 101$^{st}$ Airborne Division. He was also a lawyer, a prosecutor. He was a powerful man on the military base, and he was a demanding and intimidating force when he walked through the door at home. He ruled his private domain mercilessly, and the slightest infraction was dealt with quickly and violently. David had no doubt that his father was perfectly capable of killing any one of them, and that he would get away with it.

David didn't blame his mother for leaving, but had he known that he would become her replacement, he would have boarded a bus himself and ridden it to southern Texas or Maine or the Florida keys, as far away from Clarksville, Tennessee as he could get. Michael had graduated from high school that beautiful, sunny morning in May. He was the valedictorian of his class, and David listened with pride as his brother gave a speech to his fellow graduates. David felt goosebumps when Michael later walked across the stage and accepted his diploma. He was in awe of his big brother, who was the commander of the JROTC cadets, a star on the football, basketball and baseball teams at Clarksville High School and who had already enlisted in the United States Army. Michael was scheduled to leave for boot camp in South Carolina at the end of June.

Major Christopher Craig sat silently through the ceremony. When it was over, he ordered David straight to the car. Michael was going to lunch at a friend's house. The major had not been invited. When they arrived at home, the major ordered David into the basement. He took a set of keys from his pocket and unlocked the large padlock that secured the room where David's mother had been taken so many times.

"Let's go, boy. Move," the major said, and David moved cautiously into the room. The walls were covered in cheap paneling and two fluorescent lights flickered behind a frosted panel in the ceiling. There was a small bed in the corner, a wooden chair, a bench. There were also ropes and chains and pulleys and whips and things that David didn't recognize. His father locked the door behind them.

What followed was a nightmare, a series of indignities that David knew he would never be able to wipe from his memory. He'd been in the room for perhaps fifteen minutes. There were already welts and bruises on his buttocks and the backs of his thighs. His father had raped him with something – he didn't know what it was, he only knew that it hurt. He was now tied to a chair, facing the major, who had just unzipped his pants.

"All of it," the major said. "If you bite me, I'll break your jaw."

David thought he heard a metallic sound outside the door, and suddenly a tremendous explosion ripped through the air. The wooden door splintered at the lock as the gunshot tore into it. Another shot sent the door flying open. The major turned around, and David could see his brother, Michael, standing on the other side of a cloud of smoke.

"Untie him," Michael said, leveling the shotgun at the major's chest.

"Who in the hell do you think you are, boy, pointing a damned gun at me?" the major demanded.

"Untie him, right now, or I'm going to splatter your brains all over this room."

"You don't have the guts."

Michael lowered the gun slightly and the shotgun belched fire and smoke. The major flew backward as part of his right thigh was ripped away.

"You shot me! You shot me, you little sonofabitch!" the major cried from a sitting position against the wall.

"Next one goes straight into your face," Michael said. His voice was firm and steady. David didn't know whether his father believed Michael, but David did. "Crawl over there and untie my brother, you disgusting pervert."

David turned his head and watched his father crawl across the floor. Thirty seconds later, he was free.

"Put your pants and your shoes on," Michael said. "Hurry up. Go out and get in my car. Right now."

Less than five minutes later, Michael came jogging out of the house. He tossed the shotgun into the back seat and climbed in behind the wheel.

"What are we going to do?" David said.

"The same thing Mom did. We're out of here, and we're not coming back."

# PART I

# TWENTY YEARS LATER

**D**avid Craig was urinating in the kitchen sink when he saw something move on the back porch. He staggered over to the back door and opened it. His eyes widened when he suddenly recognized the gargantuan human being standing there.

"What are you doing here?" David said as he staggered back a step. It was nine o'clock at night and David was drunk. He was drunk every night by nine o'clock.

"Just thought I'd stop by and say hello," the man said. "How long's it been? Couple of decades? I been in prison almost all that time. Just got out a while back. Thought I'd stop by and say hello to my childhood buddy."

"How did you ... how did you find me?"

"Your daddy told me where you live. He also told me you get arrested for DUI every time you turn around and that your brother keeps you up."

"You talked to my father?"

"Yeah, he sort of reached out to me when I flattened my last sentence. Listen, David, do you have a basement in this place?"

"What?"

"A basement. You know what a basement is, right?"

"Yeah, I know what a basement is, but—"

"Well, do you have one?"

"Yeah. I don't go down there much."

"Can I see it?"

"Why do you—"

The man pushed past David into the house. He walked through the kitchen and pointed at a door.

"Is that it?" the man said. "Is that the basement door?"

David leaned against the kitchen counter and nodded his head.

"I'll be right back," the man said, and he flipped a light switch and disappeared down the steps. He was back in less than five minutes.

"It ain't much of a basement, but it'll do," he said. "It's got an electrical outlet and room for an upright freezer, and that's all I need."

"Freezer? You want to put a freezer in my basement?" David said.

"I don't *want* to put a freezer in your basement. I'm *going* to put a freezer in your basement. And you're gonna help me."

"What? Why? I don't understand."

The man put a massive hand on David's shoulder.

"Listen, I'm going to be doing a little contract work and I might need to keep something in the freezer from time to time. I might not ever use it, but there might come a time when I have to. So what say you get that stupid look off of your face and help your old buddy bring the thing in here and get it into the basement? I've got a dolly and straps. It won't take long at all."

"What are you going to keep in it?" David said.

The giant man smiled and said, "If I told you that, I'd have to kill you."

# FRIDAY, SEPTEMBER 1

**M**y name is Joe Dillard, and I had come to loathe doctors over the past decade. I didn't loathe them for any particular reason other than they kept giving my wife and me bad news about her cancer. She'd been diagnosed years earlier with breast cancer and we'd gone through the initial surgeries, chemotherapies and radiation treatments. For a while, it went away. Then it came back in Caroline's bones, scattered throughout her skeletal system. More treatments: hormones, chemotherapy, radiation. Then it moved into her liver. Even more chemotherapy. On this particular day, she and I were sitting in the dull, Spartan office of a neurologist named Dr. George Stoots at Vanderbilt University in Nashville, Tennessee. He was a thin, studious-looking man with mouse-colored hair and wire-framed, reading glasses resting on his nose. He'd set a computer screen in front of us and was pointing at bright spots on the screen.

"See this?" he said. "It's a mass, a tumor that has made its way through the skull and is trying to get into your brain, Mrs. Dillard."

He then took his pen and traced a semi-circle all the way from the front to the back of Caroline's brain, which was represented on the screen.

"And if you'll notice this discoloration here, this is all cancer. It's working its way around your skull, trying to find a way into the brain. It takes a million cancer cells before they show up on a scan, so obviously, the cancer is extensive. Eventually, it will get into your brain if we don't do something."

"And if that happens?" I said as I heard Caroline begin to sniffle beside me.

"It becomes extremely difficult to treat. The brain is wrapped in meningeal fluid that insulates it and protects it. One of the things the fluid would insulate and protect the brain from would be chemotherapy. The chemotherapy drugs wouldn't be able to get to the tumors."

"And surgery is out of the question?" Caroline said.

"I'm afraid so," Dr. Stoots said. "The only option left available to you is going to be radiation. I've already met with the radiation oncology people here and what they're telling me is that you would be looking at ten radiation treatments – they call it 'whole-brain radiation' –given once a day for ten days. You'll take the weekends off. We can help you set the treatments up with your radiation oncologist in Johnson City so you don't have to drive down here and stay for two weeks."

"Risks?" I said, feeling the same sense of shock and numbness begin to creep over me that I'd felt so many times before. "Side effects?"

"The most dangerous risk with radiation is death," Stoots said flatly. "If the doctor miscalculates the dosage or radiates the wrong site, it could be fatal. I don't foresee either of those things happening, though. The side effects are pretty tough, Mrs. Dillard. You might as well know that going in. The primary side effect will be extreme fatigue. You'll spend about three weeks, maybe four, pretty much flat on your back. You'll be able to get up and go to the bathroom, you'll be able to eat, things like that, but you'll sleep sixteen, eighteen hours a day some days. There will also be hair loss at the treatment site, most likely permanent, and some skin irritation around your ears. You might experience dry mouth, maybe some nausea, some mouth sores, and you might feel addled at times, just not mentally sharp."

"Sounds delightful," Caroline said as she squeezed my hand.

"And if she decides not to do it?" I said.

"Eventually the tumor will get through, start shedding cells into the meningeal fluid, and those cells will start attaching to the brain. Once that happens, you're looking at all kinds of possibilities, none of which are pleasant. She could lose her sense of taste, she could go blind, she could lose her memory, just dozens of things."

"And if she does it and it works?"

"The hope is that it will kill the cancer in her skull and that we can then go back to managing the other areas of concern."

"Will she be herself?" I said. "Will she know me, will she be able to live a quality life?"

"She could lose some memory over the long-term," the doctor said. "Let's say she can remember ten things on a grocery list right now. In three to five years, she might only be able to remember seven."

The doctor left us alone to talk a few minutes later. I sat there looking at Caroline and felt a tear slip down my cheek. She was already crying.

"You don't have to do it," I said. "It'll be okay. You can stop all of this right now."

"Is that what you want?" she said, looking at me with glistening brown eyes.

I shook my head. "Of course not," I said. "I love you more than anything in this world, and I want you to stay here with me, with all of us. But I don't want you to suffer, either. You've already been through so much."

She reached for me and we embraced.

"Whatever you decide," I said. "If you've had enough, I understand completely."

"I'm not ready to go," she said softly through the tears. "I don't want to die. I don't care what it takes. I can handle it."

I stepped back a little and wiped tears from both of her cheeks. I forced myself to smile.

"That's my girl," I said. "Let's gear up for another battle. Sounds like this one is going to be tough."

"What about dinner tonight?" she said. My son, Jack, and his girlfriend, Charlie Story, were both practicing law in Nashville and were planning to meet us for dinner.

"What about it?"

"I'm sorry, Joe. I can't do it. I'll just wind up crying and ruin dinner and it'll be awful."

"It's okay," I said. "We had dinner with them last night so it won't be as though we just blew in and out of town without even seeing them. I'll call Jack and explain. What do you want to do?"

"Let's go back to the hotel and pack up," she said. "I just want to go home."

# FRIDAY, SEPTEMBER 15

**D**eputy Jason Whitson flipped on his blue lights as the small pickup truck continued to weave back and forth across the gravel road. He'd been following the truck since he'd come upon it by coincidence several miles down the mountain on Rock Creek Road and had seen it cross the center line twice within a half-mile. It had turned onto Beauty Spot Gap Road, which was little more than a glorified mountain trail, and was climbing Unaka Mountain. Granted, it was dark and the mountain road was curvy, but this was too much. Whitson felt he needed to do something, but he was reluctant to make the stop. He was alone and inexperienced, and it was nearly midnight. But the person driving the truck was either ill, drunk or high, and if Whitson didn't stop him now, he'd soon cross over the border into the state of North Carolina.

Whitson turned on the revolving lights; they cast eerie shadows off of the trunks of massive trees and the leaves of rhododendron bushes. The parking lot at the Beauty Spot, a popular place atop Unaka Mountain near the Appalachian Trail and the North Carolina border, was only a couple of hundred yards ahead. It would be a logical place for the truck to pull over since there were no shoulders on the rugged, narrow road. Whitson breathed a sigh of relief when the truck's brake lights glowed and it turned into the lot. It came to a stop a few seconds later.

This was the first such stop the twenty-six-year-old Whitson had made on his own. He'd only been with the Unicoi County Sheriff's Department for a year-and-a-half and had been on the road as a patrol deputy for a mere six months. Prior to that, he'd spent a year working in the jail. Before that, he served a stint with the U.S. Marines, including a twelve-month deployment to Afghanistan, and had earned an associate's degree in law enforcement from Northeast State Community College. He was working on his bachelor's in criminal justice at East Tennessee State University part time. Up until a few days ago, Deputy Whitson had ridden with a training officer, but now he was on his own, high up on the Northeast Tennessee mountain about seven miles out of Erwin. Unicoi County had only eighteen thousand residents, but it covered almost two hundred square miles of mountainous terrain. There was only one deputy besides Whitson on duty, and he was on the other side of Erwin. If something went wrong, the closest help was almost a half-hour away.

Whitson turned on his spotlight and aimed it at the back of the driver's head. There didn't seem to be anyone else in the truck. He'd already called in the tag number and told the dispatcher he suspected the driver was under the influence and was stopping the vehicle. He unfolded his lean, six-foot frame out of his cruiser slowly and cautiously moved forward. A flashlight was in his left hand and his right hand rested on the butt of the pistol that was holstered on his hip. The mid-September wind was howling like angry ghosts, and the mountain air was chilly against Whitson's cheeks. As he approached the driver's window, which was rolled all the way down, Whitson took a quick look at the truck bed. It was empty except for two plastic containers about the size and shape of large beer coolers. They were beige and sealed with black electrical tape that had been wrapped around and around each container. Beside them was a fifty-pound bag of lime. Whitson turned his attention back to the driver, whose hair and beard were a dull red. He looked to be late-forties, and he was staring straight ahead.

"Put your hands on the steering wheel!" Whitson said above the wind. The man complied with the demand.

"Is there something wrong with you?" Whitson said.

The man shook his head.

"Why are you swerving all over the road?"

The man turned to look at Whitson. His eyes were grayish-blue, swimming in pink, and he was smiling.

"'Cause I'm hammered," the man said in a thick slur.

"Hammered? Do you mean you're drunk?"

"Drunker 'n Cooter Brown."

Whitson hoped the microphone on his video camera was picking up the conversation despite the whistling wind. He ran the beam of his flashlight over the interior of the truck and spotted what appeared to be a half-empty pint bottle of Jack Daniel's whiskey sitting in plain view on the seat next to the driver.

"Do you have any weapons in the vehicle?"

"Not a one."

Whitson reached out and opened the driver's door.

"Step out," he said.

The drunk poured himself out of the truck, using the door to balance himself. By this time, despite the strong wind, Whitson could smell whiskey. He helped the man to the front of the truck and had him place his hands on the hood and spread his feet.

"Do you have any needles, any drugs, anything I need to know about in your pockets?" Whitson said.

"Mebbe a lil' weed."

Whitson searched him thoroughly. There was less than a quarter-ounce of marijuana and a small pipe in the left-front pocket of the man's blue jeans, along with a small, plastic baggie containing what Whitson guessed was about a half-gram of methamphetamine. Whitson opened the man's wallet and found his driver's license.

"Are you David Craig?" Whitson said.

"That'd be me," the man said. He was still spread-eagled against the front of the truck.

Whitson asked for an address and a date of birth, and both answers – although they were somewhat difficult to understand – matched the information on the license. He called it in to the dispatcher and set the wallet on the hood.

"Would you take a field sobriety test for me, Mr. Craig?" Whitson said. If Whitson could capture a couple of balance tests on video, there would be no doubt about his condition, and no doubt of a conviction for D.U.I.

"I ain't jumpin' through none of your hoops," Craig said.

"How about field breathalyzer? Will you blow for me?"

"How about you blow me?"

Whitson felt his temper flare, but he kept it in check.

"You're under arrest for driving under the influence, possession of controlled substances, and violation of the implied consent law, wise ass," Whitson said as he spun David Craig roughly around and pulled on his wrist. He felt Craig's arm tighten at first and thought he might be in for a fight, but then the arm relaxed and Craig allowed Whitson to cuff him. Whitson straightened Craig up and began to lead him to the back of the patrol car.

Whitson helped Craig into the back of the cruiser. He radioed the dispatcher and was informed that Craig didn't have any outstanding warrants, although he did have three previous convictions for D.U.I., the last of which was six years earlier. Whitson then asked the dispatcher to arrange for a tow truck to pick up Craig's vehicle and told her to notify the jailers that he'd be bringing in a D.U.I. suspect within the hour. Whitson walked back to the truck and searched the cab thoroughly. He found nothing but an empty beer can beneath the seat and a marijuana pipe that looked like it hadn't been used in quite some time inside the glove compartment.

He then turned his attention to the plastic containers he'd seen earlier in the bed. Whitson thought about the training he'd been given on searches incident to arrest and inventory searches. Could he open the containers? They were in plain view in the back of the truck, but they were sealed. And what was the bag of lime for? He knew lime was sometimes used to cover dead bodies because it neutralized the smell of rotting flesh. But it was also used in gardening. Was he within his rights as a police officer to open the containers? He began tugging on one and was surprised by its weight. He lifted it over the side of the truck and dropped it onto the ground. It landed with a dull thud. He decided to go for it. Whitson removed his folding knife from his pocket and set about slicing the tape. When he removed the top from the container, he discovered three black trash bags, all knotted, inside. Whitson cursed quietly under his breath, and when he began to untie one of the bags, he noticed it was cold.

Whitson opened the bag, stared for a few seconds. He felt his stomach tighten and his legs weaken as he let go of the bag and staggered backward.

"Jesus," he said. "Sweet Jesus help me."

# FRIDAY AND SATURDAY, SEPTEMBER 15-16

Jason Whitson had recovered from the nausea, but not from the shock of what he'd found a short time earlier in the back of David Craig's truck. He was back at the sheriff's department headquarters in Erwin now, watching through a two-way mirror as Sheriff Steve Sherfey and Chief Deputy Buck Garland faced off with Craig. Sherfey had been elected only eight months earlier and had no previous law enforcement experience. He was a red-headed, belligerent, housing contractor who was also head of the county commission's budget committee when he and the previous sheriff had become involved in a nasty, public dispute over funding for the sheriff's department. The previous sheriff, a dim-witted redneck named Henley, had resorted to mud-slinging and name-calling in the local papers and on the local television stations, and Sherfey had retaliated by resigning from the county commission and filing papers to run in the next sheriff's election. He'd spanked Henley in the election, had turned his construction company over to his son, and was now the high sheriff of Unicoi County.

Buck Garland was a childhood friend of Sherfey's who was running a lumber yard in Unicoi when Sherfey decided to run. He worked hard to help Sherfey get elected and was rewarded with the chief deputy/lead investigator's job. He went through the academy training in Nashville and also received some training in investigation and was now Sherfey's closest confidante in the sheriff's department. Garland was a bruiser of a man, dark-haired, wide-shouldered and thick-necked. He wore bib overalls to work most days. He still ran the lumber yard; he just didn't spend as much time there.

When Whitson had called Sherfey and given him the news of what he'd found in the containers, he could hear excitement in the sheriff's voice. A cut-up, frozen body? That would mean only one thing – front page headlines and the lead on the local TV news programs. Sherfey certainly didn't mention anything about law and procedure. When Whitson got David Craig to the sheriff's department, the sheriff and Buck Garland were waiting. They'd already talked Craig into waiving his right to have an attorney present and his right to remain silent by convincing him they were there to help him and that they had a great deal of pull with the district attorney. Craig had scrawled his signature on a waiver and was willing to talk.

"So David," the sheriff said, "why don't you start by telling us who is in those bags we found?"

"Name's Fletcher Bryant, I believe," Craig said. He was slurring his words, obviously still very, very drunk, which made Whitson uncomfortable. Even he, as inexperienced as he was, knew that confessions or statements made to police had to be voluntarily and knowingly given. A confession obtained from an intoxicated person could be challenged in court as being involuntarily and unknowing. The sheriff and Garland should have let him sleep it off before they tried to question him, and they hadn't even bothered to take him to the hospital for a forced blood draw to determine his level of intoxication. The D.U.I. case, which was the reason for the initial stop, was being totally ignored.

"And did you have some kind of relationship with Fletcher Bryant?" the sheriff said.

"You mean outside of you finding him dead, chopped up and bagged in the back of my truck?"

"Yes, outside of that," Sherfey said. "Did you know him?"

"Nope."

"But you just said you killed him, correct?"

"Did I?"

"I believe you did. Would you mind telling us why you killed him?"

"I'm surprised you ain't ever heard of him," Craig said slowly. "He wrote the opinion that set a sex offender free. I can't remember the guy's name right now. Williams, Weems, maybe. Anyway, he was convicted five times for sex crimes and he just got released from prison because the Supreme Court overturned his last conviction on a technicality. Know what the technicality was?"

"Can't say that I do," Sherfey said.

SCOTT PRATT

"The thirteen-year-old boy the dirt bag drugged and raped committed suicide rather than go through a trial. The Supreme Court said the dirt bag didn't get to confront his accuser and let him go, even though a jury heard the evidence and packed him off to prison where he belonged and the appeals court upheld the conviction. Damn Supreme Court, though, bunch of liberal prima donnas, reversed the appeals court. Fletcher Bryant wrote the opinion. He won't be writing any others."

"So you're telling me that the man stuffed into those plastic containers in the back of your pickup truck is a Tennessee Supreme Court justice?" Sherfey said.

"Did I stutter? I may have slurred a little 'cause I'm drunker than a big monkey but I didn't stutter. Justice Fletcher Bryant is his name. He lived in a fine home in Nashville in the Bel Meade neighborhood."

"Then this was a vigilante killing," Sherfey said. "You're a vigilante."

"This was a protection killing. He won't be setting any more rapists free."

"Excuse us for a second, Mr. Craig," Sherfey said, and he and Buck Garland got up and walked out of the room.

"Isn't this the fourth one?" Sherfey said in an excited tone as he looked at Garland and Whitson. "Isn't this the fourth judge that has disappeared in the past six months or so? Two criminal court judges, one out of Knoxville and one out of Jackson, one Court of Criminal Appeals judge – a woman who lived in Knoxville – and now a Supreme Court judge. Nobody's found a trace of any of them."

"I believe it is," Garland said. "This is going to be huge, Steve. We better start getting ready for what's coming. Our faces are going to be on every television screen in the country by tomorrow morning. This place will be crawling with media. We're going to wind up talking to Nancy Grace on her show. My God, my wife will pee all over herself. She loves that woman. I think what we have sitting in there is a serial judge killer. Gives me goose bumps just thinking about it. Do you know that every law enforcement officer in this state has been looking for this dude for months? And we've got him, right here in little ol' Unicoi County. Me and you, old buddy."

"Let's get back in there while he's still talking," Sherfey said. "See what else we can get out of him."

Two minutes later, Sherfey and Garland were back at the table while Whitson continued to watch through the two-way mirror. David Craig was puffing lazily on a cigarette (there was no smoking in the jail, but the sheriff was making an exception) and looking down at the table top. His eyes were half-closed.

"It's interesting to me," Buck Garland said, "that you were so precise about the way you cut him up. He was frozen, for one thing, which means you most likely didn't kill him tonight."

"He was killed two days ago," Craig said.

"Where did you kill him?" Garland said.

"He wasn't hard to find."

"You cut his legs into two pieces and his arms into two pieces and removed his head. Then you bagged him and boxed him up very meticulously. It makes me wonder whether you've ever done this kind of thing before."

"I reckon it would," Craig said.

"You reckon it would what?" Garland said.

"Make you wonder."

"Have you?" the sheriff said. "Have you done other ... what'd you call them? Protection killings?"

"I haven't ever killed a soul that didn't deserve it."

"So you have, then. You've killed others."

"Maybe."

"Let's just talk about this theoretically, then," Sheriff Sherfey said. "Let's just assume, without you actually admitting to anything, that you've killed before. How many might we be talking about here? One? Two? More?"

Craig ran his fingers through his greasy red hair and said, "Theoretically? In the judge category? Maybe four."

"Including this one, this Fletcher Bryant?"

"He'd be number four in the judge category."

"How many other categories are there?"

"I'd say several."

"So, again speaking theoretically, you've killed several people."

"It's possible that several people have been killed."

"Where were you taking him?" Buck Garland said.

"Who? The judge?"

"Yes. Where were you taking him?"

"To an old exploratory mine shaft."

"You just dump the containers in and cover them with lime?" Garland said.

"I would've dumped the bags. I ain't gonna waste good containers."

"Would you mind showing us?" the sheriff said.

Craig folded his arms on the table and dropped his head on them.

"I'm drunk and I'm sleepy," he said. "I might tell you in the morning. I think I best take me a little nap now."

Whitson watched as both Sherfey and Garland began prodding and poking Craig's head, neck, shoulders and back, but soon he could make out the unmistakable sound of a loud snore. Sherfey pushed himself away from the table, stood, and turned toward the mirror.

"Deputy Whitson," he said through the glass. "That was one hell of a bust you made tonight. Looks like you went up on the mountain and bagged yourself a serial killer."

# SATURDAY, SEPTEMBER 16

Of all the crazy things I could have done at the age of forty-six, I taught myself to play the drums. I think I was looking for a way to filter away some more of the stress of my wife's ongoing battle with metastatic breast cancer. I still worked out a lot – I ran and I lifted weights – but I'd always wanted to play some kind of musical instrument. When I was young, though, my mom had always vetoed the idea of my learning an instrument, primarily because we always lived in a small house and she didn't want to be tortured by listening to me practice. So I took some of the money I'd made defending a music executive in Nashville on a murder charge, built a room above my garage (it wasn't entirely sound proof, but it was solid) bought myself a small set of Pearl drums, a hi-hat and a couple of cymbals, and started banging away. I also put a stationary bike in the room and some dumb-bells so I could exercise when the weather was bad, and I put a desk and a computer in there so I could work if I wanted.

After several months, I'd become decent enough on the drums that I could play along with a lot of songs. I'd put a set of headphones on, plug them into my phone or

Ipod, and go to it. The Saturday Caroline came walking in holding a cell phone up in the air, I was beating the hell out of the drums to a song called "Get Your Buzz On" by The Cadillac Three, a band my son, Jack, had turned me on to. That was one of the many things I loved about having kids. Even though they were older now and had moved out of the house, they still suggested new music all the time and I kept an open mind about it.

Caroline was wearing a bright, purple scarf wrapped around her head because her hair had fallen out a couple of weeks earlier. Six weeks prior to going to Vanderbilt and learning about the brain radiation, we'd learned her breast cancer, which had metastasized but had been confined to her bones for nearly three years, had moved into her liver. It was devastating news, but her doctor at Vanderbilt assured us that new treatments were being developed all the time and that Caroline still had a long, long way to go. She had prescribed a chemotherapy drug called Taxol, though, and within a few weeks, Caroline's beautiful, auburn hair had fallen out. We'd been to the radiation oncologist in Johnson City to set up her brain radiation appointments, but the treatment program wasn't scheduled to begin for another week.

"You need to take this call," Caroline said when I took the headphones off.

"Who is it?"

"A doctor named Michael Craig. He says his brother has been arrested in Unicoi County."

"For what?"

"Joe, don't you think I've been doing this long enough to know when a phone call is important and when one isn't?"

"A little grouchy, are we?"

She walked toward me, holding out the phone.

"Gimme a kiss," I said, and she did.

I put the phone to my ear and said, "Joe Dillard."

"Mr. Dillard, my name is Dr. Michael Craig," a baritone voice said over the phone. "I'm a surgeon in Johnson City. My brother, David, has been arrested in Erwin and it's imperative that an attorney go to see him right away. I've asked around, and you seem to have the best reputation. I was hoping you would agree."

"What's the charge, Dr. Craig?" I said.

"Don't you listen to the news or read the papers?"

"I try to avoid it."

"They're accusing him of being a serial killer. They're saying he confessed to killing four judges."

I was silent for a few seconds. I'd paid enough attention to know that three judges had gone missing over the past several months and there was a huge investigation and hunt going on for whomever was responsible. If there was a fourth, I hadn't heard about it. But I'd never before been asked to defend a serial killer, and didn't know whether I wanted to accept the challenge.

"Who is 'they?'" I said. "Who says he confessed to killing four judges?"

"The sheriff of Unicoi County. Everything I've gotten is from the papers and the television. My brother hasn't called me."

"Would you be the person he would call?"

"I think so, yes. We're pretty close. I'm telling you, Mr. Dillard, this doesn't make any sense at all. David is gentle by nature. He drinks too much, but I can't imagine him harming anyone or anything, let alone being some kind of psychopathic killer. And there's just no way he would kidnap and kill a judge, any judge. I mean, why would he do a thing like that? He doesn't know anything about the law and doesn't seem to care much about anything other than getting high. I know him better than anyone. Will you go and see him, please? I'll pay the fee, whatever it is, if you'll represent him."

"If they charge him with killing four judges, probably in four different jurisdictions, it's going to be a pretty sizable fee, Dr. Craig."

"Doesn't matter. He's my brother, I'm absolutely sure he didn't do this, and I can afford it."

Those words were music to any defense lawyer's ears. The prostitute in me decided right then and there it was worth a look.

"I'll go see him," I said. "Is he in the Unicoi County Jail?"

"That's what they're saying. How long before you can get there?"

"An hour."

"Great then, thank you so much. Please call me as soon as you talk to him."

I disconnected the call and looked at Caroline, who was smiling.

"The judge killer?" she said. "I heard about this on the news this morning."

"And you didn't bother to tell me?"

"You've always loathed judges. I didn't think you'd mind if somebody did away with a few of them."

"I don't. But this guy has a rich brother who's willing to pay for a lawyer."

"Do you think you can tear yourself away from your John Bonham routine long enough to practice a little law?"

I did a loud roll on the snare and crashed one of the cymbals. She covered her ears.

"I should have been a Southern rock n' roller," I said. "It's in my soul."

# SATURDAY, SEPTEMBER 16

S heriff Steve Sherfey was the first person to greet me after I made it past the guard into the tiny Unicoi County Jail. At five-feet, nine inches tall, Sherfey stood about six-inches shorter than me and always seemed to be trying to hold in his stomach and puff out his chest.

"Well, if it isn't the mighty Joe Dillard," he said in a snide voice as I cleared security. "Come to see our serial judge killer, I understand."

"Why are you calling him a serial killer?" I said. "Did he sign a confession?"

"Not exactly, but he was talking in hypotheticals. Who hired you, anyway?"

"Can't see where that's any of your business, sheriff," I said. I didn't enjoy antagonizing law enforcement officers, but I didn't have any respect for Sherfey. He was a politician posing as a cop, and that was always dangerous. "Are you going to let me see my guy or do I go get a court order?"

"He's over there, in the isolation cell," the sheriff said. "You're going to have to talk to him in there, and we're going to have to lock you in there with him if you want some privacy. You comfortable with that?"

"Sure. I love being alone with murderers. We seem to bond for whatever reason. Maybe they sense I'm not that much different than they are."

"You've killed a few, from what I hear," the sheriff said.

"Never killed anybody that didn't deserve it."

The sheriff chuckled. "Maybe you do have something in common with him. That's exactly what he said. By the way, the medical examiner already has a positive I.D. on the victim. He's exactly who your boy said he was. Supreme Court Justice Fletcher Bryant."

"Speaking of what he said, would you mind showing me a copy of the Miranda waiver? Since he talked to you, I'm assuming you got him to sign a waiver."

"Yeah, he signed one. I'll give you a copy before you leave."

"How about a statement? Did he sign one?"

"Didn't quite get around to that."

"Has he called anyone? Did you allow him his phone call?"

"It was late when he got in here and even later when he went to sleep. He's been snoring in that cell all morning. You're going to have to wake him up."

"So he's sleeping off a drunk? You interviewed him when he was drunk?"

"He seemed fine to me," the sheriff said. "Buck and me and Deputy Whitson will all swear on a stack of Bibles that he was sober when he arrived at the jail."

"Buck?"

"Buck Garland, my chief deputy."

"Oh, yeah, I've heard about him. The lumberjack turned cop who is the right-hand man of the contractor turned sheriff. How did you guys get onto David Craig in the first place?"

"Deputy Whitson stopped him up by the Beauty Spot. Suspicion of drunk driving. Then he found the body in some plastic containers that were in the back of the truck."

"I'll need a copy of his incident report. Was the search incident to arrest for DUI?"

"I guess so, or inventory search is probably more like it."

"Were the containers open or did they have a cover on them?"

"They were covered and taped, but Jason – Deputy Whitson – did the right thing. He had probable cause for an arrest and he conducted a good search."

"Do you have a breathalyzer result for your DUI charge?"

"Not charging him with DUI. We're charging him with murder and abuse of a corpse."

"Any field sobriety tests on video? Do a forced blood draw?"

"No! Are you deaf? I told you we're charging him with murder."

"Got anything on video? The stop, your interrogation, anything?"

"Nope."

"Why not? I've had plenty of cases over here in the past. The cruisers all have cameras."

"Whitson's was broken."

"Take me to my client," I said.

The sheriff led me down a short hallway, turned left, went through a sliding, barred door, and then led me down another short hallway. He produced a key and turned the lock in the metal cell door.

"There you go," he said. "Have a nice visit."

"I'd stay away from the television cameras if I were you," I said. "From everything you've told me, this guy is going to walk away from this, and you're going to look like a fool in the process."

# SATURDAY, SEPTEMBER 16

Think of a hangover cliché, and that's what David Craig looked like. Death warmed over. Rode hard and put up wet. Straight off a five-day bender. Emptied the tequila bottle with a straw and then sucked the worm through.

He was thin and gaunt, his face and nose a light shade of purple. His hair was a dull red and thinning, and he had a scraggly beard that was laced with gray. He was still in his street clothes – gray jeans, a black T-shirt and black cowboy boots. When I'd awakened him a couple of minutes earlier by shoving his back with my foot, the first thing he did was stand over the toilet and urinate for what seemed like ten minutes. Even now, hours after his arrest, the gunmetal gray cell reeked of whiskey.

When he finally finished and flushed the toilet, he took a long drink out of the tap above the metal sink. Then he walked over to the concrete shelf that served as a bed and sat down. He pulled his legs up, covered his face with his hands, and said, "Who are you?"

"Name's Joe Dillard. I'm a lawyer. Your brother asked me to come and talk to you."

"Good old Mikey," he said. "I can always count on Mikey."

"How much about last night do you remember, Mr. Craig?" I said.

"Not much after I polished off the first bottle of Jack."

"Do you remember being arrested?"

"I seem to recall lights flashing at some point, but that's about it."

"What about talking to the sheriff?"

"What about it?"

"Do you remember it?"

"No. What'd I tell him?"

"You didn't sign a statement, but since they're charging you with first-degree murder and abuse of a corpse, I'm assuming you told them you killed the person they found cut up and stuffed into containers in the back of your truck."

He was quiet for a few seconds, then he rubbed his eyes and cheeks with his fingers and looked over at me. I was leaning against the cell wall a few feet away.

"Oh, that," he said. "Yeah, well, I guess that's gonna be a little bit of a problem. What exactly did I say, do you know?"

"All I can tell you is what your brother told me on the phone and what my wife told me. The sheriff apparently held a press conference early this morning and announced to the world that he had arrested the man responsible for kidnapping and murdering four judges. I'd heard about the first three, but this latest one was a Supreme Court judge from Nashville who had just gone missing. I didn't even know about it. You apparently told them that the body in the back of your truck was Justice Fletcher Bryant. They've already identified him."

"So what do I do now?" he said.

"Keep your mouth shut, for one thing. Don't talk to anybody. You're not going to get bail, so you're going to be in here a while, which means you're probably going to go through some pretty severe alcohol and maybe drug withdrawal. Don't expect much sympathy from anybody around here, but they'll at least keep a nurse around so you don't die. I'm sure they'll want to keep you alive so they can try to convict you of killing this judge and stick a needle in your arm later. There's also the possibility that they'll come to you with some kind of offer if you'll tell them what happened to the other three judges, assuming, of course, you know what happened to the other three. The offer will be something along the lines of if you'll tell them where the bodies are so the families can give them a proper burial, they might come off of the death penalty. It isn't much of a deal because Tennessee doesn't execute people anyway, and the way things are looking, I don't think it'll be long before the Supreme Court does away with the death penalty entirely. If they give you a cellmate, he's a jailhouse snitch. Don't talk to him. Now ... how did you spend your day yesterday? And if there's any killing or cutting up bodies involved, leave that part out. I'm interested in how much you had to drink, what you drank and where you drank it, and any drugs you may have consumed."

"I got up around noon and drove over to The Saddlebag," Craig said.

"That little bar by the V.A. in Johnson City?" I said.

"Yeah."

"Do you live at the V.A.?"

"No. I rent a small house between Boones Creek and Jonesborough."

"Do you work?"

"I do odd jobs for my brother. He pays me, pays my rent. He helps me out, you know?"

"He said you're close."

"We're pretty tight."

"Which one of you is older?" I said.

I half-expected him to say he was older, because he looked like he was close to fifty, but he said, "Mikey's thirty-eight. He's six years older."

"Back to the Saddlebag," I said.

"I sat in there most of the afternoon, just like I do every day but Sunday, until maybe five o'clock when the rednecks start coming in."

"How much did you drink?"

"I drank maybe eight, nine beers."

"Run a tab or pay as you went?"

"I pay as I go. Cash."

"Bartender's name?"

"Gene Collins."

"He'll remember you were there and how much you drank?"

"Reckon so."

"Where did you go from there?"

"Home."

"So since it's near Jonesborough you got home at what, five-fifteen or so?"

"I'd say that's about right."

"And?"

"And what?"

"Are you going to make me pry every bit of it out of you?" I said. "What did you do? Account for your time between five-fifteen when you got home and midnight when you were stopped. And like I said before, if any of it involves killing anybody or cutting anybody up, leave it out."

David Craig rubbed his face again and took another deep breath. I could almost see the gears in his brain turning, but they'd been rusted by alcohol and whatever else he'd used to poison himself, and the gears were grinding and turning very, very slowly.

"I watched some TV for a couple of hours and polished off a pint of Jack Daniels I had in the cupboard. When the Jack was gone, I drove over to Uncle Jim's liquor store and bought me two more. I took them back to the house, sat down in my recliner, and fell asleep. I woke up about ten o'clock, I reckon, took a shower and a hit of meth to wake up, and then I sat down for about an hour, watched some more TV and sipped on one of the pints. Finally, I loaded those containers they found into the back of my truck and headed for the mountains. Somewhere along the way I think I finished off the second pint and started on the third."

"Do you drink like that every day?"

"I drink every day. I hit the liquor and the meth a little harder than usual yesterday."

"Because of what you were doing?"

"Probably. Something like that."

"I'm sure they've searched your place by now. Are they going to find anything I need to know about?"

"Nothing serious. Little weed, little meth, some pipes, razor blades. Stuff people who use drugs have around the house."

"You said you loaded the containers into the back of your truck. Where were they before you loaded them into your truck?"

"In a freezer in my basement. A guy I knew when I was a kid came by my house a few months ago and put the freezer in there. He's huge, a crazy man. He said he just got out of prison and was going to be doing some contract work. Then he comes back the other night with this body and these containers. He told me who it was, how he killed him, everything. Bragged about it. He said he'd be back for the body on Sunday, but I couldn't stand the thought of it being in my house, so I took it out and was going to get rid of it."

"Care to tell me this person's name?"

"Not a chance. I'd be a dead man."

"Okay," I said, holding up my hands, "we'll come back to it another time. Let's concentrate on your arrest and subsequent interrogation. How much of it do you remember?"

"Flashes," David said. "I have a vague memory of the blue lights swirling and the cop getting me out of the car."

"I heard the officer stopped you at the Beauty Spot. What were you doing all the way up there?"

"Taking the body to an old, exploratory mine shaft I know about."

"Where is it?"

"I'd rather not say. The property belongs to an old buddy of mine. We used to do some four-wheeling up there. He's got nothing to do with any of this."

"Do you remember anything you said to the officer at the Beauty Spot before or after you were arrested?"

"Not really. I mean, I was drunk as hell but I'd done some meth to keep me going. I'm sure we were probably talking some, but I don't really remember, you know, the specifics."

"What about after they got you in here? Do you remember signing a Miranda waiver?"

He shook his head.

"Do you remember anything you told them?"

"Can't really say that I do."

"Do you remember who interrogated you?"

He shook his head again.

"One guy, two guys, a woman, maybe?"

"I don't remember."

The whiskey smell was getting to me in such close quarters and a thought dawned on me. I got up and started banging on the door. A guard opened it a couple of minutes later.

"Is the sheriff still here?" I said.

"He's in his office."

"Tell him my client wants to voluntarily take a breathalyzer. Right now."

The guard shut the door and I could hear his heels hitting the concrete floor outside the cell as he hurried away.

"What are you doing?" David Craig said.

"Just hang on," I said.

In less than five minutes, Sheriff Sherfey was standing in the doorway, hands on his hips.

"Just what are you trying to pull?" he said.

"I'm not trying to 'pull' anything," I said. "Give him a breathalyzer or do a blood draw and have it analyzed. You said you and your chief deputy and the road deputy are all going to swear he was sober when you interrogated him. If you give him a test and his blood alcohol content is zero, then there's a chance you're telling the truth, but this cell smells like a distillery. If you give him a test and he comes in at .04 ten hours after you arrested him, then I'll have to hire an expert and have him bring a little science into the courtroom. You know alcohol levels dissipate uniformly once a person stops drinking, right? We can get a reliable estimate of what his BAC was when you arrested him and when you interrogated him."

"His BAC is not an issue. I already told you that. We charged him with murder and abuse of a corpse, not D.U.I."

"Why did your deputy stop him in the first place?"

"He had a headlight out," Sherfey said.

"That isn't what you told me a little while ago," I said. "I can't wait to see the report. Are you really going to order your road deputy to lie?"

Sherfey's eyes narrowed and his cheeks flushed.

"You best watch who you call a liar around here," he said. "This isn't Washington County."

"You're right about that. We have a real sheriff in Washington County. Guy named Leon Bates. Maybe you've heard of him."

"Visit's over," he said. "Pack up and get out."

"I'm not finished with my client."

"This is my jail," he said. "Walk out the door right now, or you're going to find yourself in a cell of your own."

I could have told him to stuff it and let him lock me up. Had he done that – and he probably would have – I would have eventually bankrupted his county. But I decided to choose the spot for the next battle, so I picked up my briefcase and walked toward him. I hesitated in the doorway, looking down on him.

"This is nowhere near over," I said. "I'll see you in court real soon."

He wadded up a piece of paper he was holding in his hand and tossed it on the floor at my feet.

"There's the Miranda waiver he signed," Sherfey said. "I'm sure you know where you can stuff it."

I bent over and picked up the wad of paper. I opened it and looked at the signature. It was a sloppy mess. I was looking forward to comparing it to David Craig's signature when he was sober, or at least relatively so.

"What about the incident report?"

"Can't seem to lay my hands on it."

"So you're going to get your deputy to write another one that fits your new facts. Perjury's a felony, sheriff. Remember I told you that when they shut the cell door on you."

I started walking toward the door, and then stopped and turned back to face the sheriff. His face seemed to be smoldering.

"And one more thing. Give my guy his phone call. Let him out of that dungeon for an hour a day. Make sure he has medical care when the DT's hit him. Treat him like a human being, or I'll haul your butt to federal court and make you wish you'd never run for office."

# SATURDAY, SEPTEMBER 16

Dr. Michael Craig, at least in physical appearance, was his brother's polar opposite. He was clean shaven and his short, brown hair was perfectly groomed. He was solidly, if not perfectly, built, his turquoise eyes were clear and intense, his skin was smooth and taut, and he carried himself with the bearing of a soldier. I called him as soon as I left the jail and he asked me to come to his office. We met in a conference room down the hall from the empty lobby.

"How is David?" he said as soon as I sat down.

"Hung over," I said. "The cell smelled like the inside of a whiskey barrel."

"Did he tell you what he was doing with a dead judge in the back of his truck?"

"We didn't really get into many specifics of what was inside the container. I was more interested in the circumstances of the stop and the search. I think the legal issues have legs. The biggest problem will be finding a judge with enough courage to rule in our favor."

"And if a judge rules in our favor?"

"He's out of it clean. They won't be able to use the body they found in the containers as evidence against him and they won't be able to use anything he may or may not have told them. He'll walk out a free man."

"What are the odds of that happening?"

"We're up against a house builder who is playing sheriff because he got pissed off at the last sheriff and managed to get himself elected. He has no idea what he's doing or what he's gotten himself into. I think he's planning to go into court and perjure himself, but I also think I can get around him."

"How?"

"Doesn't matter. Just leave it to me if you want me to represent him."

"Yes, yes, of course. How much will it cost me?"

I put my elbows on the table and laced my fingers beneath my chin. I'd been thinking about the answer to this question on the drive from Erwin to Johnson City. I let out a deep breath and said, "Normally, I'd tell you you're looking at high six-figures, maybe a million or more, but under these circumstances, I just don't see it taking that much time. I'm going to have to do some investigation and I'm going to have to twist a few arms, but if I can get it tossed out on the front end, you'll only be looking at about twenty-five grand."

A look of bemusement came over the doctor's face.

"Are you serious?" he said.

I shrugged my shoulders. "Like I said, I just don't think I'm going to have to put that much time in, and I'm not going to screw you just because he's your brother. The search of his truck was illegal. Some states might let it happen, but not Tennessee. The law in Tennessee is tough on warrantless inventory searches. The cop took a knife and cut through some tape to open up the containers without a warrant. He didn't have probable cause to do it unless your brother blurted out that he had a body in the back of the truck, and even if he did, he was so drunk they wouldn't be able to use anything he said in a probable cause determination. They should have waited until he sobered up."

"Do you really think he's going to get out of this scot free?"

"I think the charges will be dismissed eventually. It might be early in the process, or it might be later on appeal. If the judge denies all of my motions and we wind up in Criminal Court and we have to go through a trial because the Criminal Court judge denies the same motions, the fee is going to go way, way up. If we go to trial and he gets convicted, then we appeal, and you'll still be paying. But let's say the first judge, the General Sessions Court judge, rules everything inadmissible and the case gets dismissed. He still isn't really out of it. They'll probably take it to a grand jury and indict him. Then we wind up in Criminal Court in front of one of two judges, both of whom actually have brains. The old judges, Ivan Glass and Leonard Green, are out and the new judges haven't caught the black robe fever yet. They probably will, but not yet. I think either one of them will have the courage to rule our way. But your brother still had the dismembered body of a sitting Tennessee Supreme Court justice in the back of his truck. Three other judges are missing. There will be consequences. The legal system can't allow people to kidnap and kill its judges and get away with it."

"What are you saying?"

"Let's assume one of the Criminal Court judges has the stones to follow the law and the rules and dismisses the case. I think somebody will kill David, or at least try to. Maybe the real killer will come after him, because David knows who he is."

"He does? How do you know that?"

"He told me. Somebody put a freezer in the basement of his house with the express purpose of storing bodies in it. When that somebody finally came along and actually put a body in there, David couldn't take it. He got the body out of the freezer and was going to dispose of it. I think the killer was going to come back for it, and now David has gotten himself arrested with the body. The real killer will be afraid David will give him up, and he'll kill him."

"So he told you who did it?"

"No. He's afraid. He wouldn't say who did it. But the guy will come after him. Either that, or someone sitting in a high place will send a soldier, be it a TBI agent or a Highway Patrol trooper or just a thug hit man, and they'll put a bullet in David's brain."

"I'll protect him," Michael Craig said. "I was a Green Beret and then moved on to Delta for four years. I can take care of my brother."

"I knew you had to have a military background," I said. "I can tell by the way you carry yourself."

"What about you?" the doctor said. "Serve your country?"

I nodded. "Ranger."

"Combat?"

"Some."

"I saw a ton of combat," he said. "As a matter of fact, if I wasn't too old, I'd love to be in the Middle East right now sitting in a sniper's nest sending Jihadists to paradise."

"So we're getting a little off track here," I said. "Just answer one question for me."

"Absolutely."

"Since you say your brother didn't do it, do you have any idea who might have killed that judge?"

# SATURDAY, SEPTEMBER 16

I spoke with Michael Craig for about an hour at his office, but he was little help when it came to an explanation for the body in the back of the truck. He simply had no idea, he said. He reiterated that his brother was non-violent, that he had never wanted to serve in the military because he ultimately didn't think he would have the stomach to kill someone if the need arose. Their family was fractured, father and mother split up when Michael was a teenager. Their father, Michael said, was a military JAG officer – a lawyer and a prosecutor – who had eventually left the military and had become an assistant district attorney in the Third Judicial District (Hancock, Hawkins, Hamblen and Greene Counties) and was now a Criminal Court judge in that same district. He lived on a large farm outside of Greeneville, about thirty miles to the southwest of Johnson City. Michael said his father had always been cold and distant and demanding, and they had no contact with him. Their mother, Michael said, was deceased. When I asked him what happened to her, he said he'd rather not talk about it, so I let it go.

After I finished at Dr. Craig's office, I stopped at Dixie Barbecue for some lunch and to shoot the bull with the owner, an old buddy named Alan Howell who was about to retire and close up the place. Alan was a student of local history, especially the Civil War era, and he loved to tell stories. I loved to listen as much as he loved to talk, so it worked out well. Caroline's dance studio was only a couple of miles from the diner, so after I was finished at Alan's, I stopped by there to tell Caroline what was going on with the new case and to say hello to my daughter, Lilly, who had pretty much taken over the studio since Caroline's cancer had caused her to become less active. They were getting ready for a competition and were holding a Saturday rehearsal.

I knew something was wrong as soon as I walked through the door into Caroline's office. Both Caroline and Lilly were in there. Lilly looked as though she'd been crying, and Caroline looked as though she was on the verge of killing someone.

"What's going on?" I said.

I didn't stop by all that often, so they were both surprised to see me. The place was usually a madhouse with music blaring and girls dancing around and Lilly yelling above the music. Parents were often vying for Caroline's attention in the waiting room or in the office, so it wasn't exactly a place that made me feel welcome.

"We're having a problem," Caroline said.

"What kind of problem?"

"I'm not sure I should tell you," she said.

"Why?"

"Because I know you. I know how you are."

"You're not making any sense," I said. "What's going on?"

"Do you promise you won't get angry if I tell you?"

"No," I said. "If it's something I should get angry about, then I'll probably get angry."

"At least promise me you won't do anything rash."

"Like what?"

"Like hurting anyone."

"The place is full of teenage girls, Caroline. Do you think I'm going to start breaking their legs?"

"There's a young man sitting in a red Mustang out in the parking lot," Caroline said. "His name is Jimmy Carr. He's a senior in high school, the quarterback of the football team, and he's been dating Lyndsey Woods for a couple of months. You know Lyndsey, right?"

"Yeah. Blonde. Pretty. Good dancer. You've always said she's a good kid."

"She is, but she's gotten herself into a bad situation. She's trying to break up with this boy, but he won't stop harassing her. This is the second time he's showed up here. Lyndsey went out to his car to talk to him, and she wound up getting in. Lilly looked outside a little while ago and saw Jimmy slap her."

That immediately made my blood boil. I don't care about modern gender stereotypes and whether boys or men should be seen as protectors of girls or women; I have a very simplistic attitude about males beating on females. They don't get to do it, at least not if I have a say in the matter.

"Did you call the police?" I said.

"We were just about to when you walked in, but there's more. As soon as Lilly saw him hit Lyndsey, she went straight out the door. I was in here and didn't even know what was going on. One of the girls came and got me."

Caroline looked at Lilly and said, "Tell him. Tell him what happened."

"Are you sure?" Lilly said. "Maybe we should just call the police."

"What happened?" I said. "Did he touch you?"

"I went out and went up to the car," Lilly said. "Lyndsey's nose was bleeding, dad, and she was crying. She was trying to get out but he had ahold of her arm and wouldn't let her. The window was down and I told him I saw what he did and that he couldn't slap her like that. He told Lyndsey to stay put and he got out of the car and got right in my face. He said I needed to keep my nose in my own business before I wound up getting hurt. Then he pushed me hard against the car that was parked next to him and told me to get the f--- out of his sight. I saw Mom coming out the door and I ran over and grabbed her and pulled her inside. I was afraid she'd go after him and that he might hurt her. Her bones are so weak ... the cancer ..."

Lilly's voice trailed off and I immediately spun and headed out the door.

"Joe! Wait!"

It was Caroline, but she was too late. The Mustang was a little ways across the lot, about thirty feet away. I could feel adrenaline surging through me as the anger began to intensify. The thought that this bastard had slapped a young girl, threatened and pushed my daughter, and may have injured my wife was just too much for me to handle. My vision tunneled. All I could see was him.

I walked up to the driver's side of his car. He looked at me with a stupid smirk on his face until I reached in and grabbed a handful of the black, man bun that was sitting on top of his head. I pulled him straight out of the car through the window and had him on the hood of the car next to him before he knew what was happening. He was a big kid, probably six feet one, two hundred pounds, but I was so full of rage and adrenaline he felt like a rag doll.

"Go inside," I said to Lyndsey.

I climbed onto the hood of the car and straddled the quarterback. I punched him in the face four times as hard as I could. The fourth punch broke his nose and blood began to spray.

"You think you can come to my wife's place of business, slap Lyndsey, threaten and push my daughter, and scare all these girls, you worthless piece of shit?" I growled.

"Joe! Joe! Stop it! Stop it!" Caroline was yelling. I could also hear Lilly begging me to stop, but I wasn't finished.

I grabbed him by the collar and started picking his head up and banging it back down against the hood. After the fourth or fifth bang, his eyes rolled back in his head and I stopped. I got off of him, lifted him to his feet by his shirt and leaned him against his car. I started slapping his face until I saw enough light in his eyes that I knew he could understand what I was saying to him.

"You are going to stay away from Lyndsey Woods," I said. "You got that? She's off limits to you from now on. Say it! Say it out loud!"

He mumbled that he would stay away from Lyndsey Woods.

"And if I ever hear of you being on this property again, if you ever touch or threaten or even look cross-eyed at my daughter or wife again, I'll kill you with my bare hands and I'll enjoy it. You got that, big boy? Say it. Say, 'yes, sir.'"

He said it clearly enough that I was satisfied, so I opened the door to his car and shoved him inside.

"Get the hell out of here," I said. "Go bleed someplace else."

He started his car and drove slowly out of the lot. After he'd disappeared, I turned to see Caroline, Lilly and a group of about twelve teenage girls all staring at me wide-eyed. I started walking toward my pickup truck.

"Boys don't get to beat on you," I said loudly before I climbed into the cab. "Remember that. Boys *do not* get to beat on you!"

# SATURDAY, SEPTEMBER 16

Caroline pulled into the garage less than ten minutes after I did. I was in the kitchen, sitting at the table. I'd grabbed a beer out of the refrigerator and was guzzling it, trying to calm myself. My hands were still shaking from the adrenaline and my chest was still tight. My right hand was already swelling from the blows I'd delivered to the quarterback's face.

"Don't," I said to Caroline as she walked up to the table and folded her arms across her chest. The folding of arms always meant I was about to be scolded or lectured, and I wasn't in the mood for either.

"Are you crazy?" she said. "I'm serious, Joe. Have you completely lost your mind? You just beat a teenage boy senseless. You're probably going to be arrested, and if you don't get arrested, I'm betting you're going to get sued."

"I don't care," I said. "If they arrest me, I'll beat it. There isn't a jury in the world that would convict me after they hear about him slapping Lyndsey and pushing Lilly. Same thing with getting sued. He'd be wasting his time."

I knew I was wrong about being sued. If the kid went to the emergency room and wound up with a stack of medical bills and filed suit against me, he'd probably win. I was thinking it would probably cost me somewhere between fifteen and twenty thousand dollars. I'd pay if it came to that. It was worth it in a perverted sort of way.

"You could lose your law license."

"So?" I shrugged my shoulders. "If the pencil pushers in Nashville want my law license because I meted out a little justice to a bully, they can have it. And if they take it, I'll tell them to shove it up their asses."

Caroline walked around the table and sat down directly across from me.

"I'm worried about you," she said. "You just don't seem to be yourself lately. You fly off the handle at the slightest things, you're swearing more than I've ever heard you swear, and you're quiet and moody. Do you think you should maybe see somebody?"

"See somebody? A shrink?"

She nodded. "It might help. I know your job is stressful, and I know you worry about me all the time. I think the cancer is getting to you."

"Of course it's getting to me," I snapped. "It's like a freaking roller coaster ride that never ends. Up one day, down the next. A little good news here, a dose of devastation there. It hovers over us like a giant hammer, just waiting to drop. We barely do anything together any more, do you know that? You're either at the studio, at the cancer center, or you're in bed. We can't go anywhere for more than two days without bookending the trip around chemotherapy or doctor's appointments. Now you're about to have your entire brain radiated and who knows how that's going to turn out? And you know what the worst thing is? I can't fix it! I can't do a damned thing about it. I feel so helpless and frustrated that sometimes I just want to bang my head against the wall."

"Maybe I'll die soon and your suffering will be over," she said.

"That isn't fair," I said. "You brought it up. You wanted to talk about it. Am I not allowed to be honest once in a while?"

"That's why I'm suggesting you go see someone. Be honest with them. It hurts me to hear you say those things."

I looked at her and felt ashamed. She was right. She had been through so much and had battled so valiantly for such a long, long time. She didn't need weakness from me.

"I'm sorry, Caroline," I said. "I don't know exactly what's going on."

"You need a friend," she said. "A real friend. You need Jack."

I nodded and felt a small smile cross my lips. Having Jack around would have helped, but he was still in Nashville, practicing law with his girlfriend, Charlie Story. I missed him terribly, but he'd been gone for years: first college, then a couple of years in minor league baseball, then law school. I had this storybook dream that he and Charlie would get married and come back to Johnson City and we could all practice law together and chase windmills, but I didn't get the sense from him that he wanted to come back. He seemed to like Nashville, and he and Charlie, from everything he'd told me, were getting along extremely well.

"I do miss him," I said, "but he has his own life. I have to let him live it. And I have Leon. He's still my friend."

"Leon's busy being a sheriff and a politician," she said. "How often do you even talk to him?"

"Not much," I admitted. "It's my fault. I don't reach out to him, and I'm sure he thinks I've got my hands full dealing with our ... our situation."

"You mean my cancer?"

"It's our cancer. It affects me as much as it does you."

"You're lonely," she said. "You miss me because I'm sick, you miss Jack because he's gone, you miss Lilly because she's raising a child and you know she's about to move away with Randy."

"Thanks for the reminder," I said.

My son-in-law, Randy Lowe, was about to graduate from medical school and move into his residency program. The problem was that the residency program – which was oncology – was in Charleston, South Carolina. He, along with my daughter, Lilly, and my grandson, Joseph, would be moving at the end of the school year, and they'd be gone for at least three years. The dance studio would remain Caroline's, but she'd be relying on other people to help her run it. She already had several people helping, and they were all excellent, understanding, wonderful people, but I knew, and Caroline knew, that it just wouldn't be the same without Lilly around.

"Maybe I'll start hanging out with Sarah," I said.

Caroline shook her head. Now it was her turn to smile. Sarah, my sister, was working about twelve hours a day at her little diner in Jonesborough. She'd moved to a small farm in the Horse Creek area of Greene County that was about as far off the grid as one could get. The only time I saw her was when I ate at the diner, and I hadn't seen her daughter, Grace, in two months.

"We all used to be so close," Caroline said, the smile leaving her face. "It's hard to believe everything has become so broken."

"Nothing's broken," I said. "We might not be as close as we once were because the kids have grown up and have their own lives, but we still love each other. I'd still take a bullet for anyone in this family."

"Let's hope it doesn't come to that," Caroline said. She moved around and sat next to me at the table. She reached out and took my hand.

"You haven't said a word about your visit to the jail," she said. "Are you going to take the case?"

I nodded and said, "Yeah, I'm going to take it on, but it's going to be as bizarre as any case I've ever had. I always think every case I take will be my last one. This one might really be it."

"Did he kill this judge?"

"Who knows?" I said. "The evidence certainly points in that direction since the judge was butchered and frozen like a steer and stuffed into containers that were in the back of his truck. But I don't see a motive. His brother says he doesn't care about much of anything but getting wasted and he doesn't know anything about the law. Why would he suddenly start killing judges, and why would he go all the way to Nashville to kill a particular judge? And the other judges? He had to hit the road to kill them, too, if you believe the whole serial killer theory. You also have to believe he's a brilliant, clever bad ass who was somehow able to subdue and murder these people without anyone catching so much as a glimpse."

"Is it that much of a stretch?" Caroline said.

"Wait until you see the guy. Lilly would give him all he could stand. Sarah would beat the crap out of him."

"You'll figure it out," Caroline said. "You always do."

"Maybe," I said, guzzling the last of the beer, "but no matter what happens, I'm going to make a bunch of serious enemies in this one, as if I haven't made enough in the past."

"People around here know you. They know you do a job that's difficult, and that you do it for the right reasons."

"It isn't the people around here I'm worried about," I said. "This is going to bring in heavy hitters from all over the country. Judges are the primary symbol of one of the most powerful institutions we have in America – the criminal justice system. Killing them threatens the very existence of the institution. Somebody's going to pay for that. I just have to figure out a way to make sure that someone isn't innocent, and I have to make sure it isn't me."

# PART II

# SUNDAY, SEPTEMBER 17

**W**hen I woke up at 5:30 the next morning, they were out there. They'd apparently started coming during the night, as soon as word got out that I was going to represent David Craig. I was making myself a cup of coffee when I glanced out the kitchen window and saw them. It was still dark, but their lights were on. I went into the garage and walked to the windows that looked out over the driveway. Television news vans and trucks were parked up and down the road for a quarter-mile in both directions. This was a phenomenon I had never understood. Why would these idiots do this? Why would they camp out at a lawyer's home? Did any of them really expect me to come out and play nice with them? Even worse, were they pointing their zoom lenses at every window of our home, including the bathrooms and bedrooms?

I'd only dealt with this kind of situation once before, and I decided to deal with it just a little differently than the last time. My German shepherd, Rio, who I usually let out first thing in the morning, began to go nuts. I quieted him quickly because I didn't want him to wake Caroline. She was taking a lot of prescribed drugs and could sleep through most anything, but Rio was loud, especially when he was excited or angry, and he was both. He was well-trained, though. I'd spent a lot of time and a lot of money training him as a protection dog, primarily because I'd dealt with so many dangerous people during my career and I never knew when one of them might come back to haunt me. Rio responded to my commands, but he could also work things out for himself if the need arose. I took him by the collar and led him back through the house, and he remained quiet. I dressed quickly in a gray University of Tennessee sweatshirt, jeans and running shoes, and went back out through the garage, grabbing Rio's leash and a flashlight along the way. I hooked Rio up to the leash, hit the button that opened one of the garage doors and walked quickly up the driveway toward the morons. I stopped about twenty feet from the end of the driveway. They began to scramble toward me, reporters and camera people and whoever else was out there with them.

"Don't come onto my property!" I yelled.

"Mr. Dillard, can you tell us ... ? Mr. Dillard, did your client confess to killing the judge? Is he a serial killer? How many has he killed? Where are the other judges? Mr. Dillard! Mr. Dillard!"

I held up my flashlight to quiet them and said loudly, "I accept that because of my profession I'm a public figure and you jerkoffs can do and say pretty much whatever you want. But this is my private residence, my wife is ill, and I'm not going to stand for this. Now ... I want all of you to meet Rio. He's a very friendly guy, unless someone he doesn't know invades his territory, and his territory is this property I'm standing on and that house behind me. If any one of you sets foot on this property, I'll let him off the leash or out the door and he'll light you up. I'm not going to answer a single question any of you has regarding David Craig or any other case I'm handling. If you want answers to questions, you go to press conferences, you attend the hearings in open court, you work your sources, you *do your jobs the right way.* Hanging around out here at my house will only ensure that I ignore you completely and that – if you make a wrong move – a hundred-pound German shepherd is going to take a bite out of your ass."

"So you're threatening us?" a female voice said from somewhere in the darkness. "You're on camera, on the record, and you're threatening the press?"

"I'm threatening anyone stupid enough to trespass on my property. I'm threatening anyone stupid enough to disturb my wife, who has absolutely nothing to do with any of this and doesn't deserve to be treated like a virus under a microscope."

A large, male reporter stepped forward, right at the edge of driveway.

"That dog of yours is a dangerous animal," he said. "If he tries to attack me, I'd be well within my rights to kill him."

"You kill this dog, you better kiss your mother, and your own ass, goodbye before you do," I said.

"Did you just threaten to kill me?" the man said.

"Hurt my dog and see what happens to you. Now get the hell out of here, all of you. There's nothing for you here, nothing to see, nothing to report, nothing to do."

"I think you're wrong about that," the male reporter said. "You've already given us plenty."

I whispered a command to Rio and let him off the leash. He issued a low growl but remained frozen. I turned back toward the house and walked down the driveway. As I got to the garage door, I yelled another command and Rio streaked down the driveway and stopped at my feet. I looked down at him and said, "She's right, buddy. Caroline's right. I'm losing my mind."

# SUNDAY, SEPTEMBER 17

A t 7:00 a.m. that morning, I was sitting at the Waffle House in Boones Creek with the esteemed sheriff of Washington County, Leon Bates. I knew Leon was an early riser, so I'd called him right after my little confrontation with the news folks.

"You're looking a little ragged around the edges, brother Dillard," Leon said in his smooth drawl. He was tall and lean with an angular jaw, wearing his ever-present khaki uniform. He'd removed his cowboy hat and set it on the seat beside him in the booth.

"A lot going on."

"I take it Ms. Caroline isn't doing well," he said.

I told him about the brain radiation, about what we might be facing.

"She's actually doing okay, Leon," I said. "At least mentally. It seems to be wearing on me worse than her for whatever reason. I mean, it doesn't make any sense. She's the one who's sick and I'm the one who's going to hell in an emotional hand basket."

"I heard you tuned up a teenager yesterday afternoon outside your wife's dancing school," Leon said.

"How could you possibly know that?"

SCOTT PRATT

"I have eyes and ears everywhere."

"Seriously. How did you know?"

"One of the dancers' father is a friend. She told him and he called me. He said he thought you did the right thing, but that you might need some help if this young feller tries to jam you up."

I shook my head and took a sip of coffee. "I don't know, Leon. I've always been a little edgy, but lately I feel like I might lose it at any second."

"It's just because you care about her and you're scared. I know you'd fight a circle saw. Hell, I've seen what you're capable of doing and I'd never doubt your courage, but this cancer is something different. You're afraid you're going to lose the person you love more than anyone you've ever loved and right now you're not handling the stress all that great. Nothing to be ashamed of."

I felt tears welling in my eyes and fought them back. It was something that was happening to me more and more frequently when I talked about, or thought about, Caroline.

"I appreciate that, Leon, but I didn't really call you for a therapy session."

He nodded as the waitress set our breakfast down in front of us. "All right then, what can I do for you?"

"You've heard that I'm representing David Craig, the alleged serial killer of judges?"

"I have, and I commend you for taking on such an unpleasant task. Did he do it?"

"No. I really don't think he did. I don't think he's capable."

"So how do I fit into this?"

"I need a favor."

"Is it legal?"

"Yes."

"Will it get me beaten in the next election?"

"Nothing will get you beaten in the next election."

"What's on your mind?"

"There's a young deputy in Unicoi County named Jason Whitson. He made the original stop on my alleged judge killer and did an illegal search. I've done a little checking on him, and he's a good kid. Ex-marine, tour in Afghanistan, working hard to better himself. Sheriff Sherfey is going to pressure him into lying on the witness stand, into committing perjury. He's also probably already pressured him into changing his written report of the stop. I'd like you to reach out to him and have a little talk with him about the importance of integrity in law enforcement and how once you cross that line, you can't go back."

"I can do that," Leon said. "Be more than happy to."

"There's one more thing."

Leon raised his eyebrows.

"When I file the motions I need to file and we have a hearing in a month or so, if Whitson tells the truth, Sherfey is going to fire him."

"I'm sure he will."

"I need you to give him a job."

Leon shoved a large fork full of scrambled eggs into his mouth.

"We pay better over here and have a department that's ten times better than those wannabes," he said. "Send him on over. If you recommend him, he's hired."

"Thanks, Leon," I said, "I knew I could count on you."

I watched him chew the eggs for a second and said, "Leon?"

"Yessir?"

"I'm afraid I'm going to have to ask you for one more thing."

"Uh-huh." His expression didn't change.

"After I get my client out of this, I'm going to want to find out who is killing these judges. You know I don't care much for judges, but we can't just have somebody going around killing them."

"And?" Leon said.

"I want you to help me find whoever's responsible. I know you don't have any jurisdiction outside of the fact that my client lives in Washington County so we might step on some toes along the way, but who cares? We haven't worried too much about doing things the conventional way."

Leon drained his coffee and gave me a long look. His mouth was set, but his eyes were twinkling.

"You're crazy, brother Dillard, do you know that?"

"I've been hearing that a lot lately."

"Well, I've been known to indulge in a little insanity myself. Consider it done. Whatever you need."

As we walked up to pay our bill a few minutes later, Leon pointed to a television on the wall behind the cashier. I was on the screen with Rio, threatening the reporters. Leon chuckled.

"Subtlety never has been one of your strengths, brother Dillard," he said. "Give me your check. Breakfast is on me."

# MONDAY, SEPTEMBER 18

I was back at the Unicoi County Jail early the next morning. David Craig had been given the opportunity to take a shower and was now in a striped jumpsuit. He looked ridiculous, but at least he – and the cell – smelled better. He was due to be arraigned in front of the Sessions Court judge in twenty minutes.

Caroline was making arrangements for his brother, Michael, to pay my fee, so as far as I was concerned, I was locked and loaded, ready to fight for this man. When I walked into his cell, the first thing he said to me was, "What are the chances of you smuggling a little alcohol in here for me?"

"Zero," I said.

"C'mon, man, you're supposed to be my lawyer, my friend. You're supposed to be on my side. I really, really, really need a drink."

"Sorry, David, but it isn't going to happen. I'm not risking going to jail, losing my law license, or anything else for that matter, so you can get high. I'm not judging you and I feel badly for you, but just don't ask because I'm not going to do it."

"So what the hell are you doing here?" he snapped. I noticed his right hand, which was hanging loosely near his thigh as he sat on the bed, was trembling.

"You have an arraignment in twenty minutes, and we need to talk some more," I said.

"About what?"

"A lot of lawyers don't do this, but I've decided to just go ahead and ask you some tough questions. Feel free to tell me the truth. Tell me again how that dead judge got into the back of your truck."

"I pulled him out of my freezer and put him there. I couldn't stand the thought of him being in my house."

"So you knew he was in the freezer. And you also knew who he was, right?"

"Yeah, because the guy who killed him told me."

"So this guy killed him, cut him up and bagged him, brought him to your house, put him in the freezer, and told you all about it. Is that right?"

David shook his head slowly. He was sitting on the edge of his concrete bed, staring at the floor.

"It didn't exactly happen that way," he said.

"So how did it happen?"

"The guy who brought him in cut him up in my basement. He made me watch. Said it made me an accomplice or something."

"You need to tell me who this person is."

"I'll never tell you or anybody else who he is! Never!"

The force of his answer surprised me, but I pressed on.

"Why not?" I said. "It'd be your ticket out of this cell. You'd be back at The Saddlebag before you know it."

His head swung up and he stared at me, wide-eyed.

"I wouldn't be back at the Saddlebag," he said. "I'd be cut up and thrown in a hole somewhere is where I'd be."

"So is this a person you've known for a long time?"

"I've known him long enough to know he'd cut my head off and never give it a second thought."

"How did you meet him?"

"I ain't saying. Stop talking about him. Ask me whatever else you want, just don't ask me about him."

"Okay, David," I said, "just calm down."

He was becoming agitated, and I didn't want to lose him. The criminal defense lawyer/client relationship is tough enough when the lawyer and the client get along. When the lawyer becomes the enemy, things go straight downhill.

"I won't talk about him," I said, "but I'd like to talk about the circumstances just a little more. When did he put the freezer in your basement?"

"I'm not sure of the exact date. Not even sure of the month. Less than a year ago, maybe six, eight months."

"So he's been planning this judge thing for a while. Did he tell you he was going to store bodies in the freezer?"

"No, but I knew he was up to something bad."

"Why didn't you just tell him no? Why didn't you refuse to allow him to put the freezer in your basement?"

"I didn't have a choice."

"Does that mean you thought he would kill you if you refused?"

"It means I didn't have a choice."

"So when he brought Justice Bryant into your house, when was that, exactly?"

"It was Thursday night around ten o'clock when he showed up. He said he needed to leave somebody in my freezer for a day or two. He didn't say some*thing*, he said some*body*. Then he told me who it was, why he'd killed him, how he'd killed him, the whole bit. He was almost as high as I was. He was proud of what he'd done. Said he'd killed three other judges already and would probably kill a bunch more before it was over. Then he made me watch him cut up the body."

"Did he say how he killed the judge?" I asked.

"Strangled him with his bare hands. He said that's how he likes to do it. He likes the intimacy of it, he likes watching their eyes almost pop out of their heads while he's choking them. He said he did the same thing to the others."

I hadn't seen the preliminary autopsy report yet, so I had no idea whether the judge had really been strangled.

"Did he leave any of the others with you?"

David shook his head. "This was the first one."

"Did he say why he was leaving him?"

"He said he grabbed the judge up and killed him late Wednesday afternoon and stayed in Nashville Wednesday night. He had him in his van under a tarp, but when he got to Knoxville Thursday morning, the van's transmission started giving him trouble. So he checked into a hotel room, stashed the judge, and took the van to a repair shop. It took them a day and a half to get the parts and get the van fixed. He said he had to be in Asheville in two hours and that the judge was really starting to get ripe. So he dropped him in the freezer after he cut him up with that saw. He said he'd be back Sunday to get him, but I couldn't take it. I had to get the body out of my place."

David's hands were beginning to twitch again and I noticed his jaw tightening involuntarily, so I decided to end the questioning there. We'd have plenty of time to talk in the future.

"Can you hold up through this arraignment?" I said.

"What do I have to do?"

"Nothing. Just walk in and stand at the podium next to me. Expect it to be a zoo. There will be media everywhere. The judge will read the charges, ask how you want to plead, and I'll tell him you're pleading not guilty. He'll ask when we want a preliminary hearing, and I'm going to tell him we want to waive it so we can get this up to Criminal Court as soon as possible so I can challenge the search in front of a judge that matters. If I get the Sessions judge to declare the search illegal, toss all the evidence, and let you out of jail, they'll just indict you in two days and arrest you again. You're going to Criminal Court whether you like it or not so we may as well just waive the preliminary hearing and get on with the case. The county grand jury meets in two days, so we can go ahead and get your indictment over with and get you arraigned in Criminal Court in about two weeks. I'll try to get a motion hearing set a couple of weeks after that and see if we can get you out of here."

"So I'm going to be in here for a month?"

"At least, maybe longer. It just depends on how things go with the judge that gets assigned to your case. If things go badly and we wind up going to trial, you might be in prison for the rest of your life."

# MONDAY, SEPTEMBER 18

I was right about the arraignment. It was a zoo. Sessions Court was always somewhat crowded because so many people managed to get themselves arrested for stupid, petty offenses, but on this day there were reporters and cameras everywhere. The courtroom was completely filled with lawyers, defendants and their families, victims and their families, inmates from the jail, sheriff's deputies and curious gawkers.

The judge was a man named David Stults. Stults was laid-back, in his early fifties. He was tall and lanky with a long, handsome face and bright, blue eyes. He usually wore blue jeans, a white, button-down shirt with no tie, and tennis shoes beneath his black robe. He'd been on the Sessions Court bench in Unicoi County for twenty-five years and by some miracle, had managed not to turn into a complete ass.

When court opened and he strolled up to his seat on the bench, he nodded at me and looked around the room.

"My goodness," the judge said. "Don't think I've ever seen it quite this crowded in here."

The judge's clerk had already told me we would be up first because the judge wanted to get rid of the reporters as quickly as possible, so I was standing at the podium when he walked in. David Craig appeared in a doorway to my left a few seconds later. He was handcuffed, waist-chained, shackled and flanked by four deputies and the sheriff. He shuffled his way toward me and stood next to me at the podium.

Sitting at the prosecution table was Fred Brooks, the assistant who usually handled cases in Unicoi County Sessions Court, and Tanner Jarrett, the First Judicial District Attorney General. Tanner had been an assistant in the D.A.'s office when I was there several years earlier, and he had run for the office on the same day Steve Sherfey, the sheriff, was elected. I'd always liked Tanner, even though it would have been easy not to care for him. He was strikingly handsome, he came from privilege – his father was a wealthy state senator – and he wore bow ties, which I'd always found to be pretentious and silly-looking. But Tanner was bright, reasonable and level-headed. He could evaluate a case at face value, and if the case was weak, he wouldn't necessarily go to the mat with it simply because a police officer had made an arrest. He also knew the law and the rules of evidence, which wasn't always the rule of thumb among elected district attorneys. His office was in the courthouse in Jonesborough, which was roughly fifteen miles away in Washington County, but I wasn't surprised to see him there. He was, after all, an elected official and the top law enforcement officer in four counties. He'd have been crazy to miss out on this public-relations opportunity.

I looked back out over the crowd and was reminded of just how white Unicoi County was. There wasn't a single black face in the courtroom, not even among the reporters. I'd always heard stories that Erwin was a "sundown town," and that a sign saying, "Nigger Never Let the Sun Set on You Here," used to stand at the Erwin city limits, but I'd never seen concrete evidence, like a photograph, for instance. But the fact remained that the black population of Erwin in the twenty-first century numbered less than ten citizens. It wasn't exactly a place known for its diversity.

The town was also infamous for having hanged a five-ton, Asian elephant named Mary in 1916. The elephant was part of a traveling circus, and had been mistreated by an inexperienced trainer in Kingsport a day earlier. She'd become enraged and killed him. The next day, she was taken by rail to the Clinchfield Railroad yard in Erwin and hanged from a railcar-mounted industrial crane. On the first attempt, the chain they were using snapped and the elephant fell to the ground and broke her hip. They finally got it right, though, and managed to hang her in front of more than two thousand spectators, many of them children. They buried her next to the tracks.

I was thinking about the injustice Mary had suffered and the parallels with the circus and this case when the judge suddenly read the case number and I snapped back to the real world. "State of Tennessee versus David Craig, who, I assume, is represented by Mr. Joe Dillard," the judge said. "Is that correct, Mr. Dillard?"

"It is."

"Mr. Craig, you're charged with especially aggravated kidnapping, first-degree murder and abuse of a corpse. Would you like for me to read the incident report?"

"We waive reading the report," I said, "although I'd like the court to make one available for me when we're finished here. The sheriff wouldn't share it with me yesterday."

I looked over at Sherfey and saw his cheeks flush.

"No problem, Mr. Dillard," the judge said. "How does your client plead?"

"Not guilty."

"What about bail? Do you want to address bail, Mr. Dillard?"

"Is there any point?"

"Absolutely none. He had a sitting Supreme Court justice frozen and cut into pieces in the back of the vehicle he was driving. The defendant is ordered held without bail. Do you want me to set a date for a preliminary hearing?"

"We're going to waive the prelim and let them take their case to the grand jury," I said.

"I love it when a lawyer makes my life easy," Judge Stults said. "Mr. Craig, the court will enter your plea of not guilty for the record, and I order you held without bond in the Unicoi County Jail. Your case is bound over to the next session of the Unicoi County Grand Jury, and your next court appearance will be in Criminal Court – right here in this same courtroom in front of a different judge – two weeks from today. Anything else from anyone?"

"No, sir," I said.

"Nothing from the State," Tanner Jarrett said.

Judge Stults smiled. "Alrighty then. Next case."

I turned to the prosecution table and walked up to Tanner.

"Can I talk to you in private for a few minutes?" I said.

"Sure," he said. "We can use the judges' office."

When we got into the small office that was used by the Criminal Court judges when they were in town, we shook hands and engaged in a little small talk. Tanner took a seat behind the desk and I sat across from him.

"What's on your mind?" he said.

"I have a lot of respect for you, so I'm going to give you a heads up," I said. "My guy didn't do this, and your sheriff is going to perjure himself in Criminal Court when we have a hearing. When he does it, I want you to charge him and make an example of him."

Tanner's eyes became larger for a few seconds. He started to speak and then stopped. He laced his fingers on the desk and leaned forward.

"Would you repeat that, please?" he said.

"My client didn't kidnap or kill or cut up or freeze the judge," I said. "Eventually, I'll find out who did it, or at least I'm going to *try* to find out who did it. But in the meantime, I'm going to file a motion to have the case thrown out as soon as we get into Criminal Court. I think I'll win, and I'm sure Sheriff Sherfey is going to get on the witness stand and lie about several things. I plan to prove he's lying during the hearing, and when I do, I want you to make an example of him. I want you to charge him with perjury and prosecute him. I know law enforcement has taken a knock on its reputation lately, but a lot of it is because of guys like Sherfey. He has no business being a sheriff, let alone handling a case this important."

"What do you think he's going to lie about?" Tanner said.

"Pretty much everything that happened from the time they stopped my client until they either finished interrogating him or he passed out."

"What makes you think I won't give the sheriff a heads up about what you're planning?"

"Two things. I think you're a good prosecutor and a good person and once you find out what he's done, you'll want him gone, too. And secondly, you don't know what I'm planning."

"We can't just throw up our hands and quit because you say your client isn't guilty, Joe. This is going to have to play out in court."

"I understand that. You might want to let one of your assistants handle the motion hearing, though, because I'm not sure you want to be out in front of this one. If there's someone in the office you don't like very much, that would be the person I would suggest."

Tanner smiled.

"So it looks like you have someone in mind," I said.

He nodded. "I have just the person."

# FRIDAY, SEPTEMBER 22

Jack Dillard and Charlie Story were sitting at Ruth's Chris steakhouse on West End Avenue in Nashville. It was Friday, the place was packed, and it had been a long week. Their law practice, which was still in its fledgling stage, consisted strictly of criminal defense work. Both of them worked misdemeanors and felonies in both state and federal court. Both of them accepted appointed cases from the various judges in Nashville. Both were young and relatively inexperienced, but neither was afraid to reach out to other lawyers for assistance. They called Jack's father, Joe Dillard, on occasion, but they were reluctant to do so. Part of the reluctance was stubbornness, but part was that they didn't want Joe to know just how little they knew about the practice of criminal defense law. He'd been doing it forever. He was a walking criminal defense encyclopedia. Both of them wanted to be just like him some day.

Jack was in a maudlin mood. They'd finished dinner, and he'd just taken his first sip of the third vodka martini he'd ordered. He usually drank one beer with dinner on Friday. He'd done some heavy drinking a few times in college and in minor league baseball, but he'd never really cared much for drinking. He preferred to face life sober. His mom's illness was weighing heavily on his mind, though, and he knew it was a terrible burden to his dad. He felt guilty about not being home, about not helping his dad care for his mom, and he felt helpless against the disease that had afflicted her for so long. When his mom and dad had visited a week earlier, she had looked so thin, almost emaciated, and although she'd put on a smile and was wearing make-up and a wig that looked perfectly natural, he could see pain in her eyes, and the memory was haunting him. Then his mom and dad had abruptly left Nashville without saying goodbye after she'd received the news that she needed to undergo brain radiation. Jack had always kept his dad's advice in mind when it came to Caroline: "Remember, she's the one who's sick. Not you. Don't feel sorry for yourself." But the thought of her suffering was causing him a fair amount of suffering, too.

He looked across the table at Charlie, so pretty and as tough as his mom. She'd been through plenty of heartache in her young life, but to look at her you'd never know. She soldiered on with an air of optimism and unrelenting forward momentum. She rarely spoke of the past. It was always the future with Charlie, what it might hold, how good it might be. She was Jack's beacon of light in the dark world of the American criminal justice system, and now he was planning to lean on her through this emotional upheaval with his mom's cancer.

Jack lifted his glass toward Charlie, and she lifted her glass of red wine. The glasses clinked, and Jack said, "To courage. To my mom."

"To courage and your mom," Charlie said, and they both turned the glasses up. Jack drank deeply while Charlie sipped. She was almost finished with the only glass she'd ordered that evening.

"I'm driving," she said.

"I know."

The conversation during dinner had been stilted and sporadic, which made Jack feel even worse. It was his fault that the evening had been so dull.

"Jack," Charlie said after the check had been paid and they'd started toward the door. "Will you do something for me?"

"Sure. What is it?"

"Stop beating yourself up. What's going on with your mother isn't your fault. Cancer is as random as a tornado blowing your house away. There's no way to predict, and there's no way to prevent."

"I know," Jack said. "I just feel like I should be there. I feel like I should be helping."

"Then go," Charlie said as they stepped up to the valet station and she handed the ticket to the attendant.

"What do you mean?"

"Go home if it would make you feel better. I can hold the fort down here for a while. Go to Johnson City and stay with your parents. You can help your dad take care of your mom, you can work with your dad if you want. It'll be good for you."

Jack shook his head. "Can't do it," he said. "That would be leaving you in the lurch."

"We're not exactly setting the world on fire here," she said.

"But we have too many cases for one person to handle. You can't be in two places at one time."

The valet attendant pulled up in Jack's Jeep, and Charlie climbed in on the driver's side. She pulled onto West End Avenue and headed for I-40, which was a couple of miles to the north.

"How would you feel about going back there?" Jack said. The vodka was thickening his tongue, and he felt warmness in his throat and stomach.

"To visit?" Charlie said.

"No. I mean moving back there. How would you feel about it? We could practice law with my dad. You practiced law with him for a little while, you know what he's like."

"I love your dad," Charlie said.

"So do I. He's a great teacher. He's patient and he'd get us more work than we could handle. He turns away dozens of cases every year because he's pretty much seen everything at this point and he doesn't need the money. We could take those cases. We could live anywhere you want. We could even go back up to your place on the mountain if you think you'd like that."

Charlie shook her head as she turned onto I-40 heading east. They shared a house in Hermitage with Charlie's dog, Biscuit. Her horse, Sadie, was boarded at a nearby farm.

"I don't think I'm ready to go back to the mountain," she said. "The gold is still up there. It would be calling me like a siren. I know it's blood money like you said it was, but I'd still think about it."

"Then we could find a place close to Johnson City, maybe in Jonesborough. Rent a small farm, maybe, until we get enough money together to buy a place."

"I don't know, Jack," Charlie said as she pulled off at exit 221. She turned north onto Old Hickory Boulevard. "I mean, that area is my home, too, and I'd like to go back someday, I'm just not sure if I—"

Jack saw a bright flash of light to his left and thought he heard a terrible, loud crash. His final thought before he blacked out was of Charlie.

# SATURDAY, SEPTEMBER 23

The man who unintentionally nearly killed my son and his girlfriend was named Clarence Beals. He was fifty-five years old, a life-long smoker, and he had a heart attack while driving along Central Pike at Old Hickory Boulevard in Hermitage. When the heart attack hit Mr. Beals, he accelerated through a red light and T-boned Jack's Jeep on the driver's side.

Jack wound up with a severe concussion, a fractured sternum, a separated right shoulder and two fractured ribs.

It was much worse for Charlie.

Both of her legs were broken, compound fractures of the femurs. She, too, suffered a severe concussion and four broken ribs. She also wound up with a broken nose, a lacerated kidney, a collapsed lung and a ruptured spleen.

When I received the telephone call from Nashville that Jack and Charlie had been in an accident and were in surgery, I called a man who owned a manufacturing company in Greeneville. I'd helped a friend of his out of a sticky situation about a year earlier and I knew he had a Lear jet. I told him about the accident and asked him if he would fly Caroline and me to Nashville. We were in the air within forty-five minutes and we were at TriStar Summit Medical Center two hours after I received the call.

Jack didn't require surgery, but because of the concussion, he was in the ICU ward and was heavily sedated. It was awful seeing my son, who was so strong and so tough, lying in a hospital bed, helpless and drugged, with tubes running into him and monitors all around him. We were only allowed to stay in his room for a few minutes each hour, so we moved to the ICU waiting room until Charlie finally came out of surgery. I'd told one of Jack's nurses that Charlie had no immediate family and that we were as close to her as anyone besides Jack, so when she finally came out of surgery, one of the doctors who had worked on her came into the waiting room to talk with us. He was surprisingly young, early-thirties, with chestnut brown hair that he combed straight back and brown eyes. He said his name was Jackson Wendle, and that he had repaired Charlie's collapsed lung and removed her spleen.

"An orthopedic surgeon set her legs and her nose. There's really nothing we can do for the ribs other than help her manage the pain. When the ribs broke, it didn't do any damage to any of the surrounding organs, but she's going to be in a lot of pain for a while. Same with her legs. Both of her femurs were snapped in half. They'll heal, but they're going to hurt. A neurosurgeon put a drain in her skull to relieve pressure on her brain from the concussion. We don't foresee any problems, but we'll keep a close eye on it. The laceration on her kidney will heal up over time."

"How long is she looking at in terms of recovery?" I asked.

"She's young and fit, so she'll heal fairly quickly, provided there aren't any complications with infection. But we're still looking at a couple of weeks in the hospital, unless the concussion is more serious than we think. The legs will take about a year, maybe more to heal fully and regain their strength."

"Are you telling me she won't be able to walk for a year?"

"She'll be able to use crutches or a walker fairly soon, and then gradually she'll have to relearn walking, especially from a balance standpoint. She'll need a solid physical therapy plan and she'll need to follow it strictly. My best guess is she'll be walking without assistance in about six, seven months, but if you're talking about running or skiing or weight lifting or those sorts of things, she's looking at about twelve to eighteen months."

Caroline and I left the hospital and checked into the Opryland Hotel a little after two in the morning. We collapsed into bed and were back at the hospital five hours later. Jack, to my surprise, was awake. When he saw us walk in, tears filled his eyes.

"It was my fault," he said.

Caroline sat down beside him and started stroking his forehead. I walked to the other side of the bed and took his hand in mine.

"Why would you say a thing like that?" Caroline said. "You weren't even driving."

"We went out to dinner and I was feeling sorry for myself and drank too much," he said. "If I hadn't done it, I would have been driving."

He turned his head and looked up at me pitifully.

"How bad is she, Dad?" he said. "The nurses won't tell me."

"She's right down the hall. She's going to be fine," I said.

"But how badly is she hurt?"

"She took a pretty good lick, Jack. She has some pretty serious injuries, but the surgeons took good care of her and she's going to be all right. It's just going to take a little while for her to heal up."

"How long?"

"It doesn't matter. We're here for her. You'll be here for her. We'll get through it together. And I don't want to hear any more talk about it being your fault. The nurses say the man who hit you T-boned you at a red light, he didn't have any serious injuries, and he's dead. That tells me he may have had a medical problem, which means this was just a random occurrence. Bad luck. I'm going to run down a police report and talk to a few more people this morning, but I'll bet you that's what happened. Nothing anyone could have done to change it. It was nobody's fault."

He'd calmed down considerably by that point. I think the simple fact that his mom and dad had showed up so quickly and were there for him helped put him at ease. And the guilt he was feeling? I'd been there, done that with Caroline so many times I understood it completely. He was my son, and I wouldn't allow him to torture himself for something that simply wasn't his fault. I knew it would take some time, but I'd keep working on him. I knew which buttons worked with Jack, at least most of the time. Sometimes he reminded me of me and was totally unpredictable, but for the most part, I'd always been able to reason with him.

A thought struck me and I actually almost smiled. Maybe we could make the best of this near-tragedy.

"Jack, let me ask you something," I said. "Caroline is about to go through this radiation thing and from what they've told us, she's probably going to be pretty much flat on her back for a few weeks, maybe a couple of months. Charlie is going to need a lot of attention, too. What would you think of maybe just packing it up and moving in with us? We'll transport Charlie in an ambulance when they're ready to release her. We'll turn the house into a triage center. I'll get Sarah and Lilly to help and even Randy when he can. Can you give up your practice here without causing a huge stir?"

"It's funny," he said, staring up at the ceiling. "Charlie and I were talking at the restaurant last night about moving back and maybe trying to get you to practice law with us."

"So you might consider it?" I said. I looked across at Caroline, who was looking back at me with a gleam in her eye.

"We'll talk about it some more as soon as she's able," Jack said, "but as far as I'm concerned, I'm ready. I think it's time to go home."

# MONDAY, SEPTEMBER 25

Judge Norman Watson enjoyed walking his dog, a cockapoo named Cracker Jack, from precisely 7:00 a.m. until 7:30 a.m. each morning before he went to work, weather permitting. Watson lived in a nice home in a private, sparsely-populated neighborhood near the Redtail Mountain Golf Club just outside of Mountain City, Tennessee. He rarely saw a vehicle during his morning walk. He left his driveway, went to the end of the road, walked around the cul de sac, and returned to his house.

Watson was the General Sessions Court Judge for Johnson County, a rugged, beautiful, mountainous area located at the Northeast tip of Tennessee. Watson was a jovial, chubby fifty-year-old who enjoyed fine wine and travel and had been elected to the judgeship fifteen years earlier after practicing primarily divorce law for ten years in Mountain City. He had graduated from East Tennessee State University, where he was a decent, but not exceptional, student who majored in political science and minored in history. He had attended law school at Liberty University in Lynchburg, Virginia, which was one of the worst law schools in the United States according to the U.S. News and World Report rankings, and had finished near the bottom of his class. He failed the Tennessee bar exam twice.

Watson now presided over civil, criminal and juvenile cases. His base salary was just over seventy thousand dollars a year, and he received an extra sixty-five hundred a year for handling juvenile cases. He was married, had a twenty-six-year-old son who lived in Cincinnati and a twenty-five-year-old daughter who was married and lived in Atlanta. His daughter had borne his first grandchild, a girl, just six months earlier.

The judge had been accepting bribes in misdemeanor cases, especially driving under the influence cases, to supplement his salary for almost ten years. His fee to fix a D.U.I. case was $5,000, which was half of what a D.U.I. conviction would cost a defendant in Tennessee.

These were the basic facts about the judge. Some of them had been told to the man who was about to kill him, and others had been learned through close, careful surveillance. Not that the killer really cared about the judge's moral and legal transgressions, and he certainly didn't care about the man's family. He simply enjoyed killing people, and he enjoyed doing it with his bare hands. He enjoyed watching them cry and snivel and he enjoyed listening to them beg. He took great pleasure when they wet themselves while they were praying to God for mercy, and he took even greater pleasure in the final smell of defecation after they'd drawn their last breath.

The morning was bright and a bit breezy. There was a nice chill in the mountain air as the man in the van turned onto Redtail Road at 6:55 a.m. He passed by

Watson's house, drove to the end of the road, and parked the white van in the cul de sac. At approximately 7:15, he saw Judge Watson and his unleashed dog top a small rise about fifty yards in front of him. He put the van in drive and pulled out slowly. There wasn't a soul in sight. As he came closer, the judge moved to the other side of the road, as did his dog. The killer pulled alongside the judge, stopped, and rolled down his window.

"Good morning," he said pleasantly. "I've managed to get myself lost. Can you tell me how to get to Jake Wardner Road?"

The judge approached the van, smiling.

"You're not too far," he said. "All you have to do is—"

The killer threw his weight against the door as he opened it. It hit the judge in the face with a loud smack and knocked him to the ground. Cracker Jack scurried away. The killer, who was a huge, solidly-built man, slid the side door of the van open quickly, reached down and grabbed Judge Watson by the front of his shirt and by his belt. He picked him up off the ground and tossed him into the van onto his stomach. He hopped onto the judge's back and quickly restrained the judge's hands and ankles with plastic restraints that were already in the van. He tied a bandana tightly around Judge Watson's mouth to gag him. He removed a previously prepared syringe with a small dose of Brevital Sodium from the van's console and injected the drug into the judge's right hip. Then he climbed over the seat, put the van in gear, and drove slowly away.

# WEDNESDAY, SEPTEMBER 27

Leon Bates pulled his cruiser into the parking lot beside the Highland Church of Christ, just off Highland Church Road in Washington County, and waited. It wasn't unusual for police vehicles to park in the lot. Sheriff's deputies parked there often to fill out paperwork, and even Johnson City officers used the lot, since the city had annexed the nearby, upscale Garland Farm Estates neighborhood a decade earlier in order to collect more tax revenue. The area was definitely rural and should have remained in the county, but the city grabbed it up anyway, which meant they had to provide fire and police protection, water, sewer and trash collection. Leon had heard several officers complain about having to drive all the way out to the Garland Farm neighborhood, especially since virtually zero crime occurred there, but when they complained, Leon always shook his head and said, "Take it up with one of the pinheads on your city commission."

Less than five minutes after Leon pulled in, a blue Hyundai Elantra pulled in next to him. The driver was a young man, lean and fit, with brown hair cut closely to his scalp and brown eyes. It hadn't taken Leon much effort to get in touch with Jason Whitson, the Unicoi County deputy who had arrested Joe Dillard's client, David Craig. Leon knew everybody in law enforcement, and he knew a great many people outside of law enforcement. He had made a few discreet inquiries, obtained Whitson's cell phone number, and had given him a call. He'd had no difficulty getting Whitson to agree to meet him. Leon waved his hand, and Whitson exited his car and climbed into the passenger side of Leon's cruiser. Leon extended his right hand.

"Leon Bates," he said.

Whitson shook the hand and said, "Jason Whitson."

"Care to go for a little ride?" Leon asked.

"Sure, why not?"

Leon put the car in drive and headed for Shadden Road, which led out to Gray Station. He planned to take a drive through the country, away from prying eyes.

"So I hear you were a marine," Leon said, "so was I back when I could still bend over without sounding like a bowl of Rice Krispies. The ol' snap, crackle, pop, you know? I don't care what anyone tells you, there ain't nothing good about getting old. I'd trade the wisdom for strength, flexibility, libido and stupidity any day of the week."

Whitson gave him a nervous smile.

"You have an awesome reputation," Whitson said. "Everybody in law enforcement talks about you like you're Clint Eastwood or something."

"I like to think I'm a mixture of Dirty Harry and Ronald Reagan," Leon said. "Clean cut but a bad dude if you mess with me."

"That's not a bad way to be," Whitson said.

"I suppose it isn't. You're from Unicoi County, am I right?"

"Yes, sir. Born up on Tiger Creek. Went to elementary school there, then went into the county school system."

"Pretty good football player from what I hear."

"I did all right. Got a couple of offers from small schools, but I wanted to serve. Both my granddaddy and my daddy were marines, so I thought I should carry on the tradition."

"Well, I thank you for serving," Leon said. "You were in Afghanistan, right?"

Whitson nodded. "Twelve months. You sure know a lot about me, sheriff."

"I have good reasons to know a lot about you. One of the things I've found out about you is that you're a fine young man. You work hard, you're a Christian, you try to do the right thing, you're going to school part-time to finish up your college work, you're engaged to a nice, pretty young lady named Susan Dykes and you hope to raise children one day. How am I doing?"

"You're doing fine, but you're making me wonder why you know all of this."

Leon slowed the car and turned to face Whitson.

"Because I'd hate to see you throw all of it away because of an idiot."

"Idiot? I'm not sure I understand."

"I'm talking about your sheriff. I'm talking about David Craig. I'm talking about committing perjury in a court of law and throwing your entire career away because your sheriff is an egotistical idiot."

Whitson was silent for a full minute. Finally, he said, "I'm not sure what you're—"

"I didn't know anything until Joe Dillard came to see me," Leon interrupted. "It was after he'd been to see his client over at the jail. He also talked to your boss. You see, Dillard and I have been close friends for a long time. Real close. We've been in some sticky situations together, and there isn't anybody I'd rather count on in a pinch than ol' brother Dillard. He's the kind of guy you'd want in your foxhole with the enemy closing. He's razor sharp – doesn't miss a thing – and he isn't afraid of the devil himself. Now, listen to me. Brother Dillard knows what your sheriff did. He didn't see him do it, he didn't hear him do it, but he knows, all right? He knows. He knows Sherfey put you up to changing your incident report the night you arrested David Craig and he knows Sheriff Sherfey is going to pressure you to commit perjury when you testify in court next week. He knows David Craig was drunk when you arrested him and he knows he was drunk when Sherfey and that wood cutter interrogated him."

Whitson shook his head. "I really shouldn't be talking to you about any of this," he said.

"You're wrong," Leon said. "I'm exactly the person you should be talking to. Because if you do the right thing, I'm going to take care of you. If you go into court and tell the truth, you and I both know that not only will Sherfey fire you, he'll come after you with guns blazing. He'll try to have you arrested for perjury, and he'll try to ruin your name in the law enforcement community. He'll try to fix it so that you can never work as a cop anywhere, ever."

"Damn straight he will. He'll ruin me and everything I've worked for."

"Unless..." Leon said, "...unless you have a friend who's willing to help. A powerful friend. A friend who has been around for a long, long time and has an excellent reputation. A friend who will take you under his wing, give you a better job, and set you up in a program that will help pay for your college expenses while you're working. We have a program like that for our employees at the Washington County Sheriff's Department. Paid for it with money we've seized from drug dealers over the years."

"Are you offering me a job, sheriff?"

"Depends. Are you willing to tell the truth in court?"

Whitson took in a long breath and released it slowly.

"To hell with Sherfey," he said. "Tell me what you need me to do."

"I already did. Just tell the truth."

# TUESDAY, OCTOBER 10

Caroline went through her radiation treatments, and the doctor was right. She began sleeping sixteen to eighteen hours a day, and when she was awake, she was like a zombie. She was also in a tremendous amount of pain. It was difficult for all of us to watch her suffer, but she simply gritted her teeth and took it.

And then we almost lost her to the third leading cause of death in the United States. Medical mistake.

I sat down on the edge of the bed next to my wife at six-thirty on a Thursday morning and gently pushed her shoulder. Her eyes opened slowly, but I could tell they weren't focused.

"Caroline?" I said.

She finally looked at me without recognition.

"What's your name, baby?"

A blank stare.

"Do you know who I am?"

Same result.

"Can you talk, Caroline? Say 'yes' if you can talk."

Her eyes rolled and she murmured, "Yes."

"Okay," I said. "We're going to the emergency room."

It had started the previous Friday, when I took her to the Regional Cancer Center for her weekly chemotherapy treatment. They'd taken a urine sample and told her she had a urinary tract infection, something that was becoming more and more frequent. Several months prior, a tumor had developed on her tailbone. That tumor began pressing on a nerve that caused her to lose feeling in her sexual organs and become incontinent. The doctors eventually radiated the tumor, some of the feeling came back, the incontinence went away, but she was left having to insert a catheter into her bladder each night before she went to bed in order to fully empty the bladder. Caroline apparently didn't take all of the precautions necessary for complete sterility of the catheterizations – primarily because she did them at bedtime after a day full of heavy pain medication – and as a result, the infections kept popping up. When they did, she became what I called "loopy." She said and did strange things. She asked me once if my clients were paying me in pirate gold.

The doctors had prescribed antibiotics on Friday for the infection, and I'd make sure she'd taken them. But she would have no part of me being in the bathroom while she did the caths, and who could blame her? Besides, to be honest, I didn't want to be in there. As the week progressed, I noticed her "loopiness" wasn't really improving. I also noticed on Monday night that there didn't seem to be as many used catheters in the wastebasket as there should be.

I went into Charlie's room and awakened Jack. I told him I was taking Caroline to the emergency room at the

Johnson City Medical Center and that I'd be in touch. Then I packed a bag because I knew they'd admit her and I drove her to the hospital.

Seven hours later, she was finally settled into a room. Intravenous antibiotics were flowing, intravenous fluids were flowing, and pain medication was flowing. Her face had regained its color and she had come back to her senses, at least a little. She knew her name and my name and where she was, but she didn't know the date, she didn't know who the president was, she couldn't tell me the name of our grandchild, Joseph.

On the second day, the oncologists ordered a brain MRI, which made me nervous. Caroline's brain MRIs were always done in Nashville at Vanderbilt. She'd had only one in Johnson City, and that was more than a year earlier. On the third day, which was Thursday, an oncologist from the group of oncology doctors who treated her in Johnson City came in. I was there, Randy and Lilly were there, and Jack was there. It was about eleven in the morning. The oncologist was relatively young, probably mid-thirties. He was about five-nine with dark hair and a dark complexion, wearing the white coat of a doctor. I knew from dealing with him in the past that he was originally from Palestine. His name was Hasan Sirhan.

"So," he said in a thick middle-Eastern accent, "I'm afraid this doesn't look good."

"What doesn't look good?" I said.

"We're aware, of course, of the activity of the cancer around the brain," he said. "We compared the MRI results with the results from a year ago, and there has been some fairly significant progress of the disease around her brain."

"Wouldn't you expect that?" I said. "It was progressing. That's why they just did the whole brain radiation, to stop it."

"The urine culture that was done in the emergency room came back clean. No infection. So that leads us to believe that her symptoms are being caused by cancer growing in her brain. It's quite possible that the cancer was too far along for the radiation to have done any good."

"What are you saying?" I said. "Are there any options?"

"We could try to drill through the skull and get some chemotherapy drugs directly to the tumor in the brain, but I'm afraid it wouldn't be effective. At this point, I would recommend that you stop all of her treatments. We'll put you in touch with Hospice and you can take her home and make her comfortable."

I looked around the room at my family and looked over at Caroline, who was hearing this but not comprehending what the doctor was saying. I felt tears begin to burn my eyes.

"So this is it?" I said. "It's over?"

"I'm sorry," Dr. Sirhan said. "I'm truly sorry."

I was numb for a second. I felt as though my knees might give out and I'd wind up on the floor sobbing. But something inside of me refused to accept what this man was saying.

"I want to bring the Vanderbilt doctors in on this," I said. "They've been treating her for four years, and they're the ones that write the orders. Can you send the MRI to Dr. Stoots at Vanderbilt and let him look at it? He just did an MRI last month. He can compare yours to the one he just did. Let's find out what he has to say."

"I suppose we could do that," Dr. Sirhan said, "but I'm afraid it will just be delaying the inevitable."

"Delaying the inevitable is just fine with me," I said. "The longer we can delay it, the better."

So they did what I asked. The oncologists sent a disc of Caroline's Johnson City brain MRI to Dr. Stoots by overnight, express mail. Three agonizing days later, he called them and asked where it was. He'd been expecting it, and it hadn't arrived. Eventually a secretary in his office found it beneath a stack of papers. He looked at the MRI, called Dr. Sirhan, and said, "I don't see any change. Do a spinal tap. If there are cancer cells in the meningeal fluid, we have a serious problem. If there aren't any cancer cells, someone has made a serious blunder."

I don't know why Dr. Sirhan didn't have enough sense to order the spinal tap immediately to confirm his suspicions. Randy, Lilly's husband and a medical student, had mentioned it as soon as he heard what Sirhan said.

They did the spinal tap that night. It took five days to get the results.

No cancer cells in the meningeal fluid. Most likely Caroline's delirium was caused by a urinary tract infection coupled with dehydration.

I called Dr. Sirhan and told him that before he ever told a family again that their wife and mother and grandmother was dying, he needed to be absolutely certain.

Then I told him in the future, to stay the hell away from my wife. I told him if I ever saw him within a hundred feet of her, I'd break every bone in his body.

And I meant it.

# MONDAY, OCTOBER 29

Time passed, as it always does. Jack shut down the law office that he and Charlie ran in Nashville and spent every hour possible with her until they brought her back to Johnson City in an ambulance. We had to go through some logistical challenges – getting their cases transferred to other lawyers, getting their vehicles and possessions from Nashville to Johnson City, getting Charlie's horse, Sadie, transported, and getting her massive Irish wolfhound, Biscuit, settled in. He and Rio were both alphas, although they had both been neutered, and I worried that there might be problems. But both dogs seemed to sense their masters were having problems and they needed to behave, and there wasn't a single fight. Besides, Caroline's teacup poodle, Chico, ruled the roost. The first thing Chico did when Biscuit walked into the house was to start jumping up and nipping at his ears. Biscuit did his best to ignore it.

I had a small barn built near my outbuilding and had the construction guys paint it red, and then I had a three-rail, white, vinyl fence installed around two acres near the barn so Sadie would have a pasture. It was fairly expensive, but it was quaint, almost elegant, and the look on Charlie's face when she saw it made it worth every penny.

Charlie was getting stronger every day, although I could see frustration and pain in her eyes when she attempted to get up and move around. The surgeons had used metal plates and screws to repair the breaks in her legs, and I'd been surprised that they'd encouraged her to put weight on them as soon as possible after the surgery. Jack said she was walking up and down the hall at the hospital with the aid of a walker a week after the accident. We had turned our dining room, which we rarely used, into a bedroom for her, primarily because it was on the main floor. Jack slept on a couch in her room most nights. Occasionally he would go downstairs to his old room and crash for a few hours. Lilly and her husband, Randy, and their son, Joseph, stopped by every day and helped out any way they could, and even my sister, Sarah, and her daughter, Grace, were stopping by to see if there was anything they could do. It was good to have the help, because I was neck deep into preparing for David Craig's hearing. It hadn't hurt my case that another judge, a Sessions Court judge in Mountain City named Watson who I'd always heard would fix a case if the money was right, had gone missing.

Jack couldn't play nurse full-time – and Charlie didn't want him to – so he was able to help me research the law I needed to make my arguments that the search conducted by Deputy Whitson violated both the Tennessee and United States Constitutions and was, therefore, illegal. My written motions argued that any evidence gathered as a result of the search was inadmissible, and that David

Craig should go free. Everything I filed was immediately seized upon by the media and reported. The prosecution was not required by the local judges to respond in writing, which was something that had annoyed me for two decades. If I had to file written motions and back them up with memorandums of law, the prosecution should have to do the same. But the prosecution had always argued that their case load was simply too large to allow them to file written responses to defense motions, and the judges had always agreed. The judges wound up doing their own research on the legal issues – which wasn't necessarily a bad thing – but in essence, the judges did the prosecution's work, which, in my mind, made them an advocate for the State.

Six weeks of sobriety and not being able to smoke had done wonders for David Craig, both physically and mentally. He looked, spoke and acted like an entirely different person than the one I'd met in the dingy cell at the Unicoi County Jail. It was like watching a person age backward, like he was drinking from the fountain of youth. His withdrawal from alcohol had been terrible. I'd driven over to Erwin to check on him almost every day to make sure the sheriff and his staff were taking care of him, and during the first week, he could barely speak. He went through bouts of nausea, fever, chills, anxiety, and he had delusions. The nurses on staff at the jail, both men and both prickly, were entirely unsympathetic. They did just enough to keep themselves, and the jail, from getting sued. I was convinced that had I not stayed on top of them, they very may well have let David Craig die in that cell.

When the date for the hearing finally arrived, Jack and I drove over to the Unicoi County Courthouse. I had subpoenaed Gene Collins, the owner of The Saddlebag bar, Jerry Conerly, who had sold David Craig the liquor the night he was arrested, Sheriff Sherfey, Chief Deputy Buck Garland and Deputy Jason Whitson, just in case Sherfey tried to tell Whitson to stay away. We'd drawn Judge Gwen Neese, whom I'd known for many years as a lawyer. I had one particularly vivid memory of her at a Christmas party twenty years earlier. I was standing less than ten feet from her with a few other men. She was a "frosty blonde," which is what they called highlights back in those days, and she was an attractive, voluptuous woman who happened to be monumentally intoxicated that evening. At one point one of the male lawyers said something to her that caused her to lift her red sweater above her substantial breasts (she was wearing a sheer, red bra beneath the sweater) and she said, "Eat your hearts out, gents. All this and brains to boot." I liked her even more after that. I hadn't been in her court since she'd been elected judge, but I'd heard good things about the way she handled herself, her docket and the people who appeared before her.

David Craig came in flanked by four deputies. He was shackled, waist-chained and handcuffed, and the first thing I did was ask Judge Neese if she would order the deputies to remove his cuffs. To my surprise, she granted the request. Craig whispered into my ear, "I need a pen and a piece of paper." I slid a legal pad in front of him and handed him a pen. He turned away and wrote something down, then turned back to me.

"I want you to promise me you won't read this unless something happens to me," he said. "Do you give me your word?"

I nodded, and he handed me a folded piece of yellow paper.

"Seal it up in an envelope. If I get out of this and something happens to me, open it up and read it."

"If you're sure that's what you want," I said.

"That's what I want."

I stuck the paper in my briefcase and looked around the room. The place was packed again, standing room only, as Judge Neese had her clerk call the case. Sitting at the prosecution table was a red-faced, overweight, balding man named Paul Carpenter. Carpenter was a surly, hard-drinking, bitter waste of human flesh who had been banished to the far reaches of the district in Johnson County. He'd been a career prosecutor – he was there when I worked in the D.A.'s office. People complained constantly about his attitude and his demeanor, but I knew his teenage son had committed suicide two years before I became the D.A. and he had two other children, so I couldn't bring myself to fire him. For some reason in the ensuing years, Carpenter came to believe he should be either a judge or the district attorney. He'd run for both Sessions and Criminal Court judgeships and had been soundly defeated. He'd also run against Tanner Jarrett in the election for district attorney general, and Tanner had thrashed him. Tanner hadn't fired him, though, which I thought said a lot about Tanner. Tanner was, however, about to make Carpenter a sacrificial lamb by feeding him to a wolf, and that wolf was me.

The motion I'd filed was vague enough that Sherfey would have no idea what I was about to do, but it alleged enough factual disputes that the judge granted an evidentiary hearing. The two primary focuses of the motion were the suppression of evidence due to what I said was an illegal, warrantless search of the containers in the back of David Craig's vehicle and the suppression of any statements Craig may have made to any law enforcement officer due to his level of intoxication the night he was arrested.

"I ask for the rule, your Honor," I said.

Rule 615 of the Tennessee Rules of Criminal Procedure allowed me to ask the judge to exclude witnesses from hearing the testimony of other witnesses. Since Sheriff Sherfey was the primary law enforcement officer in Unicoi County and it was his case, he could testify and sit at the prosecution table, but Buck Garland and Jason Whitson had to stay outside. I had no way of controlling who Paul Carpenter would call first, but I was hoping Sherfey's ego would have caused him to insist on being the first witness.

"Anyone who is going to testify in this matter will have to wait out in the hall with the exception of the primary parties," the judge said. "Mr. Carpenter, call your first witness."

"Call Sheriff Steve Sherfey," Carpenter said, and I breathed a sigh of relief.

Sherfey took the oath, gave his name and experience, and then he and Carpenter got down to business.

"Sheriff, on the night and early morning of September fifteenth and sixteenth of this year, did you come into contact with the defendant, David Craig?"

"I did," Sherfey said. "He was arrested up at the Beauty Spot by Deputy Jason Whitson for first-degree murder and abuse of a corpse after Deputy Whitson found the body of Supreme Court Justice Fletcher Bryant in containers in the back of David Craig's pickup truck. I interrogated him along with my chief deputy, Buck Garland, at the sheriff's department headquarters about an hour after his arrest."

"And prior to your interrogation of Mr. Craig, did you advise him of his Miranda rights?"

"I did."

"Did he sign a waiver of those rights?"

"He did."

"May I approach the witness, your Honor?" Carpenter said as he held up a piece of paper.

"You may."

"Is this the original of that waiver?"

"It is," Sherfey said. "It's signed and dated. That's his signature right there."

Carpenter asked the judge to admit the waiver as evidence and the judge granted the request.

"And did Mr. Craig appear to understand that by agreeing to speak with you without a lawyer present, that anything he said could be used against him later?" Carpenter said.

"He understood perfectly," the sheriff said. "He knew exactly what he was doing. He wanted to co-operate."

"Did Mr. Craig appear competent to be questioned? Was there anything wrong with him?"

"Nothing that I noticed."

"Was he drunk?"

"He didn't appear to be. He wasn't slurring words, his eyes weren't red. He appeared normal, perfectly rational, and I didn't smell any alcohol on him."

Sherfey, the most powerful law enforcement officer in Unicoi County next to the district attorney, was lying through his teeth. I was seething at the defense table. It was all I could do to keep from doing what I'd done to that football player with the man bun. I wanted to pull him off the witness stand and punch him in the face.

"Did Mr. Craig make any statements during your interrogation that were against his own interest?"

"He said several things. He said he'd killed Judge Bryant because Judge Bryant had written an opinion that let a sex offender out of prison. I said something about it being a vigilante killing, and he said it was a protection killing. Those were his exact words. He said he'd done it before, and that he'd do it again. He said the judge lived in a fine home in the Bel Meade neighborhood in Nashville, which turned out to be true. He said he'd never killed anyone that didn't deserve killing. He said he was taking the body to an old, exploratory mine shaft across the North Carolina border. He said he'd killed four judges and several other people."

"Sheriff Sherfey, do you know how it happened that Deputy Whitson first came upon Mr. Craig?"

Carpenter was about to get into hearsay evidence. Whitson was available and I could have objected, but I kept my mouth shut. If he wanted more rope with which to hang himself, I was more than willing to give it to him.

"I wasn't there, but from the report Deputy Whitson filed, Mr. Craig had a taillight and a headlight out. He came upon him not far from the Beauty Spot, where he was going as part of his routine patrol route. He stopped Mr. Craig and when he walked up to the window, Mr. Craig seemed extremely nervous. He was sweating, even. Deputy Whitson asked him a few questions and then asked him what was in the containers in the back of the truck – he had two plastic containers bound with black electrical tape in the bed of the truck along with a bag of lime – and Mr. Craig just blurted out that there was a body in there and that he was real sorry, that he didn't mean to do it. So Deputy Whitson asked if he could open one of the containers and Mr. Craig told him to go ahead. And inside the containers was the frozen, dismembered body of Judge Bryant. Deputy Whitson made the arrest and called it in."

When Carpenter was finished with the sheriff, I stood up and said, "Just to be clear, your sworn testimony is that Mr. Craig was as sober as a judge, is that right?"

"I don't think that's funny, Mr. Dillard," Sherfey said, "but yes, he was stone cold sober."

"Did he sign a confession or a statement of any kind?"

"No. He wouldn't sign anything but the Miranda waiver."

"Isn't it a common practice for law enforcement officers to videotape interviews with suspects, especially people suspected of violent crimes?"

"We didn't video the conversation."

"But isn't it a common practice? It keeps people from questioning what may or may not have been said or what may or may not have happened. It protects the police from false accusations of coercion and abuse, things like that."

"It may be common practice in some places, but the FBI doesn't do it and neither does the Unicoi County Sheriff's Department."

"And there is no video of Deputy Whitson's stop and the conversation he had with Mr. Craig, correct?"

"Deputy Whitson's video camera wasn't working that day."

"Mighty convenient for you. Sheriff Sherfey, did you order Deputy Whitson to change his incident report completely after you bungled the interrogation of an extremely intoxicated suspect, specifically my client, David Craig?"

"Are you accusing me of a crime, Mr. Dillard?"

"Absolutely. Answer the question."

"I didn't order Deputy Whitson to do anything. He came in, he wrote his report, and he filed it."

"Isn't it true that Deputy Whitson initially stopped Mr. Craig for suspicion of driving under the influence, and that he arrested him for that offense?"

"I don't know where you get your information, Mr. Dillard, but whoever is filling your head with such ideas is playing you for a fool."

"I guess we'll see about that, won't we? Does your department have a vehicle-impound policy, Sheriff Sherfey?"

"Of course we do."

"Was it followed in this case? Is there paperwork?"

"I assume there is. Deputy Whitson would have filled out the paperwork and filed it."

"But you haven't seen it?"

"No."

"Because you're on top of this case, correct?"

"Objection," Carpenter said. "Argumentative."

"Sustained," Judge Neese said. "We can do without the sarcasm, Mr. Dillard."

"No more questions," I said, and Sherfey stepped down from the witness stand and stalked over to the prosecution table, staring at me every step of the way. I smiled at him and winked.

Carpenter called Buck Garland next and went through the same questions he'd gone through with Sherfey. He got the same answers. They were so close to Sherfey's it was obvious to me they'd been rehearsing. On cross-examination, I did the same thing, with one exception.

"Chief Deputy Garland," I said, "are you aware of the penalty for aggravated perjury in the state of Tennessee?

"What?" Garland said.

"Do you know the penalty for the offense of aggravated perjury in Tennessee? Do you know whether it's a felony or a misdemeanor? Do you know the elements of the offense?"

"Objection," Paul Carpenter said. "I don't see the relevance of the question."

"I was just wondering if Mr. Carpenter's witness knows he just committed a Class D felony, punishable by two to twelve years in prison and a five-thousand-dollar fine," I said to the judge.

"If he didn't, you just informed him," Judge Neese said. "You're making some serious allegations, Mr. Dillard. I hope you have something to back them up.

If you don't, you're looking at a contempt charge and a hearing before the ethics board."

"We're not finished, your Honor," I said, "but that's all I have for this witness."

"Mr. Dillard may not be finished with this charade, but we are," Carpenter said. "The State rests."

I knew it. I knew they'd try to keep Jason Whitson off of the witness stand, fearful that his youth and inexperience – and perhaps his honesty – would expose their lies. That was exactly why I'd subpoenaed him.

"Any witnesses, Mr. Dillard? Is your client going to testify?"

"I'm not sure about my client yet," I said. "The defense calls Gene Collins."

I questioned Collins about David Craig's drinking habits and whether he'd been to The Saddlebag that day. Then I called Conerly, the liquor store employee, and went through the same routine with him. Carpenter didn't have much in the way of cross-examination.

"The defense calls Unicoi County Sheriff's Deputy Jason Whitson."

I turned and looked at Sherfey. His natural cockiness had turned to uncertainty. His eyes were bulging and he was whispering frantically into Carpenter's ear. I distinctly heard, "He can't do that, can he? He can't call my deputy as a witness!"

Deputy Whitson, wearing his patrol uniform, walked into the courtroom and took the witness stand. I took him through the preliminaries and then asked him: "Deputy Whitson, were you on patrol on the night of September fifteen?"

"I was."

"And do you recognize the defendant, David Craig?"

"I do."

"Would you describe your encounter with him for the court, please?"

"I was driving southeast on Rock Creek Road, not far from Beauty Spot Gap Road, when I came upon Mr. Craig's pickup truck. He was traveling slowly, about ten miles below the speed limit, and he crossed the center line twice within a half-mile. The road is pretty curvy in that stretch, so I decided to give him the benefit of the doubt, but I kept following him. He turned onto Beauty Spot Gap Road and headed up Unaka Mountain. It's kind of tricky right in there, because you actually cross into North Carolina for a little ways and then back into Tennessee before you go back into North Carolina. So when he continued to swerve all over the road, I turned my blue lights on before he got to the parking area at the Beauty Spot, which is just off the Appalachian Trail but is in Tennessee, so I knew I had jurisdiction. He pulled into the lot there, and I called his plate number in for possible warrants. Then I got out of my car and approached Mr. Craig's vehicle."

"Excuse me, Deputy Whitson," I said. "Did Mr. Craig's vehicle have a taillight or headlight out?"

"No, sir. I stopped him because he was swerving all over the road."

"What happened next?"

"I walked up to his vehicle and told him to put his hands on the steering wheel, which he did. Then I asked him if there was something wrong with him, and he said something to the effect of, 'Other than me being hammered?' And I said, 'Hammered? Are you drunk?' And he said, 'Drunker than Cooter Brown.' So I got him out of the car and identified him by looking at his driver's license. I asked him his name and address, and the answers matched his driver's license, but his speech was extremely slurred and he smelled like whiskey. I also saw a bottle of whiskey in plain view on the front seat of his vehicle. I asked him if he had any weapons or needles or anything like that and he said no, so I searched his pockets and found a small amount of marijuana and maybe a half-gram of methamphetamine in a baggie. I asked him to perform some field sobriety tests for me and he refused, then I asked him whether he would take a breathalyzer test for me and he said something off-color so I placed him under arrest for driving under the influence and possession of controlled substances."

"What did you do next?" I said.

"I put him in my patrol vehicle and called the dispatcher to tell the jailers I would be bringing in a DUI suspect. Then I searched the passenger compartment of his pickup incident to arrest, but I didn't find anything. Then I looked at the containers in the bed of his truck. There were two of them, maybe three feet long two feet high. They were beige, wrapped in black electrical tape. There was also a bag of lime next to the containers."

"Deputy Whitson, before you go any farther, let me ask you a question. Is there any reason you couldn't have left the truck there overnight and let Mr. Craig go back and pick it up in the morning? Is that area known as a high-crime area?"

"No, I wouldn't say it's known for crime. A lot of people go through there, hikers and people who picnic up on the bald."

"So you could have locked his truck up and left it there, correct?"

"I suppose I could have, but I wouldn't have wanted to leave those containers sitting out in the open in the bed of the truck."

"But you could have put them in the cab and locked them up, couldn't you?"

"I suppose I could have. It didn't occur to me."

"Does the Unicoi County Sheriff's Department have an impound policy?"

"It does."

"Is there paperwork you need to fill out when you impound a vehicle?"

"We have to write down on an inventory sheet everything that's in the vehicle and list the owner's name and address, administrative things like that."

"Did you fill out any of that paperwork in this case?"

"No, I didn't. Once the containers were removed and taken to the medical examiner, someone must have called one of the local towing companies and had Mr. Craig's truck taken away. Everything happened so fast, and it was so unusual to find a body like that, I didn't even think about it."

"And your sheriff didn't mention the importance of impounding the vehicle properly?"

"No, he didn't say anything."

"Is Mr. Craig's truck still there? At the tow lot?"

"I don't know. I haven't driven over there to look."

SCOTT PRATT

"Do you know whether a forensic team has gone over the truck to see whether there might be evidence that Justice Bryant was in the truck while he was still alive, or that he might have been killed in the truck?"

"Again, I don't know. That information would be a little beyond my pay grade."

"So what exactly caused you to make the decision to open the containers, Deputy Whitson? Did you suspect there was evidence of a crime inside the container? Did you have reason to believe the containers were filled with contraband or anything illegal or dangerous?"

"To be honest, I don't know what made me do it. You can call it a hunch, a gut feeling, one of those clichés, but I just didn't feel right about the containers. It was probably because there was lime in the bed of the truck, too. Something just told me I should look inside."

"And so you took your pocket knife and cut the tape and removed the lid, correct?"

"That's right. I pulled one of the containers out of the bed of the truck and cut the tape with my pocket knife. There were three black, plastic garbage bags inside, and when I picked one of them up, I noticed it was really cold. So I opened the bag, and inside the bag was a severed, human head. Turned out to be Justice Fletcher Bryant."

"What happened next?"

"I called the sheriff on my cell phone and told him what I'd found. He told me to wait until help arrived, and as soon as someone showed up, to bring the suspect into the sheriff's department immediately and that he would handle everything else."

"How long did you have to wait?"

"About twenty minutes. The first person there was an investigator named Blevins who was off-duty that night but lived fairly close. He took charge of the crime scene and I drove Mr. Craig to the sheriff's department. The sheriff and Chief Deputy Garland were waiting for me, and they started interviewing Mr. Craig immediately."

"Was Mr. Craig intoxicated, in your opinion?"

"Extremely intoxicated. I remember thinking they should have waited until he sobered up before they interviewed him. His speech was slurred and he kept dropping his head on the table."

"How long did they talk to Mr. Craig?"

"For about forty-five minutes, maybe an hour, and then he passed out on the table in the interrogation room. We couldn't wake him up, so I helped one of the jailers drag him to the isolation cell."

"Deputy Whitson, I want to show you an incident report that bears your signature. May I approach the witness, your Honor?"

"Go ahead."

I walked up to Whitson and handed him a piece of paper.

"Deputy Whitson, would you describe what I just handed you?"

"It's the second incident report I filed after the sheriff told me to tear up the first one I filed and write it the way he wanted. He said to write that I stopped Mr. Craig because of a taillight and headlight being out and to remove any references to alcohol. He said to write that Mr. Craig was extremely nervous and that he eventually blurted out that there was a body in the containers in response to a question I asked him."

There was a collective gasp in the courtroom, a true Perry Mason moment. I hadn't experienced many of them over my career, and I savored it for a moment. It was a rush.

"You didn't, by any chance, keep a copy of your first report, did you?" I said.

"As a matter of fact, I did."

Whitson reached into his back pocket and produced a folded sheet of paper. He held it up.

"I knew what he was making me do was wrong, so I kept a copy just in case," he said. "I shouldn't have changed the report in the first place. I'm sorry."

"You're fired is what you are, you sorry piece of lying garbage!" Sheriff Sherfey yelled from the prosecution table.

Judge Neese stood at the bench, which was another thing I'd rarely witnessed in my career.

"That's enough!" she said. "I've heard enough! Bailiff! Place Sheriff Sherfey under arrest for contempt of court in the presence of the court. His bond is set at five thousand dollars. Get him out of here. Mr. Carpenter, I trust you'll be indicting Sheriff Sherfey and Chief Deputy Garland for aggravated perjury. I'll be your star witness."

The judge remained standing while Sherfey was handcuffed and led from the courtroom, cursing and muttering the entire time. Once he was gone, she sat down and looked at me.

"Are you finished with this witness, Mr. Dillard?" she said.

"I believe I am, your Honor."

"Mr. Carpenter, please tell me you don't have any questions for Deputy Whitson."

"No questions, judge."

"Good. Mr. Dillard, as for your motion to suppress any evidence found in Mr. Craig's vehicle due to an illegal search, the motion is granted. There is simply no way to justify opening the sealed containers in the back of Mr. Craig's vehicle based on Deputy Whitson's own testimony. A hunch – even one that proves to be prescient – does not provide justification for a warrantless search. Therefore, any evidence found in the container opened by Deputy Whitson, and the other container for that matter, is inadmissible against Mr. Craig. As for Mr. Dillard's motion to suppress any statements Mr. Craig may have made to the sheriff, that motion is also granted. I credit Deputy Whitson and the other witnesses' testimony that Mr. Craig was extremely intoxicated, and I find that any confessions or statements he may have made were not freely or voluntarily given, despite his signature on the Miranda waiver. I find, for the record, that both Sheriff Sherfey and Chief Deputy Garland have knowingly and intentionally lied to this court regarding material facts in an official proceeding, and those, General Carpenter, are the elements of the crime of aggravated perjury. I, for one, find their conduct egregious and will never be able to believe a word either Sheriff Sherfey or his chief deputy says in my courtroom. I will be communicating my concerns to District Attorney General Jarrett as soon as I get back to my office, and I fully expect the sheriff and his chief deputy to be prosecuted to the full extent of the law. Mr. Craig, the case against you is dismissed. Costs are taxed to the State, and you are free to go. If you have anything at the jail, you can pick it up at your convenience. Court is adjourned."

David Craig looked at me like a man who had just been hit by an idea that changed his entire understanding of the world.

"You have clothes at the jail," I said. "Your wallet."

"Will you get them for me?"

"I don't think the jail would be the safest place for me right now. We'll send your brother. Need a ride home?"

"Yes. Would you mind?"

I turned to Jack, who had just witnessed his old man pull off something nearly unheard of. He was looking at me with a mixture of admiration and confusion.

"Jack, do you know where the county clerk's office is downstairs?" I said.

"Yeah, I think so," he said.

"There's a door that leads to a basement that leads to another door that opens onto the street out back. I want you to tell the clerk you're my son and you'd like to use the back door. She'll let you do it. Head for the truck, bring it, and we'll hit the door running. We should be able to avoid dealing with the hyenas that way."

Jack got up and walked out the back of the courtroom. A couple of minutes later, I ushered David Craig out the same door, down a back hall to a set of stairs at the back of the courthouse. We descended the stairs and entered the county clerk's office.

"Hi Gladys," I said, "Can we use the escape hatch?"

"By all means." Gladys looked like Dana Carvey's church lady character on Saturday Night Live. "Your son already used it."

I led David to the door, and we headed out into the late October chill. We jogged up five steps to the sidewalk and ran to the street where Jack was waiting. We piled into the pickup and were gone.

Half an hour later, we'd dropped David Craig off at his small house near Jonesborough. I knew the news vans wouldn't be far behind us. As Jack backed out of his driveway, I opened my briefcase and pulled out the yellow legal paper he had given me. I'd promised I wouldn't look at it unless something happened to him, but I was almost certain something bad was going to happen to him, and I decided to be proactive rather than reactive.

"What are you doing?" Jack said.

"Breaking a promise."

I unfolded the paper and looked at it. Two words were written in the middle of the page.

"Alf Higgins."

# MONDAY, OCTOBER 29

I called Leon Bates, and Jack and I drove immediately to the sheriff's department, which was located at the Justice Center in Jonesborough. Leon's department had grown steadily over the years, which was a tribute to both his ability to schmooze the county commissioners on the finance committee and his bulldog-like attitude toward sellers of narcotics and violent criminals.

"If you sell drugs in this county," Leon had once said to me while describing his vast network of informants, "it won't be long at all before you're selling them to me. And if you sell them to me, I'm gonna take your stuff. I'm gonna seize your car, your house, your land, anything I can get my hands on, and I'm gonna sell it and use the money to make this county a safer place to live."

His department now employed nearly a hundred and fifty people and he managed a budget of close to ten million dollars. It wasn't the NYPD, but it wasn't exactly a Podunk operation, either. Leon was at his desk in his office, surrounded by computer screens. The antique-white walls of the office were freshly-painted – the faint smell of paint still hung in the air – and the room was orderly and spotless. There was some memorabilia on the walls, but nothing ostentatious. I was sure Leon had had his photo taken with every politician from Memphis to Mountain City, but he didn't display them. There were no photos of Leon pointing a gun or making an arrest or flying in a helicopter, nothing from his days in the Marine Corps. Most of the things hanging on the wall were framed certificates from the various law enforcement academies Leon had attended throughout his career.

"I ran that name you gave me through NCIC," Leon said.

"And?" I said as Jack and I took a seat across from him.

Leon looked up for the first time and noticed Jack. His eyes brightened and he smiled.

"Well, if it ain't Jack Dillard, in the flesh," he said as he leaned across the desk and stuck out his hand. "I heard about the accident. Glad to see you're feeling better. How's Miss Story?"

"Getting stronger every day," Jack said.

"And how about your mother? How's she doing?"

"Doing okay, sheriff, thanks for asking."

"So are you going to stay up here and practice law with your daddy?"

Jack looked at me and nodded. "I believe that's the plan," he said.

"Well, you can be assured of one thing," Leon said. "You won't be bored."

"I know," Jack said. "I got a taste this morning."

"How about the NCIC check?" I said.

"Alf Higgins, if he's really our guy and is also known as Alfred Eugene Higgins – and I think he might very well be – he's one mean hombre," Leon said. "He's thirty-seven years old and was just released last year after serving fifteen years for aggravated assault and attempted murder. I don't know how he might be connected to your boy, David Craig. You'll have to ask Craig. Higgins was born and raised in Clarksville, graduated from high school there, and caught his first arrest as an adult at eighteen years old. Hit a kid with a baseball bat and broke his arm. Pleaded guilty to aggravated assault and was placed on probation for six years. Choked a girl half to death a year later, so they violated him and made him serve the six, but since he was a first-timer he only served three and made parole. He wasn't out two months when he got drunk at a pool hall in Clarksville and dang near killed a soldier from the 101st Airborne Division, which is stationed at Fort Campbell right near Clarksville. Beat the guy senseless with a pool cue and then was on top of him trying to choke him to death when three of the guy's buddies stepped in and beat him off. By the time the police got there, he'd gotten a piece of all three of the guys who stepped in. He wound up doing a plea deal for eighteen years and flattened it to fifteen."

"So he isn't on parole? No supervision?"

"He's been on his own since they released him in November of last year."

"And when did the first judge go missing?" I said.

Leon waved a finger. "I knew you'd ask, so I did some digging. The first judge to disappear was Richard Keefauver, a Criminal Court judge in Knoxville. Word around the campfire was that Keefauver was addicted to painkillers and was going light on some of the female defendants who appeared before him in exchange for sex and drugs, although apparently nobody had the courage to put a stop to it. He vanished into thin air in March after he left a trailer park where he'd just finished having sex with a drug offender while her boyfriend watched, and nobody's seen or heard from him since."

"But why would this Higgins guy kill a judge in Knoxville?" I said. "If he was convicted or pleaded in Clarksville, he would have been sentenced by a Clarksville judge."

"Don't know," Leon said. "Figuring out the links between these judges is going to be the key to finding out who's responsible. The next judge that disappeared was Mason Reid in Jackson. He was a Criminal Court judge, too, who got caught masturbating while court was in session. Seemed he did it quite often. Got so bad that the sheriff's department finally stuck a hidden camera under the bench and nabbed him in the act. They didn't kick him off the bench, though. Just sent him to counseling and told him to stop choking his chicken in court."

I couldn't help but smile. Leon had such a way with words.

"He got gone in May. His wife said he left for his weekly poker game at a buddy's house and never came back."

"So we have two perverts who also happened to be judges," I said. "A pattern begins to form."

"I'm not so sure about that," Leon said. "The third judge was Andrea Black, who sits on the Court of Criminal Appeals in Knoxville. From what I've read, the speculation has been that she was killed – if she was killed, we don't know for sure since nobody's seen her since July – because of an opinion she wrote. The court reversed the death penalty sentence of a man who had raped and murdered an elderly woman, but the court ruled that the rape and murder wasn't especially cruel or heinous under the statute and didn't meet the criteria for the death penalty."

"I remember reading that opinion. Pretty liberal interpretation of the statute," I said.

"Maybe our killer's a Republican," Leon said.

"When was she last seen?"

"She lived on a farm near Strawberry Plains and liked to ride horses. She went for a ride on a Sunday afternoon and only the horse came back. She wasn't a pervert, but the case still involved a sex crime, so maybe the pattern holds. Maybe not. Same thing with Justice Bryant. He wrote the opinion that set a sex offender free because the victim committed suicide rather than have to testify at the trial. Again, liberal opinion, involved a sex crime case, but the judge wasn't a pervert. He was last seen by his wife. He had a study in a separate building in the back of their house – similar to a mother-in-law house. His wife said he went out to read some law and vanished."

"And then we have poor, ol' Judge Watson in Mountain City who was taking his dog for a walk and didn't come back. Watson wasn't a pervert, but I've heard for years – and I'm sure you have, too, brother Dillard – that he was on the take. Fix a case for five grand. So there goes the sex crime theory."

My phone started vibrating and I looked down. It was David Craig calling. I excused myself for a second and spoke with him. He was terrified, he said. He was being inundated by media. They were out in the street, hollering over loudspeakers, trying to get him to come outside and talk with them. They were parked up and down the road, causing traffic problems. His neighbors would be furious, he said. I told him to ignore them, and that I'd call him later.

I walked back into Leon's office and apologized. "So we have corrupt judges, perverted judges and liberal judges being killed," I said.

"That seems to be about the size of it," Leon said.

"And the only evidence we have is what David Craig may or may not say about what this Alf Higgins told him or what he may or may not have seen Alf Higgins do."

"Like put a body in his freezer?" Leon said.

"Like put a body in his freezer after he made David watch him cut it up and then tell him in detail how he killed Justice Bryant."

"Reckon he might be willing to talk about that?"

"I don't know. He's terrified of this guy."

"Can't say as I blame him. Why don't you bring him in tomorrow and let me have a little chat with him?"

"I will if I can," I said.

"Why wouldn't you be able to?"

"Because he might not live through the night."

# MONDAY, OCTOBER 29

As soon as I left Leon's office, I called Michael Craig, David's brother. Michael hadn't come to the hearing, which I thought was strange. He told me he had three surgeries scheduled that day and couldn't reschedule them, but after him telling me how close he and David were, I would have thought he would be in court supporting his brother.

"Congratulations," Michael said as soon as he answered. "It's all over the news. You must have done a fantastic job."

"It went my way," I said. "Sometimes it happens, sometimes it doesn't."

"Will the prosecution appeal?" he said.

"They could, but I doubt they will. I think they'll arrest the sheriff and his deputy and prosecute them for perjury."

"Wow, this is straight out of a movie," Michael said.

"Nah, you know what they say. Truth is stranger than fiction. Listen, have you spoken with David?"

"No," Michael said. "I haven't talked with him since the day he was arrested."

"Yeah, he mentioned you hadn't come to visit him."

"I just couldn't make myself do it. The thought of him being caged up like an animal was just too much for me. I didn't want to see him like that."

"Well, you'll barely recognize him. The time off the booze and drugs has made an amazing difference in how he looks and how he feels."

"Good," Michael said. "Excellent. I'm glad to hear that."

"It'd be nice if you'd reach out to him," I said. "He's holed up in his house surrounded by media. They've staked out his place. I'd feel a lot better about him if I knew he was out of there for a few days until things calm down. And there's something else I want to ask you. Have you ever heard of a person named Alf Higgins?"

Michael was silent for several seconds. "Alf Higgins? Where does he fit into this picture?"

"I'm not sure," I said. "Do you know him?"

"I haven't seen him in a couple of decades. Knew him when we were kids. He was our next-door neighbor when my dad was a JAG officer at Fort Campbell in Clarksville. My dad prosecuted soldiers from the 101st Airborne Division when they got out of line."

I nodded, looked at Jack, and winked. A connection. The plot thickened.

"What was your impression of Alf Higgins back in those days?"

"He was a sociopathic bully who was well on his way to becoming a killer. He used to build guillotines in his garage and test them out on cats in the neighborhood."

"So you were afraid of him?"

"Everybody was afraid of him. How did you come up with his name?"

"Your brother wrote it down on a piece of paper before the hearing today and told me if anything happened to him I should take a look at the paper. I decided I didn't want to wait until something happened to David and looked at the paper. Higgins's name was on it. I think Higgins may have killed the judge and put him in a freezer at your brother's house. I think Higgins planned to come back and get the body, but your brother couldn't stand having it in there and took it out himself and was planning to dispose of it when he got stopped and this whole thing started."

"So David thinks Alf will come after him now?"

"Yeah, he does. And so do I. Is there any way you might get over there and sneak him out, get him past the media and get him to a safe hotel or to your place for a few days until we can figure something out?"

"I probably can," Michael said. "I guess I should call him and then wait until dark. We could sneak out the back and through the woods behind his house. There's a road less than a mile away. I don't think it'll be all that difficult."

"Okay," I said. "I'd appreciate it if you'd let me know when you have him."

"Will do."

"And Michael?"

"Yes?"

"Be careful."

# TUESDAY, OCTOBER 30

At nine o'clock the next morning, my cell phone rang. I didn't recognize the number, which was local, but I decided to answer anyway.

"Joe Dillard," I said.

"Congratulations," a cheery voice said. "That one will go down in local legal lore for sure."

"Thanks," I said. "Who is this?"

"You don't recognize the voice of your old buddy Peckwell?"

My heart sank into my stomach. Richard Peckwell, also known in legal circles as Tricky Ricky, Rick Peckerhead, and Rick the dick, chaser of ambulances, chaser of women, advocate of rich divorce clients – preferably female and attractive – scumbag of scumbags, was calling me, and before he said another word, I knew why.

"You're calling about the quarterback," I said. "I hate to be the one to deliver the bad news, but he deserved it."

"He may have, but that doesn't give you the right to beat the hell out of a young boy. He's run up forty thousand in medical bills."

"He's eighteen, so he isn't a minor," I said. "I checked. And I'll bet you've been sending him to chiropractors, am I right?"

"He needed treatment, and you need to pay him. I think he'd be willing to walk away for a hundred thousand."

I laughed. "A hundred grand? Tell you what, if he comes to my wife's dance school and apologizes to my wife, who he intimidated, to my daughter, who he actually shoved and threatened, and the young girl he slapped across the face, I'll give him ten bucks."

"Cute," Peckwell said. "How about this? Either you pay him a hundred thousand dollars by the end of next week or I sue you before I report you to the sheriff's department, the district attorney and the Board of Professional Responsibility."

"The sheriff's department won't be a problem," I said. "For whatever reason, I seem to have some friends there, one in particular. I also have some pretty good friends at the D.A.'s office, so I don't think you'll make much progress there, either. As far as the board goes, what's that Chris Stapleton song? Oh yeah, fire away, counselor. Take your best shot. Those geniuses can't find their butts with both hands."

"I'm going to sue you, Dillard. I'm going to make you suffer for what you did to that kid. I'm going to make you suffer for being a self-righteous bully for the past twenty-five years."

"Self-righteous? Talk about the pot calling the kettle black. Haven't you gotten yourself elected president of the local bar association two or three times? Aren't you the president of the Christian Lawyers Association? Let me ask you this: are you still trading sex for divorces? Still liking those poor, country girls who don't have the money for a lawyer but are so desperate they'll let you stick your tiny pecker in them a couple of times or polish your tiny knob in order to get away from some jerk who's beating the hell out of them or cheating on them? I can think of at least three of them who have come to me over the years complaining about you. Know what I told them to do? File a complaint with the Board of Professional Responsibility. I actually helped all three of them fill out the forms. But you're still chasing ambulances, so what does that tell you about the board?"

"This is just the beginning," Peckwell said, but I noticed his tone had lost some of its bravado. "You're going to pay up, or you're going to suffer."

"Bring it on," I said, and I hung up on him.

Just then, Caroline wandered into the kitchen wearing a bulky, terrycloth robe and a stocking cap. I walked over and kissed her on the cheek.

"Who were you talking to on the phone?" she said. "It sounded kind of contentious."

"Just an old buddy," I said. "How about a hard-boiled egg?"

Caroline sat down at the table and sighed. She looked so tired. Her skin was sagging and her eyes didn't have much life in them at all.

"What's wrong, baby?" I said. "You okay?"

"I'm just in so much pain," she said. "The bones in my arms and legs ache, and my knees are so sore I can barely walk. I'm starting to feel completely useless."

SCOTT PRATT

"The docs said it would take time to recover from the brain radiation," I said. "They said it might be three months before you're feeling semi-normal."

"And then what?" she said. "What does semi-normal mean? It's like you were saying last month, this isn't living. We can't do anything together. *I* can't do anything. You do all the cooking and the cleaning and the laundry and you take me to the doctor and you go to the pharmacy and pick up meds. You give me shots, you rub cold cloths on my neck when I'm puking, you clean up after me. I've turned you into a nurse. It isn't fair."

I put a pan of water on to boil and made her a cup of hot tea in the Keurig. Charlie and Jack were in Charlie's room. I could hear them talking quietly, but I couldn't make out anything they were saying. It was just the four of us in the house.

"You and I both know life isn't fair," I said. "I took you for better or for worse, for richer or for poorer, in sickness and in health. All that. I believe in those things; I take them very seriously."

"I know you do, but—"

"No buts," I said. "I agree with you, this one has been tough. Probably the toughest we've been through as far as the toll it's taken on you. And I admit when it takes a toll on you, it takes a toll on me. But I'm willing to hang in there if you are."

She dropped her head and began to cry softly and I moved around the table, sat down and put my arm around her.

"I'm so tired of all this," she said. "I just wish things could go back to the way they were. I wish I could be healthy again."

"You will," I said. "You'll get better. Tell you what. If you'll promise me you'll bow your neck and fight, will yourself to get better, I'll build you a swimming pool in the back yard. You can lay out there and soak up the sun, maybe drink a beer once in a while, sit in the water when you get too hot. Hell, I'll use it, too. Swimming is a lot easier on the joints than running. The family will love it, we can have cook outs and parties. What do you say?"

She was still sniffling, but she nodded and looked up at me. She smiled, which melted my heart.

"Deal," she said.

I stuck my hand out. "Shake on it?"

She shook my hand.

"I'll find a contractor and get them out here this winter, have them ready to go by March or April. By the first of May, you'll be swimming out back."

"I love you so much," she said, and she leaned over and kissed me on the lips. "I'm so lucky to have you."

"You certainly are," I said, and I got up and dropped an egg into the boiling water.

# TUESDAY, OCTOBER 29

ater that evening, which was a Tuesday, Jack and I, along with Leon Bates, pulled into a driveway in a subdivision called Hayes Farm near Boones Creek. The lots in the subdivision were huge – at least five acres – and the houses all looked to be at least five thousand square feet.

"I reckon being a surgeon isn't a bad way to make a living," Leon said as we stopped and began to get out of Leon's car.

David Craig had balked at going to Leon's office, but we'd compromised and he'd agreed to talk with Leon at Michael's house. We walked along a paved walkway through a beautifully-landscaped front yard and rang the doorbell. Michael Craig had done as I'd asked. He'd gone to his brother's home around midnight the previous night and had secreted him away through the woods in back of his house. That morning, Leon had sent a horde of his deputies to descend on the media mob that was obstructing the county road, and they'd cleared them all out. I was looking forward to talking to the brothers together. It would be my first opportunity to see how they interacted and to gauge the trust they had for one another. I was also looking forward to springing my knowledge of Alf Higgins on David Craig, although I knew his initial reaction would be anger because I'd looked at the piece of paper he'd given me without his permission. But I'd done what I thought was right. Had I waited, David might have been dead.

Michael Craig greeted us at the front door and led us through a home full of expensive furniture, expensive floors, expensive art on the walls, and expensive, decorative wood molding and ceilings. Everything about the place was first-class. It nearly shouted, "I have a ton of money! I have a ton of money!" What felt strange to me, though, was that there were no family pictures, nothing that felt like the place was a home. Michael had told me he wasn't married and had no children, but the house still struck me as cold and sterile, I suppose because my place, which was nowhere near as expensively decorated as Michael's, was full of family photos. A person who walked into my house knew immediately he was in a home where people loved each other. A person who walked into Michael Craig's home knew only that Michael was wealthy. When we got to the back deck, the place became downright obscene. The deck was one of the largest I'd ever seen, built of composite and bordered by white, wrought-iron railing with intricate designs. Wide steps led to a flagstone patio and beyond that was a glistening pool. All of this overlooked a large pond in the distance, and beyond the pond, the mountains, which had begun to turn red and gold. I'd seen a fantastic mansion when I'd defended a record company in Nashville a year earlier. Michael's house wasn't at that level, but it was certainly one of the gaudiest places in Johnson City.

"Nice," I said to Michael as we descended the steps to the patio where David was sitting in a chair next to an unlit fire pit.

"Yes," he said without further comment.

There were six chairs around the fire pit, and we settled into five of them. Jack was on my right, Leon on my left, and David and Michael across from us. I introduced everyone.

"I see you made it out of there safe and sound," I said to David.

"It wasn't all that hard," he said. "You know these country roads around here. Mike just parked on the far side of the hill out back of my house and walked through the woods. We went out the back door and were in his car and gone in less than twenty minutes."

"Good," I said. "Any temptation to drink?"

"I think there will always be temptation to drink," he said. "But I'm going to do my best to resist it."

"Amen to that," Leon said. "I'm sure brother Dillard will tell you the same thing. If it weren't for booze and drugs, he and I would have to find a different line of work."

There was a momentary silence before Leon said, "This meeting was my idea. I asked your lawyer if I could meet with you. I have some questions I'd like to ask you, if you don't mind too much. I know the judge ruled in your favor and you're pretty much out of the woods as far as that goes, but you still had a dead Supreme Court justice in the back of your truck, and from what I understand, he was cut up and kept in a freezer for a little while in a home that's located in my jurisdiction, so I think I have a right to a few answers."

David Craig gave me a sideways glance, and I said, "You can trust this sheriff, David. He isn't looking to jam you up, but, like everyone else, he'd like to know who killed Justice Bryant, because that person is most likely behind the disappearances of the other four judges. We basically have a serial killer on the loose, and I can't, in good conscience, let it go on if there's anything I can do about it. So if you would, please, answer the sheriff's questions. Sheriff, will you give Mr. Craig your word he won't be charged with any crime?"

"You have my word, Mr. Craig."

"Before we go any farther, I have a confession to make," I said to David. "I wasn't willing to wait until something happened to you to look at that piece of paper you gave me."

"What?" David said. "You looked at it? Jesus. Don't you have some kind of ethical duty to do what I say?"

"Not if I think it could cause you harm. Not if I think you might wind up dead, and that's what I thought. Turns out I was probably right."

David stood up and started pacing.

"So you know who he is," he said. "What are you going to do? I mean, it would be his word against my word if you arrest him, right? You couldn't ever convict him based on just my testimony, could you?"

"Probably not," Leon said, "but I'm sure the medical examiner kept samples of different things from Justice Bryant's body. We might get lucky and get some corroborating evidence now that we know who the killer is. And just to be sure, we're talking about Alfred Eugene Higgins, your old next-door neighbor in Clarksville, Tennessee, correct?"

"I'm a dead man," David said, circling wider around us. "He'll hunt me down and he'll strangle me with his bare hands just like he did those judges. He'll cut me up into little pieces and toss me in some hole out in the woods and none of you will ever see me again. My God, I'll never forget watching him cut up the body. Right there in my basement. He had a big drop cloth with him and some kind of saw, and he just ... he just..."

"Calm down, David. I mean it. Walk over here and sit back down."

The voice was Michael's, and it stopped David in his tracks. He immediately walked straight back to his seat and plopped himself down.

"Now, for the next question," Leon said. "Do either of you two have any idea why this man would begin killing judges?"

"Because he's freakin' crazy, man," David said. "I'm talking psychopath crazy." He looked over at his brother. "Do you remember what he used to do to cats?"

Michael nodded. "I told Mr. Dillard."

Leon looked over at me and raised his eyebrows.

"I thought you should hear it from them," I said.

"What?" Leon said. "What did he do to cats?"

"He built a guillotine in his garage and used it to cut their heads off," David said. "He asked me to come into his garage one day when I was about seven or eight and he showed me this guillotine. Next thing I knew he produced a cat from a bag in the corner. It was all tied up and it was screaming, you know? And Alf, he'd fitted this wooden box to the guillotine and he stuck the cat in there and the next thing I knew the blade fell and that cat's head dropped straight into a bucket. I started puking all over the place and Alf slapped me across the face and made me clean it up."

"Didn't this guy have parents?" Leon said.

"He's huge," Michael said. "He was huge even when he was a kid. His parents were as terrified of him as everyone else. None of the kids would tell anyone because he told anybody who knew about the guillotine that if they told and he found out about it, he'd refit it and chop *their* head off."

"How long did this go on, this cat killing?" Leon said.

"I'm not sure," Michael said. "People didn't go around him too much. I know he spent a lot of time hunting around Clarksville when he was a teenager. He told me once he loved cutting up animals. Whatever he'd kill, he'd bring it home to his garage and basically dissect it. I don't think he ever ate anything he killed. He'd just cut it up and then get rid of it, take it to the dump or something."

"Did you guys ever tell your parents about what was going on?" I said.

David shook his head.

"I told my dad," Michael said in a flat tone. "He said he hated cats, if some kid wanted to cut their heads off, it was fine with him. He also told me to keep my nose in my own business and that tattletales usually wound up getting their asses whipped."

"I wish Dad would have gone over there and tried to stop him," David said. "Maybe Alf would have killed him and saved us all a lot of grief."

Leon and I looked at each other and then back at the brothers.

"What kind of grief are you talking about?" Leon said.

"It doesn't matter," Michael snapped. "It's all in the past. We don't have any contact with our father and don't want to. It's pure coincidence that we wound up living within thirty miles of him. I graduated from high school and went straight into the military. As soon as I got out, I went to college and med school, and then I came here as a general surgery resident at the Johnson City Medical Center Hospital through the Quillen medical school. David moved here about the same time. I liked it here and eventually joined the group I'm with now. We didn't have any idea our father was living thirty miles down the road, although I knew it was possible. My father's family were some of the earliest settlers in Greene County. They owned thousands of acres, and a lot of it eventually passed down to my father. He has this almost delusional perception of himself, this idea that he's had to work for everything, that he's all about self-discipline and honor, but he's really just an entitled, ridiculously wealthy country boy who spent twenty years in the JAG Corps because it gave him automatic authority and control over other people's lives. He loved sending soldiers to prison, absolutely lived for it. The harder he got to come down on someone, the better he liked it."

We let it go at that. We were getting off track, but I planned to revisit the separation from the father – and the mother – later on if it became necessary.

"All right," I said. "Sheriff Bates has an idea – you might even call it a plan – but in order to put it into motion, David is going to have to go home in a couple of days."

"Wait a minute," Michael said. "Are you talking about using my brother as bait?"

"Think of it as a sting operation," Leon said. "I know at first it will sound a little risky, but trust me, I've done this kind of thing before and so have several of my guys. Michael, brother Dillard tells me you were a Delta sniper, is that right?"

"It is," Michael said.

"I'd love to have you join the party, but if a civilian shot another civilian, there'd be hell to pay for me. But if it makes you feel any better, two of the guys on my S.W.A.T. team were military snipers. They'll be backing me up."

"So you're planning to arrest Alf?"

"If everything goes right."

"Then what?"

"Not sure," Leon said. "I haven't really thought it through that far."

# SUNDAY, NOVEMBER 3

Alf Higgins parked his van in the lot of an apartment complex about three-quarters of a mile west of David Craig's house. When Higgins saw on the news that Craig had been arrested, he was furious. Craig was a drunk, a coward, and Higgins was certain Craig would immediately cave and tell the cops about him. But a lot of time had passed since Craig went to jail, and not a single cop had come sniffing around. He hadn't heard a word about the cops looking for him. And then, a miracle of miracles, Craig's lawyer, some hotshot named Dillard, had gotten him out of it clean. Higgins's employer was still furious with him for leaving the body at David's house and allowing even the possibility of a complication to occur, but Higgins had assured his employer that the loose end would be tied up quickly and permanently.

As soon as Higgins heard about David Craig being released, he'd made his way to Craig's house outside Jonesborough, but the place had been surrounded by news vans and trucks and SUVs. When they left the next day, Higgins broke in that night, only to find that Craig wasn't there. His clothes were there, even his toothbrush was there, but he was gone.

Higgins figured he'd probably gone to his brother's, and some cursory surveillance had proven him right. But dealing with Michael Craig and dealing with David Craig were two entirely different things. David was a pussy and Michael was a bad ass. David had told Higgins about Michael being both a Green Beret and a Delta operator in the Army. He figured Michael would have plenty of weapons around his house and would know how to use them. He also figured the security at Michael's incredibly expensive house would be top of the line.

So he'd decided to sit back and wait a few days. Sooner or later, David would go home. He'd taken a room at a flea bag motel between Jonesborough and Greeneville, registered under a fake name and paid cash. Each day, he'd go for a drive and each day, he'd eventually drive by David's house. He'd made two more nighttime visits, picking the lock on the back door and wandering through the house just to be sure nothing had changed.

On the fifth day, something changed. David Craig's pickup, which Higgins assumed had been impounded by the police, was in the driveway. Higgins drove back to the flea bag, drank a six-pack of beer, took a four-hour nap, and at ten o'clock that night, he drove back to Hairetown Road and parked at the apartment complex. He walked along the shoulder of the road for about a hundred yards and then cut into the woods. He made his way up the ridgeline, skirting a few houses along the way, and walked slowly and quietly the rest of the way to Craig's house, stopping to listen every fifty yards or so. When he was at the edge of the tree line, he crouched in the shadows, listened some more and watched. Leaves fell around him each time the wind gusted. A thick blanket of clouds had rolled in over the mountains earlier in the day and the night was chilly and dark. Higgins could see the glow of a television inside the house, and five minutes later, he saw a shadowy form move into the kitchen, stand over the sink for a short time, and walk back toward the television. Higgins decided not to wait until David Craig was asleep. He would surprise him and deal with him now.

Higgins came out of his crouch and lumbered slowly across David Craig's back yard. There were three concrete steps leading to a door that opened into the kitchen. Higgins turned the knob, and to his surprise, the door was unlocked. He stepped in and closed the door behind him. He walked through the kitchen and filled the opening that led into David Craig's den. David was sitting in his recliner immediately to Higgins's left. Even in the dim light, Higgins was surprised by the change in David's appearance since the last time he'd seen him.

"What took you so long?" David said. His voice was steady.

"Been here a few times. You've been at Mike's."

"Yeah, well, I didn't want to move and I figured I couldn't hide forever. Have a seat."

"I'll stand," Higgins said. "What'd you tell them about me?"

"I didn't tell them a thing. Nada. Zilch. Didn't have to. Mike hired a good lawyer and he told me the first day to keep my mouth shut. He said he thought he could get me out of it. So I kept my mouth shut, and he got me out of it."

"How'd he do it, anyway?"

"The lawyer? Technical legal stuff. I was drunk when they arrested me and when they interrogated me, but they lied about it. The cop that arrested me grew a conscience and came into court and told the truth. They arrested the damned sheriff, can you believe that?"

"I heard," Higgins said. "So you didn't mention my name, not to anybody?"

"Nope."

"Not even to your lawyer?"

"Nope."

"What'd you tell him about what was in the back of your truck?"

"I didn't tell him anything. He didn't seem to care."

"I don't believe you," Higgins said.

David shrugged his shoulders. "Nothing I can do about that," he said. "You can believe me or not believe me. You can kill me or not kill me, but bottom line, all of this was your fault. You're the one who brought that judge here in the first place. I couldn't stand it. It was like having a ghost in the house. I had to get rid of it."

"You wearing a wire, Davey?" Higgins said. "The cops got this place bugged?"

"The cops don't want to have anything to do with me," David said. "My lawyer just made them look like fools. As far as the cops are concerned, I got away with killing a bunch of judges. So the best thing for you to do is just walk away. Get out of here and don't ever come back. I've never met you, don't even know who you are."

"I don't think I can do that," Higgins said. "I think you're going to have to come with me."

"If I disappear, Mike will come after you," David said. "I lied to you a minute ago when I said I didn't mention your name to anybody. I told Mike."

"That's too bad," Higgins said. "Too bad for Mike."

"Mike will kill you, just like you killed all of those judges. He isn't afraid of you. We aren't kids anymore."

"I'll worry about Mike when the time comes," Higgins said as he stepped through the door and loomed over David. "You want to die standing up looking me in the eye or do I have to bend over and choke you in that chair?"

Just then, Higgins heard a door hinge creak to his right, followed by the unmistakable sound of a pistol hammer cocking.

"Back away and get on your knees," a voice said. "You're under arrest."

# SUNDAY, NOVEMBER 3

Leon Bates was telling the truth when he told Michael Craig he wasn't sure what he was going to do with Alf Higgins if he arrested him. It was a delicate matter, because Leon didn't believe for a second that Higgins was choosing the victims. He believed someone else was choosing the judges and paying Higgins to do the killing and to get rid of the bodies. In Leon's mind, the primary suspect was Michael Craig, because there was just something unsettling about him. He was too perfect. He reminded Leon of Jeffrey MacDonald, the Green Beret doctor who murdered his pregnant wife and two daughters back in 1970 and who had gotten away with it for almost ten years. The audacity of his home and the perfection of his narcissistic appearance bothered Leon. And Dillard said Michael had made a comment about wishing he could still be killing people in the Middle East. Another thing that made Leon think Michael might be involved was that the judge in Mountain City went missing while David was in jail. Judge Watson didn't fit the pattern of sexual misconduct or allowing sex offenders to walk, but he could have easily been a throwaway. Michael's brother had been arrested, Michael knew he was innocent, so he picked somebody close that Alf Higgins could get to quickly.

But how could Michael have known Watson was on the take? Had he picked him randomly, or was there perhaps something Leon didn't know about Judge Watson? Another thing Leon couldn't figure out was why Michael would be choosing these particular judges. Had he been sexually molested as a child? And even if he had, would he routinely put in the study and the work it would take to choose the victims that had been chosen?

In order to try to get some answers to his questions, Leon had decided to handle Alf Higgins unconventionally. There were very few people who knew Alf had been arrested. There were the two S.W.A.T. sniper teams who watched Alf Higgins's approach to David Craig's house and reported every movement to Leon, who had been waiting in David's bedroom. All four of those guys were rock solid. They wouldn't say a word to anyone. David Craig knew. Leon had told him to tell nobody, including his brother, but he couldn't be certain about David. Joe Dillard knew. Leon had called him within ten minutes of Higgins's arrest so Dillard would know his client was safe. But Dillard wouldn't tell a soul. No problem there.

Leon had cuffed and shackled the massive Higgins – the guy stood six feet, eight inches tall and had to weigh more than three hundred pounds – on David Craig's floor, gagged him with a bandana, placed a black, cloth bag over his head and then led him outside. One of the snipers had jogged the mile to where three unmarked sheriff's department vans were parked and had driven one of them back to David Craig's. Leon had secured both Higgin's cuffs and his shackles to iron rings in the back of the van, had climbed in behind the wheel, and had driven the van to a secluded house in northern Washington County, followed by the four S.W.A.T. members who caught up to him and trailed him in the other two vans. When they arrived at what Leon affectionately called "the farm," – an old farm house Leon had seized from a meth dealer – Leon and the four S.W.A.T. officers, all of whom were wearing black ski masks, got Higgins out of the van and took him inside to a room that Leon had designed and largely constructed himself. A single, hundred-watt lightbulb hung from an exposed beam in the middle of the room, and Leon flipped on the switch as he entered. The floor was concrete and the walls were cement block. Everything was painted a dull gray. There were no windows. A stainless steel bench ran along the wall opposite the solid, steel door. One steel rail ran just above the bench, while another was bolted into the floor beneath the bench. In the corner to the right was a wire-mesh cage, basically a five-foot cube. The three-foot-by-three-foot cage door was secured by a large padlock. Inside the cage was a black, five-gallon bucket. There was one metal chair pushed against the wall to the left.

Leon and his S.W.A.T. teamers pushed Higgins into the room and shoved him down hard onto the bench. They secured his handcuffs to the rail above the bench and his shackles to the rail beneath the bench. Once Higgins was secure, Leon said, "You boys go take a break. Me and my buddy Alf are gonna have us a private discussion."

The deputies filed out and the door slammed shut. Leon walked over to Higgins and said, "I'm gonna take this bag off of your head and take that gag out of your mouth. If you spit on me, I swear on my mother I'll take the butt of my pistol and knock every tooth you have out of your head. Nod if you understand me."

The bag bobbed up and down and Leon pulled it from Higgin's head. His hair was thick and shaggy and covered his ears. His forehead was ridged at the eyebrows and his nose was long and wide. He had a thick stubble of beard covering his face, and his dull, brown eyes betrayed nothing.

"Put your chin on your chest," Leon said.

Higgins followed the command. Leon untied the bandana and turned and walked to the chair. He pulled it away from the wall about ten feet from Higgins and sat down.

"My name's Leon Bates," he said. "I'm the sheriff of the county where you cut up a dead judge and put him in a freezer. I'm also the sheriff of the county where you just committed an aggravated burglary. You know walking into David Craig's house like that with the intent to commit a murder is an aggravated burglary, right, Alf? With your record, you're looking at fifteen years just for that. But I don't want to see you do fifteen more years in prison, because you'll still be young enough to kill more people when you get out. So basically, there are three things I want from you. I want you to admit to killing those fine, upstanding judges, and I want you to tell me where they are. And then I want you to tell me who hired you to do it. I'm not promising you anything other than you'll walk out of this room alive. You might spend the next ten years on death row. Then again, they might speed up the process for you since your victims were all judges. You might get the needle in five years. Or even better for you, the district attorney might cut some kind of deal with you and let you spend the rest of your miserable life in a maximum security prison in exchange for you telling him where all of the bodies are. I can't speak for him. So, there it is. What do you have to say for yourself?"

Higgins looked at Leon coldly and said, "I want a lawyer."

Leon smiled and shook his head. "That kind of talk will get you nowhere," he said. "Look around you, Alf. You see that little cage over there? I'm going to put you in it if I don't get what I want from you in fairly short order. You're a big man and I imagine you're going to be real uncomfortable in there. After me and my boys stuff you inside, we're going to go away and let you think about things for a day or so. You see that speaker up there in the corner? I've got the volume set real loud, and I've got an evangelical preacher on a digital file that'll blast away at you the whole time I'm gone. It's about an hour-long sermon, but I've got it on a loop so it plays over and over and over and over. He talks about redemption and the wages of sin. I'm sure it'll hit home for you. You aren't going to get any food or water and all you'll have for a toilet is that bucket in the cage. It's going to be mighty unpleasant for you, Alf."

"You can't torture me," Higgins said. "People will find out. You'll be the one who winds up in prison."

"I think you're wrong about that. I also think you're not thinking big enough, Alf. You're not thinking outside the box, no pun intended. You see, I'm not just going to torture you by depriving you of sleep and water and food and humane conditions. If I come back tomorrow and you still won't give me what I want, I'm going to put a bullet through your right kneecap. And if that doesn't work, I'll put a bullet through your other kneecap. And if that doesn't work, I'll just keep finding places to put bullets until you eventually either tell me what I want to know or you bleed out. And if you bleed out? I'll treat you just like you treated those poor judges and who knows how many others. I'll get rid of your body. I'll put you in a place where nobody will ever find you."

"You're bluffing," Higgins said. "You don't have the balls."

"Who hired you to kill the judges?" Leon said.

"Go to hell, bumpkin."

"I probably will for what I'm about to do to you. Try thinking about this, old buddy. Nobody knows you're here except for people I trust, and they're not going to tell anybody. You think the person who hired you to do these killings is going to come looking for you? He isn't, or she isn't, and if you don't tell me who this person is, then you're going to wind up rotting in a grave somewhere. That's a promise. You think your momma and daddy are going to come looking for you? They never once came to see you in prison. I looked at your records pretty thoroughly. You've spent nearly all of your adult life in prison and haven't had a single visitor. Now what's that tell you? You know what it tells me? It tells me nobody gives a tinker's damn about you. Nobody. If you up and vanish, nobody will care. Not one single person. That's really pretty pathetic, Alf. So let me ask you again, who hired you to kill the judges?"

"Lawyer." Higgins spat defiantly onto the floor.

"I ought to make you lick that up," Leon said calmly. "But just so you know I'm understanding what you're saying, just so you know that I'm really trying to be *communicative* with you, what I believe I'm hearing is you attempting to assert your right to counsel under the Sixth Amendment to the United States Constitution. Am I right? Yeah, I'm right. You're trying to assert one of your constitutional rights. But what you need to understand is that between these walls, in this room right here, there is no constitution. I hate it for you, I really do, but sometimes extreme circumstances call for extreme measures. It's like the CIA dealing with terrorists after nine eleven. They had to do some things they weren't proud of in order to keep the country safe. Now I'll admit it, Alf, I'm not going to be proud of what I'm going to do to you if you don't give me what I want, but you also have to understand that I view you as a domestic terrorist, just like ol' Timothy McVeigh. You know who he was, right? Gutless coward that bombed the federal building in Oklahoma City and killed more than a hundred and fifty people, including several children. You've attacked a powerful institution in the state of Tennessee, the judiciary. When you think about it, you've attacked an entire branch of our government. Now as far as I'm concerned, terrorists check their constitutional rights at the door when they decide to become terrorists. You decided to become a terrorist, so by my way of thinking, you don't have any constitutional rights, and if you say the word 'lawyer' again, I'm going to cut your scrotum off. Now ... one more time ... who hired you to kill the judges?"

"I want a lawyer, you redneck sonofabitch!"

Leon stood and pointed his finger at Alf.

"I don't believe I care for your attitude," he said. "And don't say I didn't warn you."

Leon turned and walked to the door. He opened it and yelled, "One of you guys go out to the van and grab a waist chain! Then all of you come on in here!"

Leon turned back and walked to the chair. He took his cowboy hat off, set it on the chair, and smiled at Alf.

"Wouldn't want to get blood on my hat," he said.

A few seconds later the four S.W.A.T. deputies walked through the door, wearing military fatigues, web gear, boots and the black ski masks. Leon noticed Alf's eyes widen as he saw them come through the door.

"Wrap that chain around his waist, through his cuffs, and lock it down tight," Leon said to the deputies. "I don't want him squirming around. And gag him. Don't want to listen to him scream, either. After you get him secured, take his pants down, underwear and all, and spread his legs for me. I'm about to turn this bull into a steer."

Leon reached into his pocket and pulled out a folding knife. He opened it, walked up to Higgins and knelt.

"My goodness, you'd think a feller this big would be packing a little more meat," Leon said. "Just goes to show, you never know who'll get one. Say goodbye to your testicles, Alf."

Leon reached his hand slowly toward Higgins when Higgins suddenly began to babble through the bandana. Leon stopped what he was doing and looked up into Higgins's eyes.

"You got something to tell me, Alf?"

Higgins' head began to nod furiously.

"It better be good. After having to look at that ugly sack, I ain't going to give you a second chance."

# MONDAY, NOVEMBER 4

It had been about seven weeks since Charlie and Jack's accident. Jack was fine; he'd recovered quickly from everything but the rib injuries, but even they had stopped bothering him to the point that I hadn't heard him complain about pain for more than a week. He was asserting himself the way Jack had always done, pouring himself into the skeletal remains of my law practice, helping to care for Caroline, and doting over Charlie, with whom, I could tell, he was deeply in love. Jack and Charlie and I had had many discussions, hours of discussions, over the direction the law practice should take. My sense was that he and Charlie wanted very much to follow in my footsteps. They wanted to practice criminal defense law. They wanted to delve deeply into constitutional principles, which were the foundation of criminal defense. Both of them were skeptics when it came to the American criminal justice system. Jack's skepticism stemmed from being around me for most of his life, and Charlie's stemmed from her father – who had lost part of an arm in Vietnam – being incarcerated for more than twenty years for growing marijuana. Neither of them trusted law enforcement officers, prosecutors or judges. Neither of them believed the system was fair. They believed it to be stacked against the poor and the uneducated, and I couldn't disagree.

I tried to talk them out of criminal defense. I truly did. I was completely honest about the constant moral dilemmas criminal defense attorneys face. I talked to them about not being able to trust their own clients, about getting up every day and walking out the door to do battle with a cop, a judge, an FBI agent, a prosecutor, a jailer, a witness, their own client. The constant fight would wear them down, I said. It had worn me down on many occasions, so much so at one point that I quit practicing criminal defense and went to work for the district attorney's office. But that had ended badly when I realized that the game was the same whether you were a prosecutor or a defense attorney. It wasn't about justice. It was about winning.

On a bright, calm Monday morning early in November, I was sitting in the kitchen reading legal opinions on a laptop (I couldn't help myself), drinking a cup of coffee, when Charlie cruised in on her crutches. Jack had gone to my small office near the courthouse in Jonesborough to begin the process of hiring a competent legal secretary/paralegal. I received calls all the time from people asking me to represent them, but I'd become extremely adept at saying, "thanks, but no thanks." That was about to change since Charlie and Jack were coming on board, and they would need a buffer, someone between them and the cranks, of which there were many. Caroline had been my buffer for years, which was amazing considering the amount of time she put into her dance studio and the illness from which she'd been suffering for so long.

"Good morning," Charlie said as she made her way to the Keurig and popped in a container of tea.

"Morning," I said. "You're moving around better every day."

Charleston was her real name, but she'd gone by Charlie since she was a kid. She was, without doubt, one of the most beautiful young women I'd ever met. Her wavy, flowing auburn hair reminded me of Caroline's and she had incredibly clear, intelligent, sapphire-blue eyes. Her lips were full, her nose petite and her body was lean and athletic. She was also, like my wife, as tough as a pine knot. She'd been through some heart-wrenching tragedies in her young life, but she'd come out on the other side stronger and more determined to find her own way to happiness.

"Feel like taking a walk?" Charlie said as the cup filled and she began sipping tea.

"Why don't we go for a run?" I said. "Maybe race? I'll bet you twenty bucks I can beat you. You pick the distance. Ten yards, forty, a hundred, a mile. I can take you."

"I'll take that bet in about a year," she said, "and I'll kick your butt."

"You want to just walk down by the barn and say hello to Sadie?" I said.

"That's more along the lines of what I had in mind."

"Let me grab a jacket and put my shoes on."

I went into the bedroom and laced on a pair of old running shoes and pulled on a jacket. Rio could tell I was going out, so he started whining and his tail started banging against the wall, and when Rio's tail started banging, Chico started yelping, and when Chico started yelping, Biscuit started howling. By the time I managed to get the second shoe laced and walk back into the kitchen, there was a cacophony of dogs assaulting my ears. We went out through the garage – which was the easiest way for Charlie to navigate with the crutches – and when I hit the garage door opener button, all three dogs exploded into the morning sunshine. It was a clear morning with virtually no breeze, the temperature in the mid-forties. Charlie and I turned left out of the garage and made our way slowly across the yard toward the barn. The red barn, the white, three-rail fence, the lake far below in the background and the brilliant reds and golds of the leaves that remained on the trees made for an idyllic scene. We leaned against the fence as Sadie came over and Charlie slipped a couple slices of apple into her mouth.

"Do they hurt, Charlie?" I said. "Your legs? How painful is it?"

"I wouldn't recommend it," she said. "They hurt all the time. It's hard to get comfortable in any position for any length of time."

"I never hear you complain," I said.

"And I never hear your wife complain."

"You're both fighters," I said. "I admire you."

"I wanted to tell you ... well ... I haven't really thanked you," Charlie said. "This barn, the fence, letting Sadie and Biscuit stay here, taking care of me. It's really too much, Joe. Thank you. I mean it."

"Just part of my evil plan to get you and Jack back up here where you belong," I said. I smiled at her and winked. "You know you don't have to stay. Sometimes I feel like I hijacked your life in Nashville. Took advantage of your situation. As soon as you're well enough, strong enough, you can go back and there won't be any hard feelings. I'll help you haul your things."

She smiled back at me and then looked up at Sadie and started rubbing the horse's ears.

"You're a kind man," she said. "The way you are with Caroline is beautiful. And this? This barn and this pasture? What you've done for me here? This is just an incredible gesture. You're generous and you're kind, and your son is just like you."

I immediately felt my face flush from embarrassment, so I acted like I was distracted by something and looked away for several seconds. When I turned back toward her, I said, "It's going pretty well between you and Jack, am I right?"

"Spoken like a true defense counsel cross-examining a witness. A statement followed by a question designed to affirm the statement. You realize you're not supposed to ask those types of questions unless you know the answer in advance?"

"I do realize that, and I do know the answer. I see the two of you, I watch, I listen. You're great together."

"I'm very much in love with him," she said, and it was all I could do to keep my jaw from dropping. One of the things I'd always admired about Charlie was her directness and her honesty, but she still sometimes surprised me.

"I'd appreciate it if you'd stop beating around the bush, Charlie. Say what you mean."

"It took me awhile to trust myself again after what happened to Jasper up on the mountain. The gold made me greedy and I did things and made decisions that ultimately cost Jasper his life. I had to forgive myself and learn to move on. I also had to learn to trust myself again. I've known I was in love with Jack for a long time, but I was afraid I would do something that might hurt him, the same as I did with Jasper."

"Charlie, that gold was absolutely unforeseeable," I said. "Here you were, just a kid fresh out of law school, and you get this incredible fortune dumped in your lap. The circumstances of how that gold got there in the first place, how it wound up being willed to you, and the fact that it came from a gangster in Philadelphia eighty years ago and his gangster thug descendants came looking for it? I mean, things like that just *don't happen*. You handled it the best you could under the circumstances. I don't have any idea how I would have handled it, but there just weren't any good outcomes. That gold was cursed. It would have hurt anyone who touched it."

Charlie's eyes had taken on a dreamy look, almost misty as she stared beyond Sadie into the clear, blue sky above. She nodded her head softly.

"I know all that now," she said. "But thank you for saying it. It means a lot coming from you."

"So back to hijacking your life," I said. "Are you comfortable here now? Are you sure you want to stay?"

"I want to practice criminal defense law. I want to do it well and be successful. I want to be with Jack. And being surrounded by a family would be something I've never experienced. All I ever had was my grandparents and Jasper. I've thought it through from every angle, and finally, I just asked my heart."

"And what did your heart tell you?"

"My heart said, 'These people want to love you, Charlie. Let them.'"

# MONDAY, NOVEMBER 4

A s Charlie and the dogs and I were walking back toward the house, I saw a black, windowless van pulling into the driveway. I was alarmed at first, but then I made out Leon Bates's angular features behind the wheel and I relaxed. Leon parked the van while I put the dogs in the house. Charlie said she was going to rest for a little while and then get on the computer and Skype with Jack. His first appointment with a prospective secretary/paralegal wasn't until ten, and she wanted to be a part of the interview process.

I walked back out to the driveway just as Leon was walking around the van.

"Coffee?" I said.

"No thanks," he said. "Let's maybe head out that trail where you run all the time. I've got some things we need to chew on."

There was a trail on property owned by the Tennessee Valley Authority adjacent to my house that ran along a bluff overlooking Boone Lake. I'd run thousands of miles along that trail over the past twenty years. I stuck my hands in my pockets, and Leon and I began strolling slowly along the trail.

"How'd it go?" I said, referring to Alf Higgins.

"I took him to the farm, thought it was best."

"The farm" is what Leon referred to as his department's safe house or "black site." He used it rarely, I knew, only when extreme measures were called for with a suspect or he needed to hide someone – a witness or a potential victim – for a short time. Just over a year earlier, a young boy had gone missing from a trailer park in the South Central community of Washington County. A registered sex offender lived less than a mile away. Leon found the boy and had him returned to his parents in four hours. He told me he did it by taking the sex offender to the farm and using some "advanced interrogation techniques." He wasn't bragging about it and I knew he wasn't proud of it, but he saved a young boy's life.

"What'd you do to him?"

"I convinced him to admit he killed the judges. I convinced him to tell me where he hid all of their bodies. And I convinced him to tell me who hired him to do it."

"Damn, Leon, that's a pretty good night's work. Care to tell me how you got all of this information out of him?"

"I basically threatened to turn him into a eunuch, and I did it with his family jewels exposed and a knife in my hand while he was restrained by handcuffs, shackles, a waist chain and four of my guys."

"I sort of wish you hadn't told me that," I said.

"Then you shouldn't have asked."

"So where are the bodies?"

"They're burned. Ashes tossed in a creek and a pond on a big farm in Greene County."

The words "big farm in Greene County" tickled my memory, but I didn't quite grasp the meaning at that moment.

"So you're not going to find them," I said.

"Probably not, but we might find some remains in the incinerator Alf says is also on the farm. But there's a lot more to it. Alf says he was hired by somebody that's a straight-up psycho, brother Dillard. Sexual sadist. There are more bodies than the judges."

"More bodies?"

"Women, mostly runaways and prostitutes. Alf was hired to do more than just kill a few judges. He's been taking sacrificial lambs to the altar, and he suspects there were probably many more before he got involved. There could be dozens of dead women, maybe a hundred, who knows?"

"You said he told you who hired him. Who was it?"

"This is where it gets really complicated."

"How so?"

"Because I have a confession that was coerced. Because I don't really have any solid evidence against anybody other than this coerced confession, and because the ashes and the incinerator and the torture chamber – assuming Alf is telling the truth – are outside of my jurisdiction, which means I have to either bring in the Greene County sheriff, who I don't trust, or the TBI, who will take over everything and shut me out. And the worst of it all is – again, assuming Alf told me the truth while his nut sack was exposed to an extremely sharp knife – the person responsible for all this plotting and killing is a powerful man."

"Who is he?"

"Take a guess."

"Michael?"

"Close, but no."

"David isn't powerful, so he's out." And then it dawned on me.

"Their father? The judge?"

"Christopher Allen Craig, former prosecutor for the U.S. Army Judge Advocate General, former assistant district attorney in the Third Judicial District, and currently a Criminal Court judge. He was also appointed last year to The Board of Judicial Conduct, the judges who are supposed to police other judges."

"Now I understand why you look the way you do," I said.

"There's more," Leon said. "The judge has an accomplice besides Higgins."

"Not another judge," I said.

"A woman. A woman who's as perverted as he is. Alf says she found and picked up the girls before he came along, and she takes part in the sexual stuff. She helps kill these girls and helps get rid of the bodies. Alf said the judge must have been tracking him in prison, because as soon as he flattened his sentence and went back to his home place in Clarksville, the judge showed up and asked him if he'd like to make some money and have some fun doing it. They talked a while, and Alf figured out that the judge was wanting him to kill some other judges, some judges that Judge Craig didn't think were worthy of continuing to sit on the bench, or even live for that matter. So Alf did the first one, and then the judge brought him in on this girl thing. He asked Alf to start picking up girls for him and his girlfriend 'to have a little fun with,' is the way Alf said he put it. They had dealers in place. Pimps. Sex traffickers."

"Did the judge pay Alf?"

"Ten thousand a pop for the judges. The women cost a thousand apiece, and the judge added three hundred for Alf's trouble. All cash."

"Any of the money left? Can you get fingerprints?"

"There's some money. We already have our hands on some of it. But I don't think we'll find prints. Alf said the judge is an extremely careful man."

"There might be some record of him withdrawing money from a bank account or an investment account somewhere," I said.

"Maybe. We'll see."

"You don't seem too optimistic, Leon," I said. "You're not going to let this guy get away with killing a bunch of people, are you?"

Leon stopped walking and turned to face me.

"I've got a bad feeling about this," he said. "Not counting the judge your client had in the back of his truck, I've got the ashes of four dead judges and who knows how many women laying out there somewhere in another jurisdiction, and I have to figure out a way to find enough bone matter or hair to even begin to prove that any of them were there. I also have to figure out a way to gather enough evidence against this judge to get a warrant, and then gather enough evidence to make sure we can put him and this woman away. The logical thing to do would be to wire Alf Higgins up and send him down there, but I can't. He's just too dangerous. I can't trust him, and I wouldn't be able to stay close enough to him to guarantee that he wouldn't tip the judge off or murder somebody else while he was loose. The judge is going to know something has happened to Alf because Alf won't be checking in with him. Alf said he used throwaway cell phones and called the judge every day. The judge won't know exactly what happened to Alf because I'm not going to book him into the jail. I'm going to keep him at the farm because I don't want anybody leaking anything to the media about me having another suspect in the judge killings in my jail. I need to act quickly because I'm afraid if the judge figures out that Alf has been collared, he might bug out on me. So I figure this is where you come in."

"Me? How do I fit into any of this?"

"We go at the judge through his flesh and blood. We use your client."

I turned and started walking again, and Leon sauntered along beside me.

"I think you need to slow down a little," I said. "David has already been through a lot. I don't know that he'd be up for this kind of thing. So let's just think it through some more. You're right, you can't go charging into Greene County onto this guy's property without a warrant, and you can't get a warrant without going to a judge. People will have to know. I say bring in the TBI. I know they're politicized, but so are you, at least to a degree. I've met some bad TBI agents, but I've also met some who are excellent. Do you remember Anita White and Mike Norcross?"

"The black gal and the guy they called 'Thor?' Yeah, I remember them. They were both good agents, good folks, too."

"I haven't seen Anita in four years, but I'm sure I can find her. I'll give her a shout and see what she's up to. Maybe she can help us. Same with Mike. I just have to find them. And as far as leaving Higgins at the farm, you just can't do it, Leon. You have to have him arraigned within seventy-two hours or you risk losing him altogether. Book him into the jail and put him in your max unit. He has a record of violence, so housing him there won't raise any concerns. What can you charge him with?"

"Aggravated burglary."

"Perfect. If anybody reads the report and sees that David Craig is the victim, you can always tell the press that Higgins is a nut job who thought Craig got away with murder. You can say he was angry because he did a bunch of time for beating up some soldiers and this guy murdered four judges and walked away."

"And then the judge here will appoint a public defender and Alf will tell the public defender about our little session at the farm."

"No, he won't."

"Why not?"

"Because you're going to tell him that if he does, he's going to commit suicide in his cell. If you threatened to cut his balls off, he'll think you're crazy enough to stage a suicide."

"You can be a devious man, Joe Dillard."

"That's what I hear. I'm just looking to buy some time until we can figure out a way to get to this Judge

Craig. After we do that, you can come back and charge Higgins with the kidnappings, the murders, the mutilations, whatever you can prove or whatever he'll confess to. You can charge him with conspiracy to commit murder on the women if we find any of them. He *is* a killer, after all."

"But he's not a serial killer," Leon said. "He's a hired killer, a hit man. I looked into his prison record, and he didn't kill anybody during all those years he was inside. In fact, I don't think he ever actually killed anyone until the judge put him up to this. The judge and his woman, on the other hand, are serial killers. They act on irresistible impulses and act out sexual fantasies. From what Alf says, that judge and his woman are as evil as it gets."

"I'll find Anita and talk to David and Michael," I said. "They obviously haven't been completely honest about their father."

"And I might take a trip to Fort Campbell and see what I can dig up. It's time I learn everything I can about Christopher Craig."

"There's one more thing you should probably do, Leon," I said.

"What's that?"

"See if you can find David and Michael's mother."

# MONDAY, NOVEMBER 4

As soon as Leon left, I walked up the driveway toward the mailbox. On the way, I called David Craig and told him I needed to meet with him and his brother.

"Why?" he said. "Alf's in custody. It's over, isn't it?"

"Afraid not," I said. "Get a hold of Michael, arrange a time when all three of us can meet, and call me back."

"How does this involve Michael?"

"It involves both of you, all right? Just call him and call me back."

I disconnected the call and opened the mailbox. On top of the small stack of mostly junk mail was an envelope with the return address of Richard C. Peckwell, Attorney-at-Law. I opened the envelope as I walked back toward the house and read what was inside. It was a demand letter. It said if I didn't pay Mr. Man Bun (Jimmy Carr, the quarterback who slapped Lyndsey Woods) a hundred thousand dollars within thirty days from the date of the letter, I would be sued. I sighed deeply and put the letter back inside the envelope. I still didn't think Peckwell stood a chance of forcing me to pay a bunch of money, but I didn't need the aggravation a lawsuit would bring.

When I walked into the house, Caroline was sitting at the kitchen table with a cup of hot tea in front of her and nibbling on a piece of toast. It was good to see her up and moving around so early in the day. The brain radiation had really rocked her.

"Good morning," I said as I walked over and kissed her on the cheek.

"Morning, baby," she said.

"Well, you called it," I said.

"Called what?"

"That kid I beat on, the one who slapped Lyndsey? He lawyered up a while back. I didn't want to say anything to you because I thought it might go away, but the lawyer is asking for a hundred thousand dollars. I just got the demand letter in the mail. Says if I don't pay up in thirty days they're going to file suit."

"Who's the lawyer?" Caroline said.

"Sleazebag ambulance chaser named Rick Peckwell."

"I don't think I've ever heard of him."

"That's a good thing," I said. "Trust me."

"I wouldn't worry about it too much," Caroline said.

"Really? That's a different tune than you were singing the day it happened."

"I got to thinking about it," she said. "And what you did, while I don't necessarily condone it, was probably right. He assaulted two women inside of three minutes and didn't think a thing about it. He would have done the same thing to me if Lilly hadn't kept me from going out there."

"Which would have resulted in me facing a murder charge instead of a lawsuit."

"You're probably right. But anyway, after thinking about it, I decided to do something that might help you out in case this happened."

"Are you serious?" I said. "What did you do?"

"Hang on a second."

She got up from the table and disappeared into the bedroom. A couple of minutes later, she was back with a piece of paper in her hand.

"What's that?" I said.

"Your ticket out of the mess you created by being a hothead."

"Stop being coy," I said. "What is it?"

"The kid is a bully, correct?" she said. "Like I said, he put his hands on two girls in my studio parking lot in three minutes and would have shoved or slapped me if he'd gotten half a chance. So I figured he had to have done it before."

I started shaking my head slowly as a grin crossed my face.

"You didn't," I said.

She nodded. "Oh, yes. Yes, I did. I asked Lyndsey if she knew about any other girls he'd assaulted, and she did. And I asked her to talk to those girls and see if they knew about any other girls, and so on and so on. And then I asked her to get me some phone numbers, and I made some calls."

She handed me the paper with a flourish.

"And right there, my hotheaded, beloved husband, are the names, addresses and phone numbers of seven girls who have been assaulted by Jimmy Carr. Every one of them is willing to testify in court if it comes down to it."

"Have I told you lately how much I love you?" I said.

She didn't say a word. She simply winked at me and raised the teacup to her lips.

# TUESDAY, NOVEMBER 5

**M**ichael Craig's estate was the natural place for the three of us to talk. He didn't have a wife or kids and his closest neighbor was almost a quarter-of-a-mile away. We could talk there openly and privately.

We'd set the meeting for seven in the evening, the day after I'd called David. I'd cooked for Caroline and Jack and Charlie earlier, and when I left they were cleaning up. Michael and David were out back, this time sitting by Michael's pool, when I arrived. Michael was drinking what appeared to be a martini, while David was drinking a bottle of water. It pissed me off immediately to think that Michael would be so callous, knowing the struggles his brother had faced – and continued to face, I was certain – with alcohol and drugs. I'd been through the same thing with my sister, Sarah. She'd been clean for years and didn't mind if the family imbibed in a little wine at holiday gatherings, but back when she was in the throes of her addictions, I would never have tempted her.

"So what's so damned important?" Michael demanded without even saying hello.

"Good evening," I said to Michael. "David, nice to see you again."

Michael's brow was furrowed and David had the look of a frightened child.

"I'm serious," Michael said. "I have better things to do than sit out here and talk to you. I hired you to do a job. You did it. It's over, or at least it should be. I don't understand why you're here."

"Mind if I sit?" I said as I motioned toward a nearby chair.

"I don't care whether you sit or you stand, but one thing is certain," Michael said, "you're not staying long."

"I hope you don't think the hostility bothers me," I said. "I'm a criminal defense lawyer. Everybody hates criminal defense lawyers, at least until they need one."

I pulled the chair over and sat down, a smile on my face.

"Care to tell me why you're so worked up?" I said to Michael.

"I already told you. I have better things to do."

"Like what? Drink in front of your alcoholic brother?"

Michael's lips tightened and his face reddened. "That's the kind of wisecrack that will get you tossed off of my property in a heartbeat," he said.

"Why do you think I'm here?" I said.

"I assume it has something to do with Alf Higgins," Michael said, "and I want to make it crystal clear to you that I no longer wish to think about, discuss, or in any way acknowledge that Alf Higgins is still breathing his share of our air."

"He was going to kill your brother, you know. So whether you like it or not, he's going to be a part of

David's life for a while. If he doesn't wind up making some kind of plea deal, David will have to testify against him."

"So what does that have to do with me?" Michael said.

"I'm here for one reason," I said. "I want both of you to come clean with me about your father. Alf says your father sent him to kill David. Alf told the sheriff that your father hired Alf to kill all of those judges that went missing, and Alf says your father has been torturing and killing young women for quite some time. The problem the sheriff has is that Alf's word is his only proof, and Alf doesn't exactly have a ton of credibility. So I was hoping maybe you could give me some sense as to whether Alf is telling the truth, maybe offer some kind of corroboration. You've both told me you aren't close to your father. What was he like when you were around him?"

There was silence for a full minute, and then David suddenly began to sob.

"Be quiet, David," Michael said. "I mean it."

"He raped me!" David blurted in a high-pitched wail. "He raped my mother and she ran away! And then he raped me and Michael shot him and we ran away, too! But he found our mother and he killed her and got away with it. He's a monster! I'm telling you, he's a monster!"

Michael rose from his seat, stepped quickly over to David, and slapped him across the head.

"Shut your damned mouth!" he yelled. "Not another word."

I got up and took a step toward Michael. I held my hands up and said, "Take it easy, please. Can we all just take a step back and calm down?"

Michael looked at me with fire in his eyes.

"Is this what you came for?" he said. "Are you getting what you want? The lurid history of our deranged father? Are you enjoying yourself? Does the pure prurient nature of what our father became give you some sort of sick satisfaction?"

"It gives me no satisfaction and it gives me no pleasure," I said. "I'm sorry for both of you."

"I don't want your pity," Michael said. "David has been wallowing in self-pity for more than twenty years, but I refuse to give in to it. The truth is, if my father showed up on my doorstep, I'd shoot him on sight and do the same thing to his body that Alf supposedly did to those judges. But I'm not going to become involved in any kind of investigation or help you in any way."

"Why?" I said. "If he killed your mother like David said. If he's a sexual sadist and a murderer, why wouldn't you help put him away?"

"Because as far as I'm concerned, he's already dead," Michael said. "He died the day I caught him raping David and nearly blew his leg off."

"You don't feel any responsibility towards the others he's killed or might kill in the future?"

"I don't feel anything at all when it comes to him," Michael said. "Now get off of my property, and don't come back."

# TUESDAY, NOVEMBER 4

Judge Christopher Craig took a sip out of his glass of scotch and looked out over the mountains. Dark thunderheads loomed in the west. They were marching toward him like an evil army, and he wondered whether they might be some kind of omen.

"Alf has done something stupid again," he said to the woman who was sitting next to him with a glass of bourbon in her hand. Her name was Loretta Jilton, and she'd once been a defendant in his court, charged with possessing a small amount of methamphetamine. The judge instinctively recognized something in her, and since she was out on bond, he'd looked up her address in the court file and paid her a visit. Eventually, he'd dismissed the charge against her after ruling that the prosecution couldn't prove the meth was hers since it was beneath the passenger seat in a car she was driving but didn't own.

Loretta was fifty, brunette, petite, and would have been attractive had it not been for a life filled with sexual abuse, alcohol and a litany of drugs. The judge looked over at her and involuntarily shook his head slightly. She had pale, blue eyes that crinkled when she smiled and a tiny, upturned nose. Sometimes, especially in poor lighting, she actually looked cute. Looking at her, the average person would never imagine the predator that lie beneath the exterior. She shared the judge's unusual sexual preferences, which meant she received sexual gratification from inflicting pain on others. *We make quite a team*, the judge thought to himself. *"Quite a team."*

"My guess is he's been arrested," Loretta said.

"Which means he's probably told them everything," the judge said. "I should have put a bullet in his brain after the stunt he pulled. Leaving a body at David's? David was a coward when he was a child. I'm sure nothing's changed."

"How long has it been since you've seen David?" Loretta said. "You've hardly told me anything about your sons."

"They're not my sons," the judge snapped. "Leave it alone."

"Take it easy," Loretta said. "Why did Alf say he left the judge there?"

"He wanted to get to Asheville to pick up the two girls he brought us that weekend. He said the broker was getting antsy on him, that he had to drive straight from Nashville to Asheville but he had a problem with his van and was running behind schedule. The judge was starting to get ripe, so he dropped him off at David's. He'd apparently put a freezer in David's basement months ago in case he needed to store a body for a little while. He said David was terrified of him and he didn't think there'd be a problem. He also said he'd put five other freezers in the homes of people who are terrified of him around the state. That means there are five more potential witnesses out there. He said he'd kill them all, but I'm sure he hasn't done it yet."

"Anyway, he said he drove on to Asheville that day, had to wait an extra day for the girls because the broker was so paranoid, spent two nights, and when he went back to David's to get the body, it was gone. A few hours later, the news broke that David had been arrested with a dismembered body in his truck. Then they found out it was Justice Bryant and all hell broke loose."

"Wouldn't it have been sweet if they'd pinned that murder on your son who isn't your son?" Loretta said.

"Damned sheriff up there," the judge said. "Nothing but a hillbilly. David's lawyer made him look like a fool. They're prosecuting him for perjury."

"So what do we do?" Loretta said. "If Alf is telling them everything, don't you think we should get out of here?"

"Get out of here? Do you mean run? Leave the country?"

"Do you have a better idea?"

"I'm not going anywhere," the judge said. "Alf Higgins is a career criminal. I'm a decorated veteran, a criminal court judge, and a member of the Board of Judicial Conduct. There isn't a judge in this state that would sign an arrest warrant or a search warrant based on an affidavit given by Alf Higgins, especially without corroboration of some kind. And there isn't any corroboration."

"What's corroboration?"

"Independent evidence. Something that supports what Alf would be telling them. There isn't anything. I paid him cash and I guarantee there are no prints on the cash. The cash I paid him came from Mason jars that my grandmother had hidden all over this place. He doesn't have any recordings, no photos, nothing in writing. He doesn't have anything but his word, which is worth squat."

"He knows what we did with a lot of the bodies," Loretta said. "He knows about the incinerator. I'm starting to think there might be a small part of you that wants some recognition for everything we've done."

"Say that again and I'll slit your throat," the judge hissed. "Have you listened to a word I said? In order for them to come in here and search for bodies, they have to have a warrant, and they won't be able to get one."

"So you think we're okay?"

"I think we're fine."

The judge drained his glass and stood. The thunderheads were almost upon them.

"I'm thinking I'll head downstairs for a while," he said. "You in the mood?"

Loretta stood and stretched. She smiled.

"I'm always in the mood," she said, "but I'm starting to get tired of this girl."

"You're going to have to start finding them again now that Alf's gone," the judge said. "I told him to kill David, and to be careful doing it. If he was stupid enough to get caught, he'll be in prison for a long time. I find it rather amazing that Alf can be so methodical and patient and dangerous, and then turn around and do something utterly impetuous and stupid."

Loretta walked past the judge into the kitchen and set her glass in the sink. Her mind was racing, but she stayed calm. The more she thought about it, the more she believed that the judge had chosen Alf knowing that he would eventually make a blunder that would bring everything crashing down around them. Once the big crash happened, the judge would become famous, and he needed the fame to feed his insatiable ego. She knew she should get away now, tonight, before they came, but she was terrified of what the judge would do to her.

"Forget about Alf," Loretta said. "It was pretty good while it lasted. He was an efficient killer and he brought us plenty of fresh playthings."

"I just hate that I won't be able to have any more judges killed," the judge said. "I was really enjoying it, and there are so many of them that need killing."

Loretta walked over and reached between the judge's legs. She gave him a squeeze.

"We'll just have to go back to being satisfied with the others," she said.

The judge felt himself becoming aroused.

"So let's do the girl in the basement today and maybe once more tomorrow," the judge said. "Then we'll finish her."

"Sounds like a plan," Loretta said. "I want to go change first, though. I'm feeling like this might call for some leather."

# WEDNESDAY, NOVEMBER 5

Judge Christopher Craig lie on his back and stared up into the darkness. It was after midnight, and Loretta was already breathing deeply and steadily beside him in bed. The girl in the basement had fared poorly (for her, anyway) that evening, and the judge was exhausted. He'd delighted in her shrieks, immersed himself in her pain, and had climaxed intensely just before she finally passed out.

He should have been sleeping soundly, and normally he would have been, but the conversation with Loretta earlier in the evening, the one during which his sons were mentioned, kept bringing up an old memory, one that he could feel himself wanting to relive. It was the memory of his first kill. It was the memory that made him realize what he really was, and what he needed to continue to be.

She ran away from him, or at least tried to. But it didn't do her any good.

Her name was Anna (she went by Ann) Lynn Susong, and the two of them met in high school in Greene County, Tennessee. She was a small and plain girl, meek in her personality, the daughter of a minister and obedient to a fault after Chris managed to gain her trust. Chris himself was a prize, or at least that's what he believed. He was bigger, stronger and faster than most of the other boys in school, and he excelled on the football field in the fall, the basketball court in the winter and the baseball field in the spring. He was the captain of the debate team, the valedictorian of his senior class, and his family was rich.

Chris never wanted for anything, although his childhood might have been called tragic by some. His mother and grandmother doted over him throughout his early years. His mother developed serious complications while she was giving birth to Chris and was unable to have more children, so he was the center of both women's attention until his grandmother developed ovarian cancer at the age of fifty-two and died shortly thereafter. A year later, when Chris was nine, his father was gunned down by a neighbor during a boundary dispute. His father was riding his four-wheeler on the neighbor's property, it turned out, and was carrying a rifle and a pistol of his own. The neighbor was charged with second-degree murder, but he hired a slick defense lawyer who argued at trial that Chris's father was a belligerent bully and basically deserved what he got. The neighbor was eventually acquitted, and that was what ultimately drove Chris to law school to become a prosecutor. Chris's grandfather was never mentioned when he was a boy. It wasn't until Chris was a teenager that his mother told him his grandfather was afflicted with "mental issues" and was locked up in the Lakeshore Asylum for the criminally insane in Knoxville. Chris kept the information to himself.

Chris proposed to Ann the night of their senior prom, and she readily accepted. He had no problem coming up with money for a ring – his mother simply gave it to him. His mother gave him money all the time, and plenty of it. Ann donned the ring and Chris managed to seduce her a couple of hours later. She wasn't his first by any means, but he told her she was. Chris was discreet about his sexual activities. When he had time and the urge hit him – which it often did – he traveled alone to Knoxville to the blocks where the prostitutes wandered the streets like painted up pieces of candy, just waiting to be sampled. He talked to the girls and found that he could find more girls in Newport, in Chattanooga, in Asheville, North Carolina. If you had money, you could find a girl, and Chris always had money. He also had his own car, courtesy of his mother's generosity, so he could easily travel from Greeneville to Knoxville or Chattanooga or Asheville. The car and the money allowed him to never become familiar in any given place.

Two years into college at Sewanee, Michael was born and Chris forced Ann to quit school in order to care of the baby full-time. Chris's sexual appetite was insatiable, but as long as he went to church each Sunday, he knew Ann would keep trying to meet his demands. He was, after all, all she had besides the baby. He'd isolated her from her family and made sure she had no close friends. And she had no idea that he was soliciting prostitutes on a regular basis and having more intense fantasies about violence and domination.

After college, Chris gained admission to the University of Tennessee College of Law in Knoxville and graduated summa cum laude in two-and-a-half years. By that time, he'd enlisted in the United States Army. He told Ann he was motivated by a surge of patriotism following the disastrous hostage rescue attempt that ended in the Iranian desert, brought down Jimmy Carter's presidency, and embarrassed the entire United States military, but secretly, he knew the army would give him more freedom from Ann, more time to explore various options. After Officer Candidate's School, Chris soon became a part of the Judge Advocate General Corps. He kept himself in excellent physical condition, moved to several posts over the next ten years (David was born during his third year in the army) and was eventually promoted to major and assigned to the 101st Airborne (Air Assault) Division at Clarksville, Tennessee. By that time, Chris had been deployed overseas twice and had become known as one of the army's most notoriously aggressive prosecutors.

As the judge lay reminiscing, Loretta rolled and snorted. *Someday I might do to you what I did to Ann,* he thought. *Someday.*

Clarksville was where things really changed for him. He'd been able to do some extremely pleasurable things to women – pleasurable to him, at least – over the past several years. Prostitutes and runaways were easy prey, as were many of the women he'd encountered overseas, but his behavior was becoming more and more extreme, his fantasies more and more intense, his compulsions more and more irresistible, and he needed a safe and private place to indulge them. The house he'd bought in Clarksville was on a large lot – just over an acre – and it had an unfinished basement. So Chris had set about building himself a chamber. For him, it was a pleasure chamber. Others would have called it something else.

Ann had been curious as to what he was doing in the basement, but when he finally took her down there, her curiosity quickly turned to horror. It didn't matter, though. She was his wife, he said, and she would do what he told her to do. Her meek nature, coupled with the years of domination and cruelty when he was home between assignments and schools and deployments, would not allow her to resist him, and the horror gradually gave way to resignation, followed by complete submission.

Until one day, not long before Michael graduated from high school, following a particularly sadistic session, Ann disappeared. She took very little with her, not even her car. She apparently called a taxi, got on a bus, and left.

It was stupid of her to think he wouldn't know where she would go, and it was even more stupid of her to think he would allow her to humiliate him in such a fashion, but he let it go.

For a while.

Ann's father was still preaching at the same church outside Greeneville, and her sister lived alone in Mosheim, a tiny town of about two thousand souls ten miles west of Greeneville. The day the boys left – the day Michael shot Chris and tore a significant part of his left quadriceps away, Chris figured they would run straight to their mother, and that's exactly what they did. It took some time for Chris to exact his revenge on Ann because he had to treat his own gunshot wound (he couldn't very well explain it to the Army), come up with a reasonable lie for his sudden limp (he'd fallen from a tree while trimming limbs), and heal up. He asked for and received a thirty-day leave of absence, and during that time he traveled to Knoxville, rented a car for cash from a mom-and-pop outfit on Kingston Pike, and drove to Morristown, where he checked into a cheap motel, paid cash, and gave a false name.

He donned sunglasses and pulled a baseball cap down low over his eyes and immediately began watching Ann's sister's house. The sister's name was Louise, and she'd lost custody of her three boys during a divorce because she was an alcoholic and addicted to opioids. She lived in a one-story, brick house off Meadow View Road. It took Chris exactly one day to figure out that Ann had found a job as a waitress at a barbecue joint in the middle of the small town. Within a week, he knew her shifts and what she did when she was off, which was to stay home and occasionally peek out of a window. Chris never saw Michael, who had already left for basic training, and only caught a couple glimpses of David, about whom he couldn't care less.

On the ninth day of his surveillance, he got the break he'd been waiting for. Ann didn't work her usual daytime shift; instead, she went in at one in the afternoon. The restaurant closed at 9:30 p.m., and Ann walked across the deserted parking lot around ten o'clock, well after dark. She was the last person to leave, and as soon as she started across the lot toward her sister's car, which was parked in the back near the dumpster, Chris pounced. He sped up to her, screeched to a stop, popped the button that opened the trunk, and stuffed Ann inside the trunk of his car in less than ten seconds.

Chris remembered the smell of wood smoke in the lot, his wife's squeals, the pain in his leg, and the utter futility of her meager resistance. In less than thirty minutes, he was back on the family farm in Greene County. By that time, his mother was in a nursing home in a dementia-induced fog. He dragged Ann from the trunk in a clearing off an old logging road right in the middle of the thousand-acre property and pulled her, kicking and screaming, to a nearby tree. He ripped off her clothing, tore off her bra and panties. He'd come prepared, and he began wrapping nylon rope around and around her torso and the tree. Before long, she was completely subdued.

"Are you ready to die, bitch?" he said.

"Please, Chris, I'm sorry," Ann begged. "I'm so sorry I left. I'll come back to you. I'll do whatever you want. Please don't hurt me."

"Hurt you?" Chris said. "Hurt you? I'm going to do far more than hurt you."

Chris turned back to the car. When he returned, he went to work on his wife, and when he was finished, she was barely conscious.

He stepped up close behind her and whispered into her ear.

"Who's your master?"

"Major Craig, sir," Ann whispered.

"That's right, and Major Craig finds you have committed an unforgivable sin. You were disobedient and disloyal, which makes you a traitor. The sentence for treason is death."

And with those words, Major Christopher Craig wrapped his belt around his wife's neck and choked her until she was dead. It was his first murder.

The memory made him smile, and he drifted off to sleep.

# WEDNESDAY, NOVEMBER 5

I found Anita White in Knoxville. She'd become the Assistant Special Agent in Charge of the TBI's Knoxville office, and when I called her, she seemed genuinely pleased to hear my voice. I asked her if Leon and I could come down and talk to her, told her it was extremely important, and she readily agreed. We left at 7:30 a.m. on Wednesday in separate vehicles and drove to Strawberry Plains, just outside of Knoxville. After we met with Anita, Leon was planning to head to Nashville. He'd found Christopher Craig's former commanding officer – who was now retired – and made an appointment to see him. By 9:00 a.m., we were sitting in Anita's sparsely-appointed office.

She remained an attractive woman, with smooth, mocha-colored skin and clear, green eyes. She was wearing a business suit and I noticed she'd let her hair grow. It was pulled back into a ponytail that fell to the middle of her back. We small talked for a little while, and I congratulated her on her promotion. The TBI was a tough place for women to advance, and if she'd done it, she'd worked hard. She told me Mike Norcross – an agent we used to call Thor because he was so good at breaking down doors with a sledgehammer – had quit the TBI and gone to work for the FBI. He was now in Chicago, and they talked a couple of times a year on the phone.

"How much of a politician have you become?" I said. "And I don't mean that negatively, I just need to know. We have something sensitive."

I could tell from the expression on her face that the question rankled her a little, but she managed to keep her composure and retaliate with an insult.

"I'm as political as I have to be," she said. "No more, no less."

"Can we keep this between us for a little while? At least until we can come up with a definite plan?"

"Why don't you tell me why you're here?" Anita said. "I think we have enough history that you know I'm not a loose cannon."

"We think we know who has been killing all of the judges," I said. "And we think we know who hired this person to kill the judges. And the kicker is that the person who hired the killer is a judge. A respected judge who sits on the Board of Judicial Conduct."

Anita sat back in her seat and looked back and forth between Leon and me.

"My," she said. "That's quite a bombshell. I thought you got the killer off on some kind of technicality."

"My guy isn't the killer," I said. "He's the killer's son."

"Beg your pardon?"

"I know. It's one of the most insane cases of my career. If you've got about half-an-hour, Leon and I will give you the rundown."

Anita folded her arms and sat back in her chair, and Leon and I took turns going through the entire thing, from the night David Craig was stopped to the capture and torture of Alf Higgins. It actually wound up taking about an hour, because Anita asked a lot of questions. But by the time we were finished, she understood what we were up against.

"You're both right," she said. "There's no way we'll get a warrant to go on Judge Craig's property and search, at least not yet. But I can think of at least one way to get started."

"What's that?" I said.

"Old-fashioned gumshoe stuff," Anita said. "We get eyes on them from the sky first, and then we get eyes on them from the ground."

Anita looked at Leon.

"I might ask you to do some things off the books. Since you threatened to cut a guy's scrotum off, I assume you'll be okay with that."

Leon grinned like a fox.

"I certainly will," he said.

"Good. Let me get some aerial stuff authorized so we can take some pictures, determine routes of ingress and egress, get makes and models of automobiles, that kind of thing. I should be able to get it done within a couple of days. Then we'll – or I guess I should say you, Leon – will do a little clandestine work. Set some cameras, maybe get some GPS trackers on vehicles. We have black bag teams like the FBI, but I won't be able to use them without valid warrants. Do you have anything like that available to you at your department?"

"You'd be surprised what my little ol' hillbilly department can do," Leon said.

"And what about you?" Anita said, looking at me.

"This guy raped my client when he was a boy," I said. "I know what that's like because it happened to my sister. I want to be there when he goes down."

"Do you have a problem with that?" Anita said to Leon.

"This won't be the first rodeo for brother Dillard and me," Leon said. "I'd feel better knowing he's there."

"Okay," Anita said. "Let's get to work."

# WEDNESDAY, NOVEMBER 5

nita White walked into the office of Special Agent in Charge Lawrence Knight without an appointment or an invitation. She took a seat in front of him and waited until he looked up from his computer. He was a short, slight, balding man with reddish hair and a generally serious demeanor. He did, however, have a wicked sense of humor.

"Anita," Knight said.

"Larry."

"I assume there's a reason you're sitting there with a smug look on your face."

"You assume correctly. I need authorization for some air time."

"Then I need a formal, written request."

"Can't do it."

Anita now had Knight's full attention. He slid the keyboard toward the computer monitor and rolled his chair away from his desk a bit. He folded his right arm across his stomach, placed his left elbow on the arm, and rested his chin on his fist.

"Is it game time, Anita? Fifty questions?"

"I'd prefer there be no games and no questions."

"Chopper or plane?"

"The Pilatus."

"So you're serious about this."

"Extremely.

"Day or night?"

"Doesn't matter. Can you get it done?"

"Can you give me anything that would entice them to authorize the use of a multi-million-dollar surveillance aircraft?"

"As long as you don't repeat what I'm about to say."

"So you can give me something to entice them, but I can't repeat it to them."

Anita nodded. "Yeah. Sort of. That's pretty much what I'm saying."

"You're very strange sometimes, Anita. Do you know that?"

"I've been told."

"Okay," Knight said. "Tell me what I can't repeat."

"I think I'm onto the guy responsible for kidnapping and killing the judges."

"Shit," Knight said. "Sorry, I mean, wow, Anita. That's pretty powerful stuff."

"I know. Can you help me?"

"Maybe. Probably. Hell, of course I can help you. I'll figure out a way. I assume you need this yesterday?"

"Day before."

"Do you have an address, co-ordinates, anything like that?"

"I have an address in Greene County. The geeks can figure out the co-ordinates. I need everything they can get."

"They can photograph insects crawling in the dark from twenty-five-thousand feet in the air with that plane."

"Let's stick to the house, outbuildings, vehicles, people, stuff like that. And ways in and out of the place."

"Okay," Knight said. "Consider it done. I'll go to the director if I have to, but it'll be done. Immediately."

"Thanks, Larry," Anita said as she rose and walked toward the door. "I knew I could count on you."

# THURSDAY, NOVEMBER 6

David Craig had made up his mind. His father, his tormentor, the man David believed had murdered his mother and who had now hired Alf Higgins to kill judges and committed other unspeakable acts according to Joe Dillard, needed to die. And David was going to kill him.

All he needed was some courage, and he found it in a bottle.

After Dillard left Michael's house the day before, David had told Michael he was going to kill his father.

"You don't have what it takes," Michael said. "You'd hesitate, and he'd tear you to pieces. Just forget about him. Let the powers that be deal with him. With any luck at all, he'll be behind bars where he belongs very soon."

But those words had fallen on ears that didn't want to process them. David felt a smoldering rage deep inside him, a heat that would soon rip him apart from the inside if he didn't do something to quell the flames. Several years earlier, not long after he'd left the Army, Michael had given David a gift for his birthday. It was a Randall knife – a "killing knife," Michael called it – and David had been both shocked and surprised. To him, the gift was totally inappropriate. It was a beautiful knife, obviously very expensive, and from looking at it, David had no doubt that if used correctly, it could easily kill a person. But David had no intention of killing anyone, and he said so.

"Just in case," Michael had said. "You never know. Besides, if you just leave it in the box and never touch it, it'll become more valuable. It's one of the best knives in the world."

The knife was now out of the box, in its sheath and attached to David's belt near the small of his back as he cruised along Interstate 81 toward Greeneville. It was nearly eleven o'clock at night, and small droplets of rain darted like translucent minnows across the beams of his truck's headlights. At his side was a fifth of Jack Daniel's whiskey, which was about half empty. He'd had to Google his father's name on his phone to find Christopher Craig's address since David had never been there. Google Maps was leading him to an address on Liberty Hill Road, within three miles of Graysburg Hills Golf Course in rural Greene County.

The voice from David's phone told him he had reached his destination, and he turned right off of the road onto a gravel driveway. He wound through woods and past clearings for nearly a mile before an old, white farm house came into view. David was struck immediately by the foreboding condition of the house and the surrounding grounds. The person who lived here apparently wasn't much of a caretaker; it was downright creepy. The wraparound porch was sagging in one place near the left corner at the front of the house and the grass surrounding the house – at least what David could see – had turned a pale brown, was long and shaggy and was lying flat against the ground. There was an outbuilding to David's right, about fifty yards from the house. It looked like an oversized garage with the exception of a smokestack sticking out of the middle of the roof. And it wasn't a garage. Two cars were sitting beneath a carport about twenty yards from where David was parked.

David had no plan other than to kill his father on sight. He turned off the ignition and the lights and opened the door. The wind was whistling. There was a faint light coming from one of the windows as David circled the house in the cold darkness. He listened for a dog. Nothing, which seemed strange. One would think a person who held people captive, tortured them, and eventually murdered them would have dogs around for security, but David remembered his father hating animals. David's father never allowed pets around the house when David was growing up, not so much as a hamster.

As David inched closer to the window from which the light was coming, he suddenly made out his father's unmistakable shape. The squared chin, the flat forehead, the long, thin nose. Reading glasses were perched on his nose, and a book rested against his chest. He appeared to be asleep. David looked around the room and didn't see anyone else. The rest of the house was dark.

David circled the house entirely, stumbling a couple of times because of the liquor. He'd built up quite a tolerance before going on the wagon. Now that he'd been off the stuff for a couple of months, it had hit him pretty hard. When he was satisfied that no one else was moving around the house, he stepped up onto the porch. The room where his father was sleeping appeared to be a study of some kind. It was near the back of the house. There was a door on the side of the house near the study, and it was that door David tried.

It was unlocked.

As the knob turned in his hand, David felt himself begin to tremble. He thought about turning back and running, but he forced himself onward. The bane of his existence was a mere thirty feet away, sound asleep. David could rush into the room and plunge the knife deep into his father's chest before his father knew what was happening. He pushed the door open and cringed when it squeaked. David slipped inside, closed the door, and pulled the knife from its sheath.

He found himself in a short hallway. The light from the study leaked through a doorway only ten feet ahead of him to his right. Beyond that, he could see the dim outline of a staircase to his left. He willed himself forward, cringing again when the wooden floor beneath his feet let out a soft moan.

David peeked through the doorway. His father had not moved. He was breathing steadily and heavily. All David had to do now was cross the room and pounce. Plunge the knife into the chest. Pull it out and slash the throat. David looked forward to being bathed in his father's blood. He felt his pulse quicken even more, his vision began to narrow. His mind went back to the basement in Clarksville on the day Michael graduated and his father raped him.

He stepped into the room as quietly as possible. He thought about waking his father so his father would know it was he who had killed him, but he decided he would know. The initial blow would kill him, but not immediately. The last thing Judge Christopher Craig would see on this earth would be his son standing over him with a knife.

Another step closer.

And another.

Five feet to go.

And then it happened.

The man in the chair moved with the agility of a cat. Before David knew what was happening, his father's hand had reached into a drawer in the table beside his chair and when the hand reappeared, it held a pistol that looked like something straight out of a Dirty Harry movie. David found himself looking down the barrel of a pistol, one with a large, long barrel. He froze, suspended like an insect in ancient amber.

"Don't you think you should have called first?" the judge said. "Didn't your mother and I teach you any manners?"

"Don't speak of my mother," David managed to say. "You murdered her."

The judge lay his book to the side with his left hand and rose from his chair.

"Yes, yes I did," he said. "It took quite some time, as I recall. She suffered a great deal. And I enjoyed every second of it."

David felt tears burning in his eyes. A primordial wail began to emerge from his entrails and he raised the knife above his head. He lunged forward.

The bullet that killed David Craig tore through his forehead and destroyed a good portion of his brain.

He didn't feel a thing.

# FRIDAY, NOVEMBER 7

Leon Bates and I – along with two of his S.W.A.T. guys named Sexton and Walker – walked more than a mile to get to Judge Christopher Craig's property. It was after two in the morning when we topped a small ridge and I looked down on the house through infrared goggles that Leon had provided. I was surprised to see a light on in the house and some movement. A man, most likely the judge, was walking from an outbuilding toward the house. A chimney in the outbuilding was belching fire and smoke.

Leon's meeting with Judge Christopher Craig's former commanding officer had been both enlightening and alarming. The officer's name was Colonel Ruben Jones, who had retired five years earlier. He was Christopher Craig's immediate superior while Craig was stationed at Fort Campbell. Colonel Jones called Judge Craig a "split personality," and said he could be as charming as he needed to be or as mean, small-minded and vindictive as any man he'd ever known. He said Craig abruptly resigned his commission after claiming to have fallen out of a tree while cutting limbs, had put his home in Clarksville up for sale and had disappeared. He also said it was for the best. Craig had pretty much worn out his welcome in the U.S. Army.

After meeting with Colonel Jones for a half-hour, Leon had gotten back in his car and made the four-hour drive back to Johnson City. He'd called me the next morning and asked if I wanted to do a reconnaissance run and maybe get some tracking devices on the judge and his woman's vehicles. He was taking his two best S.W.A.T. guys with him, too, but I think by that point I'd become somewhat of a security blanket for Leon. We'd been through so much together, he just felt better having me along.

Caroline had crashed early, and I hadn't even mentioned to her I was going out with Leon. And as we walked slowly and quietly through the woods, I remember thinking that a part of me wouldn't have minded if the judge had the place booby-trapped and I wound up getting blown to bits. It would be a better fate than watching Caroline die slowly. And as soon as the thought struck me, I once again felt an overwhelming sense of guilt. The psychological and emotional roller coaster I was riding was something I desperately wanted to jump from, but in order to get off the roller coaster, Caroline would have to lose or give up the fight. I shook the thought out of my head and told myself to just hold on.

Leon and I were crouched within a foot of each other atop the knoll.

"That's the incinerator," he whispered, pointing to the belching chimney. "He's burning something."

"Or someone," I said.

I thought of some poor, kidnapped or coerced woman, defiled and tortured, murdered and now being cremated, and I wanted to rush down the hill and go into the house with the Beretta 1301 Tactical twelve-gauge shotgun Leon had provided for me and blow Judge Christopher Craig's brains out.

"Easy, brother Dillard," Leon said, sensing my rage.

"I'm ready to kill something," I whispered.

"Not yet. C'mon, let's go."

I followed Leon down the hill and we skirted the entire house and outbuilding, staying in the shadows and among the trees about fifty yards from the house. Leon had infrared binoculars, and every twenty feet or so, he'd stop and scan. The light inside the house went out after we'd been there about fifteen minutes. A light upstairs came on briefly, but it, too, went out after a couple of minutes.

Leon's S.W.A.T.-teamers were positioned on high ground, one to the north and one to the south. We'd done a long briefing and a Google Maps recon before leaving the office. I found it absolutely amazing that reconnaissance can be accomplished so quickly and easily in this day and time. Plug in the address, zoom in, and presto! We could see the house – which was surprisingly run-down and in need of repair – we could see the outbuilding, the rusted carport that was about thirty feet off the front porch. We could see the creeks and the pond Alf Higgins had mentioned. We figured out how we would go in, how we would get out, contingency plans if something went wrong, everything.

But even the best-laid plans sometimes go wrong. I'd seen and done enough in my lifetime to know that, and

I kept thinking that the last thing we wanted or needed was to have to kill Judge Craig that night. It would be a tough explanation.

Leon turned, gave me the high sign, and started off toward the carport on his belly. In a pouch in his web gear he carried two magnetized GPS trackers. One would be attached to the judge's old, faded silver Cadillac, and the other would be attached to Loretta Jilton's black Hyundai. I was crouched next to a sugar maple, scanning the house and the wraparound porch through the infrared sight on the shotgun, trying to ignore the annoying, tiny droplets of rain that were stinging my skin in the stiff breeze. And I kept wondering who the poor soul was that was burning inside that incinerator.

Just as Leon disappeared beneath the Cadillac, I saw movement through one of the windows in the house. I keyed the button on my headset and said quietly, "Leon, someone is moving inside. Sit tight."

A couple of seconds later, I saw a figure emerge through a side door to the house, near where the light had been on. It was the judge, and my heartbeat raised just a tick as I released the safety on the shotgun. He didn't come down the steps into the yard, however. He turned to his right and walked to the front of the house, looked around into the darkness, and then turned and walked the entire length of the house to the back, still looking out into the darkness.

"Michael!" he yelled. "Michael! Are you out there? Come on inside and get some of what your brother got!"

*Get some of what your brother got? What the hell is he talking about? Is he referring to the childhood rape? Is he drunk?*

"You're cowards!" the judge yelled into the night. "Both of you! Nothing but cowards!"

And with that, he turned and went back into the house. Five minutes later, Leon was by my side.

"What do you reckon that was all about?" Leon said.

"I don't know," I said, "but I want to check that out-building over there where the incinerator is burning."

Leon and I moved away from the house to a thicket about fifty feet away. We moved around it and came to the outbuilding, which looked to be a combination of an old barn that had at some point been converted to a garage or just a storage building. It was fairly large, maybe fifty feet by forty feet, constructed of dingy, white, concrete block that looked like it had been laid outside the old barn wood. There were no windows and two doors: one a garage door and next to it, a metal door. I tried the metal door – it was locked – so Leon went to work on it. He had the lock picked within thirty seconds and we were inside.

The incinerator was humming loudly and as I scanned the room through the infrared scope on the shotgun, my stomach suddenly tightened. Sitting inside the building was David Craig's truck.

I had no doubt that David was inside the incinerator.

# FRIDAY, NOVEMBER 7

I felt both helpless and enraged. We had to leave. We were on the property illegally. We didn't have a warrant because we couldn't get one, and if we'd gone in and arrested the judge and Loretta, stopped the incinerator and retrieved at least a little of David's remains so we could attempt to identify him through DNA analysis later, we would have lost everything. Nothing would have held up in court and the judge, just like David before him, would have walked away a free man.

All we could do was wait for them to make a mistake. Or I could set something in motion that made sure the judge was stopped.

After we left the judge's property, we headed back to Jonesborough. I got out of the S.W.A.T. van at four-thirty in the morning, drove my truck home, and lay awake next to Caroline until six. Then I got out of bed, dressed, gulped down a cup of coffee, and drove to Michael Craig's house.

He came to the door dressed casually.

"Surgery day?" I said as he opened the door. I was standing on his front porch beneath the porch light. The sun hadn't yet risen.

"What are you doing here?" he said.

"I just thought I'd let you know that your father murdered your brother last night and put him in an incinerator. I don't know all of the details because we must have gotten there right after it happened."

Michael took a couple of involuntary steps backward. His face clouded. He was confused.

"But since you said your father is dead to you and you're not willing to help in any way, I guess you really don't care, do you?" I said.

He looked at me open-mouthed for a few seconds, then quickly composed himself. This guy was a genuine hard ass.

"So I assume my father is under arrest for murder," he said matter-of-factly.

"You assume incorrectly," I said. "Like I explained to you the other day, we didn't have enough evidence for a warrant, so we were on the property illegally, looking for ways to gather evidence illegally that we might later turn into something we can use. Did David mention to you that he might pay his father a visit?"

"I told him not to go," Michael said. "I told him he didn't have what it takes to deal with our father."

"He apparently didn't listen to you," I said. "How hard did you try to dissuade him?"

"Are you trying to blame this on me?" Michael said. "Because if you are, I'm about to tear you apart."

"You go ahead and give that a try," I said. "I might be older than you, but you haven't seen crazy until you get in the gravel with me. At the very least, I promise you won't be doing any surgeries for a while. You'll have some broken bones that'll need to heal."

He looked at me like a predator, sizing me up from head to toe. I could feel adrenaline building. If he wanted to fight, he was in the right place at the right time.

"Why did you really come here?" he said.

"We'll be going after him soon," I said. "One of them will make a mistake, and we'll be on them. I'll let you know when we're going to move on the judge. You might give some thought to suiting up and making an appearance."

# SATURDAY, NOVEMBER 8

Loretta Jilton pulled into the driveway of a house off Harold Avenue in Knoxville, north of the Tennessee River. She was tired. The events of the night before had unfolded quickly and unexpectedly. A gunshot had awakened her just before midnight, and she'd gone downstairs to find the judge standing over the body of a man who the judge said was his youngest son, David. The judge said David had walked in while the judge was sleeping and intended to stab the judge to death. There was blood and brain matter and bits of bone scattered all over the room. It had taken Loretta and the judge three hours to get the body out to the incinerator and get the room cleaned up. The judge hadn't uttered a word the entire time. He'd shot one of his own children in the head and acted like he was disposing of a piece of trash. He'd frightened Loretta before, but the feeling she'd gotten last night had terrified her. Never had she felt so close to pure evil. As she had a couple of nights earlier, she thought about running. Things were escalating. Alf was probably in jail and had probably told them everything. She would be in jail herself if she didn't run soon. But she knew the judge would never let her rest. He'd come after her, he'd eventually find her, and he'd make her suffer. Jail, Loretta decided, would be better than the alternative.

The neighborhood she drove into was lower-middle-class; the houses sat on quarter-acre lots and were constructed mostly of brown brick. There was an elementary school nearby. The house where she arrived was owned by a man who dealt in the dark, secretive world of human flesh. He was a pimp, a broker, a buyer and seller of women. Loretta hated him, hated dealing with him, hated what he did and what he stood for, but she needed him and others like him in order that she and the judge might continue to indulge in their unusual habits. In prior years, Loretta had procured women by simply picking them up on the street, but there were too many prying eyes on the streets. By developing a network of brokers in different cities, she could simply place an order, drive to a house, pick up a couple of girls, and be on her way. It was more expensive, but it was simpler and it was safer. The money she paid basically bought the rights to the women. Once she paid, she owned the woman. The system operated very much like slavery, but there was no documentation, no paperwork of any kind.

Loretta was met at the door by Byron Burkett, a slim man of medium height who was in his mid-thirties. Burkett's drawn, pasty complexion was that of a crack smoker, his brown eyes were bloodshot, and his black hair was shoulder-length and unkempt.

"C'mon in, Miss X," Burkett said. None of the brokers or pimps with whom Loretta dealt knew her real name, and the car she was driving was a rental from an agency at the airport in Maryville. "Been awhile. How you been?"

"Fine," Loretta said. "Are they in the den?"

Burkett nodded. The look on his face told Loretta he got the message that she wasn't there to make small talk.

Loretta walked into Burkett's small den. The place smelled of stale cigarette smoke. There was a pizza box on a table in front of a couch, and on the couch sat two women, both brunettes, both petite, in their mid-twenties and attractive, just the way the judge liked them. One introduced herself as Tracy and the other as Missy.

"Stand up and let me take a closer look," Loretta said.

The women stood and took a couple of steps away from the couch.

"Did Byron tell you the deal?" Loretta said as she walked around them both and began the lie she'd told to so many others. "I own a couple of massage parlors in Northeast Tennessee. You'll work in the parlors, but you'll live on our farm with me and my husband. Food and board are free, but we take what you earn at the parlors. You stay with us for six months, I'll give you each a thousand dollars, and then I'll cut you loose. I won't sell you to anyone. You'll just be on your own. Either of you have a problem with that?"

Neither woman said a word.

"Good, then let's get rolling."

Loretta paid Burkett a thousand in cash for each girl and led them to her car. They climbed in completely unaware of the horrible fate that awaited them.

# SATURDAY, NOVEMBER 8

eon's black bag men were in the judge's house on Friday after he left for court and Loretta went to the grocery store. They were in and out in forty-five minutes, and the TBI and Leon's department were able to capture every word that was said in that house on Friday evening and Saturday morning. The TBI surveillance plane had actually captured an image of the judge and Loretta carrying David's dead body across the yard to the incinerator on Thursday night/Friday morning during a brief break in the storm that pelted the area most of the night. The mist and light clouds obscured the photos enough so that we couldn't positively identify the people in the photographs, but we all knew who they were.

On Saturday morning, Loretta Jilton left for Knoxville to buy some women. She was followed by Anita White and her boss, Larry Knight, Leon Bates and me, two more TBI agents, and two of Leon's deputies. I had no business being involved in a law enforcement action, and everyone there knew it, but Leon had made it clear that if I wanted to be there, I was welcome. And after what had happened to David Craig, I wanted to be there. They would have had to cuff and shackle me to the bench at Leon's safe house to keep me away. We were in four vehicles, and we took turns keeping her in sight. The GPS tracker was working perfectly, but when Loretta dropped her vehicle off at a rental car agency at the airport in Maryville and picked up another car, there was a brief moment of uncertainty. We stayed on her, though, and Leon and I followed her to a house on Clifford Street. She walked into the house, stayed in there for about ten minutes, and walked out with two women, both petite and brunette, both of whom looked to be in their mid-to-late twenties.

As soon as she left and was out of sight, the two TBI agents roared up and disappeared into the house. Their job was to coerce and intimidate whomever Loretta had purchased the women from into being a witness against her. All we knew was the name we'd heard on the tape, Byron Burkett, but that name was obviously an alias because nothing came up on a Byron Burkett when Leon and Anita had run him through the databases. The agents were to bring Burkett to the TBI headquarters in Strawberry Plains, where, after we took down Loretta, we would make certain she saw him. That way, even if he refused to cooperate, we could lie to her and tell her he'd given her up.

We followed Loretta back to the car rental agency, and she and the women got out of the rental and into Loretta's Hyundai. We had no way of knowing the exact route Loretta was going to take, so the decision as to when to take her down was left up to Larry Knight. He was the top-ranking guy (besides Leon, of course, who was an elected official) and he knew Knoxville well.

Once Loretta left McGhee-Tyson Airport and turned onto Highway 129 heading toward Knoxville, we followed her to a fairly remote spot along the road near J.C. King Park. That was where Larry Knight felt traffic would be the lightest, and if Loretta happened to have a gun and start shooting, it was the place where there was the least probability of an innocent passerby being hurt.

We hung back about a quarter of a mile, and on Knight's order, everyone sped up. Leon was driving a black SUV that belonged to the department, and he swung around Loretta and began slowing quickly. At the same time, Knight and Anita pulled up beside Loretta in the left lane and Leon's two guys got on her rear bumper. We bracketed her and forced her into the emergency lane on the right shoulder. As soon as we stopped, everyone was out of the vehicles, weapons drawn (I was carrying the same shotgun I carried at the judge's house two nights earlier.) Knight ordered all three of them out of Loretta's car – one at a time – and made them lie face-down on the asphalt. They were immediately cuffed. Loretta went into the back seat of the S.U.V. with Leon and me, one of the brunettes went with Anita and Larry, and the other went with Leon's guys. They would be interviewed and released. I knew Larry was having a T.B.I. truck come to pick up Loretta's car and haul it to a waiting forensics team. We didn't know what we'd find, but we were looking for hair, fingerprints, skin fragments, anything that we might be able to match to a missing person report, anything we could use later to solidify a case against Loretta. We had to turn her against the judge.

We'd pulled back onto the road and had driven about a mile when Loretta said from the back seat, "One of you jerkoffs mind telling me what this is all about?"

I looked over at Leon and saw him smile. He looked up into the rearview mirror so she could see his eyes.

"This is about sex trafficking, which is a Class A felony in this state punishable by a minimum of fifteen years and a maximum of life in prison," he said in his signature drawl. "This is about torture and murder, about heinous crimes, which are punishable by death. Game's over for you, Ms. Jilton. I've seen your future, and it ain't pretty."

# SATURDAY, NOVEMBER 8

I sat outside the interrogation room at the TBI headquarters in Strawberry Fields and watched on a computer monitor as Leon and Anita went at Loretta Jilton.
Earlier, they'd put her in a small anteroom with a large,
glass window and made sure she'd seen Byron Burkett,
the man from whom she'd purchased two women, and
Alf Higgins, who was cuffed, shackled, waist-chained
and wearing an orange, jail-issued jumpsuit, walk by.

When they moved her to the interrogation room,
Leon began.

"You have the right to remain silent. Anything you
say can and will be used against you in a court of law.
You have a right to an attorney. If you can't afford an
attorney, one will be appointed for you. But my sugges-
tion is that you waive your rights and tell us what we
want to know, because if you don't, you're going to wind
up with a needle in your arm."

Leon looked over at Anita and said, "Was that last
thing I said coercive?"

"Maybe," Anita said, "but it's the truth. Besides,
we're not recording anything so nobody outside this
room knows what's being said. We already have enough

to put her away for sex trafficking and murder, and the murders are bad. Raping and torturing who knows how many women? How many did Alf say Miss Jilton and the judge murdered?"

"Alf can testify to about forty over a six-month period," Leon said. "He picked up the girls, and Miss Jilton and the judge tortured and murdered them. We could hammer them all on conspiracy to commit murder, but I'm going to ask the D.A. to cut Alf a little slack since he put us onto all of this. What about you, Miss Jilton? You interested in a little slack?"

Loretta Jilton had been sitting in the straight-backed chair with her hands folded on the table in front of her. She was wearing a pair of blue jeans and a pink, leopard-print sweater. Her black coat was hung on the back of her chair. She'd been looking back and forth between Anita and Leon, but the look wasn't one of hatred or contempt, it was more of resignation.

"How long you reckon those two women you bought a little while ago would have lived?" Leon said. "Alf says some of them make it as long as a week, some just a couple of days. All depends on the judge, doesn't it?"

"I believe Sheriff Bates asked you another question," Anita said. "We'd both appreciate an answer."

"What do you want from me?" Loretta said.

"I know the judge put you up to all of these terrible things," Anita said. "My fellow agents and I have done a lot of research on you over the past few days. I know you came up as rough as anyone can come up. I know about what your father and your uncle did to you. I know about the foster homes, the abuse you suffered there. I know about the drugs and the pimps and the life you lived before the judge came along and gave you some stability. But the price for that stability was high, wasn't it, Loretta? You'd never killed anyone before you met the judge, had you? And you wouldn't have ever killed anyone if fate hadn't put you in front of him in his courtroom. I don't know what he thought he saw in you, but what he really saw was weakness and vulnerability. He saw an opportunity to take advantage of and mold someone who had been abused her entire life and simply wasn't equipped to resist. He used you, Loretta, and now here you sit, facing the death penalty. You asked a minute ago what we want from you. We want the truth. We want you to tell us what the judge did to you, and what you and he have done to others. We want you to corroborate Alf Higgins's stories about the buying, raping, torturing and murdering of women. We want corroboration about Alf's stories of the judge's plan to select and kill other judges who had committed whatever sin he imagined they'd committed. We want you to corroborate Alf's story about the incinerator, about how and where the bodies were disposed of, and we want you to lead us to the places where ashes were dumped. We want you to testify against the judge if he goes to trial. We want you to do the right thing and help us put a monster away for good."

I leaned toward the monitor. There was only one in the room, and I was the only person watching. Leon had asked Larry Knight to give him privacy, but he wanted me to watch the interview. I suspected, again, that he wanted me to watch because he trusted me. I heard a sniffle and then saw tears begin to run down Loretta

Jilton's cheeks. I felt zero sympathy for her, though. Even if the judge had taken advantage of her, she had become an evil force, capable of some of the most inhuman conduct I'd ever encountered.

"What happens to me if I help you?" she whimpered. "Will I still get the death penalty? Will I still be in jail for the rest of my life?"

"Do you know who the district attorney general in Greene County is?" Leon asked her.

"I think his name was Beller, but there was an election. I didn't pay attention. I don't know who he is. Why?"

"Because these crimes, at least the rapes and the torture and the murders and disposing of the bodies, they all happened in Greene County," Leon said. "So the Greene County District Attorney will prosecute, and he's the only one who can help you. He was sitting in the front seat next to me on the drive here. He's outside in a waiting room. Do you want to talk to him?"

My mouth dropped open involuntarily and I heard myself say, "Ah crap, Leon. Really?"

I saw Loretta nod her head slowly, and then heard Leon say, "Sit tight. We'll be right back."

The next thing I knew they were walking out of the room. I stood and Leon walked up to me.

"Showtime, brother Dillard," he said.

"And I thought I was crazy," I said.

I looked at Anita. "Did you know anything about this?" I said.

She shrugged her shoulders.

"What do you expect me to do?" I said to Leon.

"Lie, cheat, coerce, tell her what she wants to hear. Get a written confession out of her so we can get a warrant and go arrest that miserable piece of garbage. Nobody will ever know what happened in that room besides you, me, Special Agent White and that psychopath in there. When she starts saying she was tricked later on, we'll all deny it. Nobody will believe her. This is one of those cases where the end justifies the means, brother Dillard. You wanted to come along, now go do your part."

"What name should I use?" I said.

"Just make one up. Doesn't matter. You heard her. She doesn't know who the Greene County D.A. is."

I shook my head, took a deep breath, and said, "The hell with it. Let's do it."

I put on my stern, trial-lawyer face and strode through the door with Leon and Anita right behind me. There were four chairs at the square table where Loretta was sitting and I sat down in the one across from her. I looked her directly in the eye.

"I understand you have something to tell me," I said.

"Who are you?" she said.

"Who do you think I am?"

She nodded toward Leon. "He said you're the district attorney in Greene County."

"That's right."

"He said you can make a deal with me."

"That depends on what you have to say."

"I want a promise, first. I want a promise that I won't spend the rest of my life in jail."

"I'm not promising you a damned thing, Miss Jilton, until I get some answers. How many women did you and the judge kill? And if you lie to me about a single detail, all bets are off. We already have enough to try you and execute you, but if you want to give up the judge, I'm willing to listen and I'm willing to show you some consideration. But not until after you give it up – all of it."

"I don't know exactly how many," she said, "but he keeps a diary. The sick bastard likes to relive the torture over and over. He reads about the murders like they were bedtime stories."

"Where's the diary?"

"In his study downstairs by the recliner. He was probably reading it the other night when his son came in."

"David? Are you talking about David Craig?"

"I think that was his name. Chris said his son came to kill him. He shot him in the head. I helped him clean up and helped carry the body out to the incinerator."

"What else?"

"He keeps souvenirs. Panties, jewelry, bras, clothing, things like that."

"And where are those located?"

"In a hope chest, if you can believe that. A cedar hope chest in our bedroom. It's getting full."

"Did you ever hear or witness anything between Judge Craig and Alf Higgins regarding the kidnappings and killings of the judges?"

"I heard all of it. He didn't hide anything from me."

"You'll show us where the ashes from all the bodies were dumped?"

She nodded.

"Is that a yes?"

"Yes, I'll show you."

"Okay," I said. "This is what's going to happen. You're going to write all of this down in the form of a statement, sign and date it, and give it to Agent White. After we verify everything and the judge is under arrest, I'll execute the necessary documents agreeing to a fifteen-year sentence for you. By all rights, you should never see the light of day outside of prison, but under these circumstances, if you give us the judge, I'll agree to the fifteen. Do we have a deal, Miss Jilton?"

She nodded her head, and I got up.

"Agent White and Sheriff Bates will take your statement in a few minutes. Excuse us."

We walked out of the room, and Leon slapped me on the shoulder.

"Hot damn, brother Dillard!" he said. "That was an Oscar-worthy performance. You pulled it off without even giving her a name. And a diary and a chest full of souvenirs? We're gonna bury this guy now."

"How are you going to play this from here on out?" I said. "The judge is probably already wondering where she is. Her statement is going to take three, four hours at least. And at some point, you're going to have to bring the Greene County sheriff and D.A. in on this."

"I'll soothe the egos," Leon said. "I'm good at that sort of thing. As far as the judge is concerned, as soon as we get the warrant and get organized, we'll go in heavy. I assume you'll want to be there at the end."

"Wouldn't miss it," I said. "But when you say heavy, you better go extra heavy. Something tells me this guy will do more than put up a fight. I think we'll be in for a war."

# SATURDAY, NOVEMBER 8

J udge Christopher Craig listened as Loretta's voice-mail came on yet again. He'd been calling for hours, and he feared the worst. It was Alf. Alf had told them everything. They'd somehow figured out a way to follow Loretta to Knoxville. She was most likely under arrest, being interrogated, and spilling her guts to save her own skin. The judge disconnected the call and tossed his phone down on the table.

*What to do?*

If Loretta was confessing, it meant that combined with what Alf had told them, they could probably get a warrant for his arrest and to search the property. It didn't necessarily mean they could convict him, though, because Alf was a career criminal and Loretta was a whore and a drug addict. They'd make terrible witnesses. He could burn the diary and the chest full of goodies, but his hobby had been going on for so long that they might find some other things. There would no doubt be blood spatter and other forms of forensic evidence in the fun room. He couldn't possibly clean it all up without burning down the house, and even if he burned down the house, there was still the incinerator and the outbuilding. There could be bone fragments, fingernails, hair, skin fragments. He could burn that, too, but Alf and Loretta knew where most of the ashes had been dumped. They'd dig and sift and would eventually find bone fragments. The judge didn't know whether they would be able to identify any of the fragments, but it was a possibility. The case against him would be largely circumstantial, but it would bring a huge amount of media attention, especially when the dead judges were factored in. He would be publicly humiliated, probably held without bail until trial.

Should he do as Loretta suggested and run?

*No. Not going to run and not going to jail. I'd rather die.*

Then the only thing left to do was stand and fight. They'd be coming, maybe tomorrow, maybe the next day. They'd probably come at dawn.

*And I'll be waiting. I have an arsenal of weapons. I'll spread them around the property, get out into the woods, and wait for them to come. I'm a Screaming Eagle of the 101st Airborne Division. My motto is Rendezvous with Destiny. And my destiny is to kill as many of these bastards as I can.*

# SATURDAY, NOVEMBER 8

I left Knoxville late in the afternoon. Loretta Jilton had given a detailed, gruesome statement that I was sure laid as little blame on herself as possible. But the things they had done to dozens, maybe a hundred, of women, were as inhuman as anything I'd ever heard about. The judge was definitely a psychopathic murderer, and as I drove along the interstate toward home, I began to get a terrible, uneasy feeling about what would happen when Leon and the cops showed up there in force. Leon said he thought it would take a full day to get everyone organized, which meant they would hit the judge's property at daylight on Monday morning. The number of people that would have to become involved would greatly increase the risk of leaks and greatly reduce the chance for surprise and the probability that the raid would go off efficiently.

And the judge would know they were coming. He would have figured it out when Loretta didn't show up with the girls. He might run, but I didn't think he would. He was too arrogant, too egomaniacal, too damned crazy. The judge was a former member of the 101st Airborne Division, one of the Army's most fanatical units. He may have been a lawyer, but if he was with the 101$^{st}$, he was also a dangerous soldier. He would have weapons. He might have stolen heavy weapons like machine guns or grenade launchers. He might have claymores. Leon and his people could very well walk into an ambush and a bunch of them could get slaughtered.

As I pulled into the garage a little before seven in the evening, I could feel an impulse, nearly irresistible, tugging at me, and I knew I was about to do something that would make me seem as insane as the judge. I had all the gear Leon had given me stowed in my pick-up, including the infrared equipment and the tactical shotgun. I also had some weapons in the house. As I stepped out of the truck, a plan began to formulate and I took my phone out of my pocket and sent a text message.

When I walked into the kitchen from the garage, Rio mauled me, as usual. Biscuit had taken a liking to me – which was mutual – so I had to pay equal attention to two massive, alpha male dogs without ignoring the tiny Chico, who was yapping and jumping up and down like he was on a pogo stick. Jack and Charlie were fixing stir-fry in the kitchen, and it smelled fantastic. It was amazing how Charlie got around on the walker. She'd figured out ways to do nearly everything for herself. She handled the walker like it was a part of her. She used it for balance, but she did it in a way that was so natural it didn't seem at all like an impediment.

"Where's your mom?" I said to Jack.

"In the bedroom."

"Asleep?"

"In and out."

I walked into the bedroom and Caroline was lying on her back, propped up on a couple of pillows. She was rubbing her knees softly. The television was on, but I could tell she wasn't paying much attention.

"Hi, baby," I said. "Knees hurting?"

"Always," she said. "And my pelvis. I just can't get comfortable."

"Are you going to eat? Want me to bring you a plate?"

"I don't think so," she said. "I'm not very hungry."

"Milkshake?" I said. "I'll make you a shake or a smoothie, whatever you want."

"Not right now. Thanks."

"You need to eat something, baby. You weigh what? A buck ten? Less? We want to see some meat on those bones."

She looked up at me with listless eyes. The drugs.

"Thank you," she said, "but I'm fine. I just need to rest a little."

"Okay, sweetie," I said. I bent over and kissed her on the forehead. "I'm close if you need anything."

I walked back out into the kitchen and sat down with Jack and Charlie. They'd made Kung-Pao shrimp, and it was delicious. We chatted for a while. They asked about the case and I told them about some, but not all, of what had happened. After we'd finished eating, cleaned up and done the dishes, Charlie went off to her room and I asked Jack if I could speak with him privately for a couple of minutes.

"Sure," he said.

"Let's go out to the barn."

"How was your mom today?" I said as we walked through the cold darkness toward the barn.

"Kind of in and out," he said. "Sometimes things just don't seem to click."

"I've noticed. Did she eat? I couldn't get her to eat."

"She wanted fried chicken for lunch, so I went and got her some. She ate most of it, along with some fries."

We walked into the barn and I closed the door against the cold and flipped on a light. I walked over to Sadie's stall and she stuck her head out and let me rub her. Jack stood beside me and did the same. After a couple of minutes, Sadie turned away and I turned around and sat down on a bale of straw. Jack sat next to me.

"What's on your mind?" he said.

"I'm going out later. I just thought you should know."

"Out? Where?"

"You know this judge I've been telling you about? The one who's responsible for killing the judges and who has been killing women? I'm going to take him down."

"Take him down? You mean arrest him? You're not a cop, Dad."

"I mean I'm going to do whatever I have to do. If I can surprise him and get an advantage on him, I'll call Leon and have him and his boys come and get him."

"I thought you said they were going in to arrest him in a couple of days."

"They are, but I'm afraid they're going to wind up getting cut to pieces. It's gotten too big. Too many people involved. And this guy is a crazy, former soldier who is probably armed to the teeth, and he knows they're coming."

"And you're going to what? Go knock on his door and say, 'Excuse me, I'm Joe Dillard and this is a citizen's arrest? Put your hands in the air while I call the cops?'"

"Don't be a wise ass."

"Then stop being irrational."

"I'm not being irrational. I just think this is a better way to do it. And besides, this guy raped his son, who later became my client, and then he killed him."

"You're sure about that?"

"Absolutely."

Jack stood and began to pace.

"I don't know, Dad. This is vigilante stuff. I mean, I know you took care of those Colombian guys a few years ago, but they came to our house. This is different. This is you going to *his* house. What if you wind up killing him?"

"Then I leave him there and walk away. Nobody will care, and I promise I won't lose any sleep over it."

"Yes, you will. You're not a murderer."

"It won't be murder, Jack."

"Damned fine line you're treading, Dad."

"Not the first time."

"And what if he kills you?"

"Then I guess I'll be dead."

"And you won't have to watch Mom suffer any more, and you won't have to watch her die eventually."

"What? What did you say?" I stood, feeling my temper flare.

"That's what this is really about, isn't it? Think about it, Dad. You're doing something you don't really have to do. Hell, you don't really need to be involved at all at this point, do you? You can say it's because of your client all you want, but you're lying to yourself. You're looking for a way out of what you're going through with Mom. If this guy kills you, your suffering stops."

I took a step toward him.

"If you weren't my son, I'd punch you in the face right now. You're calling me a coward."

He didn't budge an inch.

"You want to punch me? Go ahead. Give it your best shot. But don't expect me to just take it. Don't forget who raised me. And I'm not calling you a coward. I'm suggesting that you might not be making very good decisions right now. Because going to a psychopath's house in the dead of night with the intention of killing him or holding him for the police is not a good decision, no matter what your justification might be. Besides that, I don't want to lose you. I love you, Dad. I need you. Mom needs you. Charlie needs you. Randy and Lilly and Joseph and Sarah and Grace, we all love you and we all need you."

"Stop," I said, holding up my hands. "I've made up my mind. I'm going. I can take this guy and save a lot of bloodshed."

"Then take me with you," he said.

"Not a chance."

"At least take Rio."

"No way I'd give him a chance to kill my dog."

"So you'll give him a chance to kill you, but not your dog."

"I know what I'm doing, Jack."

"You're getting old, Dad."

"Yeah? So is he."

"Please, Dad, don't go."

I turned toward the door.

"I just wanted to let somebody know. I'm going to get some rest and then I'm going at midnight. Don't call anyone. Don't tell anyone. But if I'm not back by morning, call Leon and tell him to come running. I love you, Jack."

# SUNDAY, NOVEMBER 9

I left at midnight, black jeans, thermal underwear, layers of black, long-sleeved thermal undershirts, a black hoodie, a black jacket, black gloves, a black ski-mask, a black stocking cap, an old pair of black combat boots, an old black web belt and harness with suspenders, and thermal socks. If it was black and in my closet, chances were I was wearing it. I'd also dug up some old camouflage paint in my outbuilding and slathered it over my face. I had the tactical shotgun, the night-vision gear, a Beretta 9mm pistol holstered in the small of my back, a Smith and Wesson .38 revolver holstered around my left ankle and a K-bar knife taped in its sheath to my suspenders. I had extra ammo in pouches on the belt. I was as ready as I could have been, but as I drove down the road, I found myself wishing I had an assault rifle and a couple of grenades. And a platoon of highly-trained Rangers.

I hadn't managed to get any sleep. The things Jack said kept rolling around and around in my mind, and as I lay there listening to Caroline's uneven breathing, I wondered if what he'd said was true. Was I trying to commit suicide to save myself the pain of watching her suffer or perhaps die? Maybe I was, but it didn't change the fact that I'd made up my mind to go after Judge Craig, and once I made up my mind to do something, I usually had a hard time stopping myself. I got to the place where I'd decided to park – about two miles west of the judge's property – about forty minutes after I left the house. The temperature was below freezing, and I could see my breath in the darkness as I moved quietly through the woods. Fast moving clouds largely obscured the moon, which was low in the west. There was a stiff breeze blowing, and the branches in the trees above were clicking and sometimes groaning. By the time I got to the knoll overlooking the judge's house where Leon and I had been the night David was killed, it was probably one-fifteen or so. I wasn't wearing a watch and I'd left my cell in my truck.

I crouched next to a tree and looked through the infrared goggles for several minutes. The house was deathly still. There were no lights. The judge's Cadillac was under the carport, though, which meant – or at least I thought it meant – that he hadn't run. He was around somewhere. I found it difficult to believe he would be sleeping if he suspected the police would be coming for him. I stayed still for several more minutes, surveying back and forth from the house to the outbuilding to the carport to the woods surrounding the house.

Nothing. So I decided to move closer.

I'd moved about thirty yards down the hill when something made me freeze. It was a light, coming from one of the windows on the side of the house. It was blood red, and it was pulsing slowly. It was one of the eeriest things I'd ever seen. I watched it for a few seconds and was about to come off of the tree and move closer when I heard a hammer cock and felt the hard steel of a gun barrel at the base of my skull.

"Welcome to the party," a voice whispered. "You seem to be the first guest to arrive. Drop that shotgun and put your hands behind your back."

I cursed myself under my breath for being so stupid. The light was nothing more than a diversion. I wondered how long he'd been watching me.

I felt handcuffs snap firmly around my wrists and then his hands were all over me. He found the pistols, he took the knife and the ammo. Before I knew it, I was disarmed and completely at his mercy.

"Walk," he said.

I started off in the direction of the outbuilding. I figured he would probably just shoot me and dump me in the incinerator if I couldn't figure out a way to get away from him or subdue him.

He shoved me in another direction.

"The house," he growled.

We walked in through the same door from which he had emerged the night Leon had been placing the GPS devices on the vehicles. The house was dark – with the exception of the pulsing red light – and smelled of mildew and stale cigar smoke. We passed the room where the red light was still pulsing, went down a hallway, turned right and took a few steps.

"Stop," the man behind me said. I hadn't yet seen his face, but I knew from the commands that he was as tall as I. He opened a door to my right, flipped on a light switch, and said, "Down the stairs."

I resisted. Something told me that if I went down those steps, I wouldn't ever return.

The next thing I knew something struck me hard in my lower back – probably his boot – and I went sprawling forward. I did a couple of somersaults, saw a bright flash as my head clipped a step, and landed with a thud and a groan on concrete at the base of the steps. I took quick stock. There was a knife-like pain beneath my right armpit. Probably a cracked rib, and I could feel blood running down my legs where skin had been torn from my knees. My head was throbbing, but I was still alive.

He jerked me off the floor and pushed me down yet another short hallway, where he opened a door and shoved me inside a dark room. When he turned on the light, it was all I could do to keep from screaming. There were ropes and pullies and chains and hooks and masks and an assortment of devices that could only be described as medieval torture tools. The judge shoved me into a wide-backed, wooden chair that was bolted into the floor and quickly began wrapping me in chains. Before long, I was completely immobilized.

He stepped back, and I looked up into the face of evil incarnated. His eyes were almost black and devoid of emotion. His hair was short, salt-and-pepper, just a little longer than it would have been had he still been in the military, and it was covered by a woodland boonie hat. He was wearing a woodland battle dress uniform with the name "Craig" stitched on a nametape above the right breast pocket of the blouse, "U.S. Army" stitched on a branch tape above the left breast pocket and the 101st Airborne insignia on his right shoulder. His pants were tucked into his combat boots and his square-jawed face was streaked with camouflage paint. He reached out and jerked the stocking cap and ski mask off of my head.

"Who are you?" he said.

"The guy that's going to kill you before this is over."

His laughter echoed off of the walls around me.

"How many are with you?" he said.

"I came alone. I was David's lawyer. He told me about you raping him when he was a boy. Of course that was before you murdered him and put him in your incinerator."

He backhanded me across the mouth and I felt my lower lip split against my teeth.

"How many?"

"Just me," I said, as I spit blood at him. "And I swear to god I'm going to kill you before this night is over."

"You might just get your chance," he said. "Because I plan to have a little fun with you before I punch your ticket."

He nodded toward the bench covered in torture devices.

"I'm going to go back outside right now and make sure you're not lying to me. While I'm gone, figure out which one of those toys you want me to stick in you first."

He smiled wickedly.

"By the time I get finished with you, you'll be begging me to kill you," he said.

"Looking forward to it," I said with a false sense of bravado, because I could feel a sense of terror and dread creeping into my loins. It was a feeling I'd never before encountered, a visceral fear that made me want to scream.

The judge turned and disappeared. I began to struggle against the restraints, but it was pointless. He'd obviously done this kind of thing before. I was wrapped in a chain from my chest to my knees, and the chain had been secured with a padlock. The key to the padlock was in the judge's pocket. I looked around the room some more, at the benches and tables and chairs, the restraints, the ropes and pulleys and devices, and I began to imagine I could hear the screams of the women who had been in this room before me. I thought about Caroline, lying home in bed, certainly asleep. I wondered what she would do without me, whether she would feel betrayed that I'd left her. I thought about Jack and the admonitions. He'd been right. I thought about the old adage, "Be careful what you wish for. You just might get it." Was I getting what I'd wished for?

I wondered whether Jack had called anyone – Leon in particular. Leon had gotten me out of more than one jam in my life. Maybe he was out there in the woods, waiting for an opportunity to pounce on the judge and get me out of this mess. I put an image in my mind of Leon putting a bullet through the judge's chest and held onto it. It was my only hope.

And it didn't last long.

Less than ten minutes after he'd left, the judge returned, this time dragging an unconscious Leon Bates by his ankles. Leon's hands were also cuffed behind his back – my guess was the judge had plenty of handcuffs

– and he had a large, purple bump on his forehead that was oozing blood.

"Friend of yours?" the judge said as he dragged Leon across the room.

"Never seen him before," I said.

"Liar. Lawyer and liar. They go hand in hand, don't they?"

"Sort of like judge and psychopath?" I said. "I've always believed anyone who wanted to be a judge had to have a screw loose. You must have all kinds of screws rattling around in there."

The judge lifted Leon onto a table near the wall and quickly and expertly tied him down, face up.

"This one's not carrying any ID either," the judge said. "Sure you don't know who he is?"

"You're finished," I said. "They're going to come rolling in here with howitzers if they have to. No matter what you do to us, you won't live another thirty-six hours."

"So they're coming tomorrow morning?" the judge said. "Thanks for the information. It'll give me a little more time to prepare."

He turned away from Leon and walked over to the table. He picked up my K-Bar knife.

"Nice knife," he said. "Did you plan to kill me with it?"

"Still might."

He smiled as he walked toward me. "You've got a smart mouth, lawyer. I think before I start shoving things up your ass, I'll just cut your tongue out. And then maybe your eyes. I can snip your fingers off real easy with those bolt cutters right there. Your toes, too.

You'll pass out a few times, but I'm patient. I'll wait for you to wake up and then go back to work on you. Or I'll work on your friend while I'm waiting for you. Either way, it's going to be a long night for you and a fine night for me."

My knife was in his left hand, and in his right, he held a device I'd never before seen. It was shiny, probably stainless steel, about six or seven inches long.

"See this?" he said as he held the device up. "This is what they call a Jennings mouth gag. Oral surgeons and dentists use it to hold their patients' mouths open while they're working on them. Some folks use them for sexual games. I'm going to shove it in your mouth and then ratchet your mouth open, and then I'm going to cut out your tongue."

As he reached for my head, I started twisting and spitting and straining. I clenched my teeth, doing anything I could to keep him from getting a hold of me, but he was strong. He managed to get the device slipped into my mouth and began ratcheting it open. Before I knew it, my jaws were popping and my mouth was agape. There was nothing I could do.

He'd set the K-Bar on a bench to his right. As he leaned over to pick it up, I saw something as surreal as anything I'd ever witnessed in my life. A figure appeared in the doorway. It looked like the creature from the black lagoon, olive-drab and shapeless. It stepped into the room and said, "Turn around."

The judge, obviously startled, turned to face the thing, and the thing raised a pistol.

And then it began to fire the pistol.

Fire and smoke, deafening noise filled the room as the pistol fired again and again and again. The judge was driven back against a wall and slid into a sitting position while the man in the Ghillie suit kept firing. After he'd fired maybe thirteen or fourteen shots, the man in the Ghillie suit walked slowly over the judge, pointed the pistol directly at his forehead, and splattered his brains against the block wall. The pistol disappeared inside the suit and he turned toward me. He knelt and looked at my restraints, then stood and removed the mouth gag.

"Where's the key to this lock?" he said.

"In his pocket. Right side."

The man, who was wearing so much face paint that I didn't recognize him, turned and retrieved the key from the now-deceased judge. He unlocked the padlock and helped me get free of my restraints. Leon began to stir just then. I saw his eyes open and heard him say, "What the Sam Hill is going on here?"

"Go," I said to the man in the Ghillie suit. "And thank you."

I watched him walk out the door, then set about freeing Leon from the rope that had been wrapped around him.

"What happened?" Leon said.

"You don't want to know. The judge is dead, though."

"Who killed him?"

"I don't know who he was," I lied. "Did Jack call you?"

Leon nodded and rubbed his forehead gingerly. "Didn't get here quite in time, I reckon. Man, somebody walloped me with something."

"It was the judge. He dragged you in here and tied you to this bench. He was going to torture us."

"Well, I reckon I'm glad he's dead, then. Never been much of one for torture, especially when I'm on the receiving end. Say you don't know who killed him?"

"I saw him, but he was wearing a Ghillie suit and a bunch of camo paint. I couldn't see his face."

But I'd recognized his voice.

I'd sent a text to Michael Craig, and he'd come to kill his father.

# SUNDAY, NOVEMBER 9

eon decided it was best if he dealt with the fallout. He was calling Anita White as I half-walked, half-stumbled out of the house and back through the woods to my truck. I arrived home around three in the morning. Jack was standing in the garage when I pulled in.

"You made it," he said as he hugged my neck.

"Barely," I said.

"You look a little beat up. Want some coffee?"

"I don't think so. I think I'll hit the sack. Thank you for calling Leon, Jack. He made it, and I was in a bad spot."

"So he saved you?"

"Not exactly, but having him there was ... well, I just wanted to say thank you."

"What happened to the judge?" Jack said.

"He didn't make it."

"So it's over?"

"Almost."

I turned away and went into the bedroom. I sat down softly on the bed next to Caroline and listened to her breathe. Before I knew it, tears were streaming down my face, and a short time later, I was sobbing. She stirred and I felt a warm hand on mine.

"Joe? Joe? What's wrong? Are you all right?"

I pulled myself together and moved around to her side of the bed. I sat down beside her and began to rub her forehead.

"I almost left you tonight, baby," I said.

"What do you mean?"

"I did something stupid, something I didn't have to do, and almost got myself killed. I'm so sorry. I swear to you nothing like this will happen again."

She sighed deeply, her eyes rolled back in her head, and I knew none of what I'd said had registered. She wouldn't remember it in the morning. So I made the vow to myself instead of to her.

I would stay in this fight with her to the bitter end, no matter how painful it might be for her, for me, or for the kids. I would do whatever it took to help her stay alive and stay as comfortable as possible until the disease finally took her or they found more effective treatments. Hell, maybe they'd even find a cure if she could hang in there long enough. I would do what a husband should do, what a father should do.

I would be strong, and I would be true.

# MONDAY, NOVEMBER 24

T wo weeks later, I was sitting in a conference room at the law office of Richard "Rick" Peckwell. He'd filed his lawsuit, and the first two depositions – those of me and Jimmy Carr, his girl-beating, man-bun-wearing client – had just been completed. Carr had run up forty-seven thousand dollars in medical bills, much of it unnecessary chiropractic work. We'd gone through the events of that afternoon fairly quickly. I'd admitted to beating the crap out of him, and he'd lied about slapping Lyndsey and shoving Lilly.

Carr and his father had just left, and Peckwell and I were waiting for the court reporter to pack up and leave when Peckwell said, "Didn't go so well for you today, did it, Joe?"

"Depends on how you look at it," I said. "Your boy's a liar."

"That'll be up to a jury, if you still want to take a chance on taking it that far. He's still willing to settle for a hundred thousand, but that number's going to go up if you continue to be obstinate."

"Obstinate? Wow, I didn't know you knew any three-syllable words."

I reached into my briefcase and slid a stack of papers across the desk to Peckwell.

"What's this?" he said.

"Notices of the next round of depositions. My office, two weeks."

He began to leaf through the notices.

"Who are these people?" he said.

"Have you noticed they're all girls? Seven of them, not including my daughter and Lyndsey. Every one of those girls is going to swear under oath that your boy either slapped them or punched them in the face. There will also be some hair pulling, a lot of verbal abuse, and at least one sexual abuse claim. He twisted one girl's breast so hard it was purple for a week. She has a photo. I'll show it to you at the deposition. He's been doing this kind of thing since he was fifteen."

"None of this is relevant," Peckwell said. There was a tone of desperation in his voice.

"He just lied to me under oath. Every one of these girls will be allowed to testify because the testimony goes to his character and because it establishes a pattern of abuse," I said. "But I'll tell you what. I'm willing to concede that I may have gone too far by sending him to the emergency room. I don't regret it, but I'm a grown man, he's still a teenager, and I overreacted a little. So I'll pay him ten grand toward his medical expenses, and we can call it a day. Your cut comes out of the ten. If he isn't willing to take that, the jury is going to hear from every one of these girls and not only will he not get a dime, he – and his lawyer – might wind up getting lynched."

Peckwell folded his arms across his chest and stared at me. He hated me, and I enjoyed bathing in the emotion.

"Write the check to my trust account," he said. "I'll sell it to him."

"And you'll draw up the order dismissing the lawsuit. No admission of fault or guilt. And don't reveal the terms of the settlement. Just dismiss it."

"Agreed," he said.

I pulled my checkbook out of my pocket, wrote the check, and that was that.

# SATURDAY, MAY 20

It was a clear, cloudless, eighty-four-degree day in mid-May when the family gathered to celebrate the opening of Caroline's new pool. It had cost me a mint and was installed over a four-week period in April by a company called Brooks Malone out of Greeneville. It was fiberglass, eight-and-a-half feet deep at the deep end, salt-water, heated (Caroline liked to keep it at ninety degrees) and immaculately landscaped with pavers and river flats and dogwoods and crepe myrtles and several other species of plants. There was a tanning deck with an eighteen-inch deep pool that spilled over into the main pool. The family was all there, along with Leon Bates and his girlfriend, a strip-club owner named Erlene Barlowe. Leon and Erlene didn't appear together in public, but they'd been invited to our little party, and they'd showed up. The older crowd was hanging out on the back deck while the younger crowd was lounging around the pool. Charlie and Jack were both in the pool, along with my grandson, Joseph, and my niece, Grace. Charlie was already getting around without her walker some. She planned to use the pool to accelerate her rehab program. We'd already eaten burgers and hot dogs, which is what

Caroline wanted served, and everyone seemed to be having a nice time.

"Did you hear that Sheriff Sherfey and Buck Garland pleaded to perjury?" Leon said.

"Yeah," I said. "Sherfey will spend three months in his own jail and Garland got probation. Then Sherfey will go back to work. The county commission over there couldn't get enough votes together to oust him."

"Yeah, well, they'll be getting what they deserve," Leon said. "And oh, I forgot to tell you, Alf Higgins got himself knifed at Riverbend," Leon said to me as he, Erlene, Caroline and I sat around a table on the deck. Riverbend is a maximum security prison in Nashville. "Tried to bully his way into some kind of gambling hustle, and they cut him up pretty bad. Last I heard he may not make it."

"Couldn't have happened to a nicer guy," I said.

The public spin from the TBI, the Greene County Sheriff's Department and the Greene County D.A.'s office on Judge Craig went like this:

Judge Christopher Craig had died from a single gunshot wound to the head in an apparent suicide after he discovered the police were onto him for mass murder and for hiring the kidnapping and murder of five Tennessee judges. Testimony provided by Alf Higgins, a violent offender who had been apprehended in Washington County during the commission of an aggravated burglary, had led police to Loretta Jilton, a woman who had lived with Judge Craig for quite some time. The Tennessee Bureau of Investigation and the Greene County Sheriff's Department had taken over the investigation at that time and secured warrants for Judge Craig's arrest and for the search of his property. Upon arriving at the scene, TBI Assistant Special Agent In Charge Anita White, working out of Knoxville, discovered the judge in a room in his basement. A forensics team found a diary in his study, and it outlined in gory detail a horrifying story of torture and murder. A cedar chest was also found in the judge's bedroom – right where Loretta had said it would be – and it contained what were allegedly souvenirs from his victims. Tiny pieces of bone fragment had been found in and around the incinerator in the judge's outbuilding, along with David Craig's pickup truck. The newspapers and TV news reported that David Craig was missing and assumed dead. More bone fragments had subsequently been discovered by sifting in and around ponds and creeks on the judge's property. Only five bone fragments had yielded positive DNA matches to victims, and it was those five victims that became the focus of the investigation into Loretta Jilton. She eventually pleaded guilty to five counts of sex trafficking and murder and was sentenced to five consecutive life sentences. Her claims that she was offered a fifteen-year maximum sentence by the Greene County District Attorney General fell on deaf ears. She was being housed in the maximum security unit at the Tennessee Prison for Women in Nashville.

The way it really happened, Leon said, was that once he got hold of Anita the night the judge was killed, she, along with her boss Larry Knight, immediately came and gathered up the judge's body. He was taken to Knoxville, where a medical examiner, working under orders from people much higher up than he, performed an autopsy that essentially ignored fourteen bullet wounds. Since the judge had no competent immediate family (his mother was in a long-term care facility with Alzheimer's and Michael was not taken into consideration), his body was cremated at a funeral home in Knoxville and his ashes were spread at Asbury Cemetery not too far from Strawberry Plains.

"Can we talk about something else?" Erlene said. Her bottled red hair was still as flashy as ever and she was wearing a tiger-striped bikini covered by a zebra-striped robe. "I hate hearing about all this killing and mayhem and what not all the time. What about you, Miss Caroline? How are you feeling, sweetie pie?"

Caroline and Erlene were vastly different, but they shared one important thing in common – toughness. I could tell they liked each other a great deal.

"I'm actually doing pretty well," Caroline said. "I feel stronger than I have in months, I've put on some weight, and I think I'm off the croak again."

Erlene's head tilted to the side just a bit.

"Excuse me, honey, did you say off the croak?"

Caroline smiled and looked at me.

"Private joke between Joe and me," she said. "When I get really sick, a lot of people gossip and Joe started saying one day that they've got me back on the croak. He'd tell me that I need to get off the croak. So right now, I'm off the croak."

"That's wonderful to hear," Erlene said. "Just wonderful."

It was a chemo drug called Eribulin and a hormone blocker called Herceptin that had slowed the cancer once again. Nothing around the brain seemed to be moving, the bone scans were stable, and the liver and lung were both stable as well. Caroline had managed to get back to the dance school a couple of weeks before the year-end recital and had been there that entire day. Lilly was the main force behind the show, but Caroline was there, and that made everyone feel better.

As I looked out over the pool, the barn, the lake and up at the brilliant sky, I couldn't help but feel a sense of peace. Randy and Lilly and Joseph would be leaving soon, but we would manage. We'd always managed. Jack and Charlie were revving up the law practice and I was looking forward to seeing what the future held for them. Sarah was in a good place, enjoying working at her diner, and Grace was happy and one of the most beautiful little girls I'd ever seen.

A smile crossed my face, and for the first time in a long time, I felt like everything would be all right. The atmosphere was one of family and friends and love and hope, and as far as I was concerned, it just didn't get any better than that.

Thank you for reading, and I sincerely hope you enjoyed *Judgment Cometh (And That Right Soon)*. As an independently published author, I rely on you, the reader, to spread the word. So if you enjoyed the book, please tell your friends and family, and if it isn't too much trouble, I would appreciate a brief review on Amazon. Thanks again. My best to you and yours.

Scott

# ABOUT THE AUTHOR

Scott Pratt was born in South Haven, Michigan, and moved to Tennessee when he was thirteen years old. He is a veteran of the United States Air Force and holds a Bachelor of Arts degree in English from East Tennessee State University and a Doctor of Jurisprudence from the University of Tennessee College of Law. He lives in Northeast Tennessee with his wife, their dogs, and a parrot named JoJo.

**www.scottprattfiction.com**

# ALSO BY SCOTT PRATT

# DUE PROCESS

By

SCOTT PRATT

# ACKNOWLEDGEMENTS

Thank you to Don Spurrell and Jim Bowman, both great friends and excellent lawyers. They're my go-to guys when I have a question about law. And thank you to Dr. Kenneth Ferslew for helping me understand the effects of GHB and the procedures involved in its detection.

*This book, along with every book I've written and every book I'll write, is dedicated to my darling Kristy, to her unconquerable spirit and to her inspirational courage. I loved her before I was born and I'll love her after I'm long gone.*

# PART ONE

# FRIDAY, AUGUST 23

**M**y name is Joe Dillard, and it was hot and muggy outside as I drove my wife's car northeast through Knoxville on our way back home from Nashville. My wife, Caroline, was in the passenger seat, sleeping. I was listening to a podcast called "S-Town" about a bipolar, suicidal genius in Alabama who probably suffered from mercury poisoning and may or may not have hidden a bunch of gold on his property.

I was listening to the podcast primarily to keep my mind off of what was going on with Caroline. The drugs that had been controlling her metastatic breast cancer had once again stopped working – the cancer was advancing in her liver – and she'd been placed in a clinical trial at Vanderbilt University in Nashville. The trial was studying the effectiveness of an immunotherapy drug that had not yet been approved by the Food and Drug Administration. She'd been on the drug for almost two months and had tolerated it fairly well. It had also shrunk the tumors in her liver, but other drugs had done the same thing, and, like lethal soldiers, the cancer eventually found a way to improvise, adapt and overcome.

She'd also recently had to have radiation on her left knee because a cancerous tumor had wrapped itself around the joint and the doctors said they were afraid the knee would snap. I wouldn't wish radiation on my worst enemy after seeing its effects on Caroline in the past. She'd had her breast radiated initially, and that put her down for several months. Later, after the metastasis, she'd had her entire spine radiated, which nearly killed her. After that, they'd radiated her brain to keep the cancer cells from getting in there. The brain radiation had left her unable to function for months.

And now they'd told us that an MRI of Caroline's brain showed the beginnings of cancer in her cerebellum, which is the part of the brain that controls balance and movement. I found that ironic and tragic, because she had been a dancer and dance teacher all of her life. The neurologist had assured us that it could be handled with radiosurgery (precisely-targeted radiation) and that there would be no side effects, but I hated the thought of Caroline going through more radiation. I hated that the disease had emaciated her, that it had taken her beautiful hair, that it had caused her so much pain and worry and heartache. I hated that she had to rely on so many drugs to survive. I hated the relentlessness of it all. I'd come to hate cancer with a passion I could not begin to adequately describe.

The worst part of the clinical trial was that we had to drive to Nashville two out of every three weeks, and Nashville was a five-hundred-and-fifty-mile round trip from our home in Johnson City. We also had to spend the night in a hotel each time, so it was expensive. Caroline told me we were spending a little over a thousand dollars a month for hotels, gas and meals, but I wasn't really concerned about the expense. We were in good shape financially, and even if we weren't, I would have spent my last dime if it helped make her feel better and prolonged her life.

She woke up as we entered Knoxville, just like she always did. The nurses at Vanderbilt gave her Benadryl during her immune-drug infusion, and it always put her to sleep. She slept through the infusion, woke up long enough to get to the car, and then slept another two-and-a-half hours until we got to Knoxville.

I looked over at her when she said, "What are you listening to?"

"It's called 'Shit Town,'" I said.

"Classy title."

"It actually fits. You'd have to listen to it to understand. You want me to turn it off and put on some music?"

"Please. I don't think I can handle Shit Town right now."

"Country?"

"Is there anything else?"

Caroline had become a huge fan of modern country music. It had come out of the blue a few years earlier. She'd spent her entire life listening to pop – the same music the majority of her dance students listened to – but one day she heard a cross-over country song that she loved, and she'd been listening to country ever since. Her favorite artist was Carrie Underwood, who Caroline said had perfected her own genre called "vigilante country." I'd listened to some of Ms. Underwood's music and had to agree with Caroline's classification of the genre. Carrie Underwood had probably killed off more men in her songs than any other artist I'd ever heard. I wondered why Caroline loved the lyrics so much, though. I'd asked her whether I should start watching my back.

As we approached one of the exits not far from the University of Tennessee, Caroline said, "You know what? I could use a beer."

Caroline rarely drank, so the statement was a surprise.

"Are you asking me to stop and get you a beer?"

"No. I'm asking you to stop and get me a six-pack. Get those little ones. What are they, seven ounces?"

"Yeah, seven ounces. What brought on this sudden thirst for beer?"

"I don't know. Maybe it's the trial drug. But I want to drink a few beers."

"Do you think it'll be good for you?" I said.

"C'mon, Joe. I have cancer in my bones, my liver and my brain. I've had it for years. I've taken every drug known to man. Do you seriously think a couple of beers is going to matter?"

I couldn't argue with that, so I pulled off I-40, went into a convenience store, and bought a six-pack of seven-ounce Bud Light bottles. I opened one, handed it to her, and headed back onto the interstate. She was digging in the bag for a second beer by the time I merged onto the highway.

"Are we breaking the law?" she said.

"Do you mean are *you* breaking the law? I'm not drinking in the car."

"Well, am I?"

"Would it make you feel good if you were?"

"It'd make me feel naughty. I don't get a chance to be naughty much these days."

"Sorry to disappoint you," I said, "but a passenger can drink a beer in the great state of Tennessee."

"I'm disappointed."

"You can pretend you're naughty. Use your imagination."

The second bottle went down almost as quickly as the first.

"You're slamming that stuff," I said. "You looking to get drunk?"

She took OxyContin for pain every day, she'd taken the Benadryl earlier, and she was already reaching for her third beer.

"I need to talk to you," she said.

"And you can't do it sober?"

"I'd rather not."

"Okay ... talk."

"You've been dreaming about me dying, Joe. You're having nightmares about it."

What she was saying was true. She'd awakened me several times over the past month, but I had no idea she knew the specifics of the dreams I'd been having.

"I'm sorry," I said. "I'm talking in my sleep?"

"You've always talked when you have nightmares, and you sweat so much the sheets get soaked. You've been having nightmares about Sarah, too, about when she was raped when you were children."

"What do you want me to say, Caroline? I don't have them intentionally."

"Do you think I'm going to die?"

"No."

"Do you want me to die? Are you tired of all this? Because I'd understand if you are. I read about this syndrome last week. It's called compassion fatigue. I think you have it."

"Did you just ask me if I want you to die? I'm not even going to answer the question. I'll just chalk it up to the drugs and the beer. And I've never heard of compassion fatigue."

"I'm not drunk and I've taken so many drugs they don't even affect me. Look up compassion fatigue when we get home. It happens to a lot of different groups of people, like nurses and doctors and police officers, but one of the other groups is caregivers within families who have to deal with the long-term illness of a relative or a spouse. You're definitely in that category."

"So? Are you saying I don't care anymore?"

"I'm saying you're tired of all this and it's stressing you out to the point that you're having nightmares."

"I think you're wrong."

"I'm not wrong. You're losing compassion. You're becoming numb. You're doing it to protect yourself because you're afraid I'm going to die."

"Fine," I said. I was starting to get angry but trying very hard to control the emotion. "But this isn't fair. Seriously, how dare you suggest that I want you to die? So you have cancer. That doesn't mean you can do or say whatever you want. Sometimes you think there are no longer any consequences to your behavior because you can always play the cancer card."

"See?" she said, her voice rising. "That's exactly what I'm talking about. You're mean to me. You were never mean to me before."

As much as I hated it, this kind of spat was becoming more frequent between us. There always seemed to be tension hanging over us. I knew it was the constant pressure and frustration from the disease, but that didn't make it any less real. And as much as I didn't want to admit it, there was probably at least a grain of truth to what she was saying. I thought she was wrong about any lack of compassion, but the more time that passed and the more the disease progressed, the more stress I felt. I found myself wondering what I would do without her, and I didn't have any answers. But I couldn't say that out loud, I couldn't talk to her about it, because I knew if I started talking about what I'd do without her, I'd start tearing up and might even cry, and that would just upset her more. As far as the nightmares went, she was probably right. The long-term stress of dealing with the disease was a contributing factor, but my confusion about and fear of having to go on living without the woman I'd loved since I was a teenager was also undoubtedly in the mix.

"Can we please not argue?" I said. "I love you. I've always loved you and I will continue to love you. I'm sorry about the nightmares, I really am. I'll sleep on the couch so I won't wake you."

"I don't want you to sleep on the couch. I want you to sleep in our bed like you always have."

"Then I'll sleep in our bed like I always have."

She took another pull off a beer and turned toward me.

"Why are you suddenly being so agreeable?"

"Look," I said. "This has been a long, hard road for both of us. For all of us. Especially for you. And now that Lilly and Randy and Joseph are gone, it's been even harder. We don't have as much help, and I've seen an emptiness in you that breaks my heart. You and Lilly were always so close, and we both had so much fun with Joseph. When they left, it was like part of your heart was torn out of your chest. Mine, too, but it's been worse for you."

My son-in-law, Randy Lowe, had graduated from medical school and was now in an oncology residency program at the Dana-Farber Cancer Institute in Boston. Caroline and I loved Randy deeply and were both extremely proud of him, but at the same time, we resented him for taking our beloved daughter and grandson to Boston. Caroline looked at me and tears filled her eyes.

"But you're still here," she said, "and I have Jack and Charlie. I just hate the thought that I'm causing you to have nightmares. And I thought the thing with Sarah was put to rest a long time ago."

"I guess it'll never be put to rest," I said. "I don't know why I'm dreaming about it, but let's just do what we've always done. Let's just hang in there and keep loving each other."

She leaned across the seat and kissed me on the cheek.

"I love you," she said.

"I love you, too," I said. "Hand me one of those beers. We'll be naughty together."

# SUNDAY, AUGUST 25

"I was raped," the girl said in a voice that could barely be heard. The Johnson City Police Officer, Tonya James, looked into her rearview mirror.

"What did you say?"

Officer James had put her passenger, a redhead who gave the name of Sheila Self and said she was twenty-four years old but didn't have any identification, into the back seat of her cruiser five minutes earlier at a convenience store on Walnut Street not far from East Tennessee State University. It was 1:30 a.m. on a Sunday morning. The passenger wore a tight, short, red spandex dress, spiked heels, heavy make-up, and looked like a hooker. Ms. Self was under the influence of some substance or was, perhaps, mentally ill. She initially made absolutely no sense at all when Officer James showed up after responding to a 911 call that reported Ms. Self was wandering around inside the convenience store muttering to herself and had refused to leave. After speaking to Ms. Self for several minutes and consulting her supervisor, Officer James determined that an involuntary mental health commitment may be in order, and she was transporting Ms. Self to Woodlawn Mental Health Facility for an evaluation.

"Do you know where I'm taking you?" Officer James asked.

"Woodlawn, but I'm not cra ... crazy. I was drugged and raped."

"Raped? When?"

"Not really sure. Hour ago, maybe? Longer?"

The woman's speech was slurred and she smelled of alcohol, but this was the first time she'd mentioned drugs or being raped. Officer James needed to pay attention in case it was true.

"Do you know who raped you?"

"Some guys, maybe three. They puh ... pulled me into a bathroom."

"Where did this happen?"

"Party. Tree Streets."

Officer James pulled into a church parking lot, turned toward the back seat, and gave her passenger her full attention.

"Tell me what happened."

"I went there to dance. I work for AAA Escort. Sometimes I do exotic dancing. They set it up."

"What time were you supposed to be there?"

"Midnight."

"And you got there at midnight?"

"I think I took a cab. It's still fuzzy, but some of it's starting to come back to me."

"Do you know the names of any of the people who raped you?"

"No."

"Can you describe them?"

"Not really. Not right now. It was dark."

"Were they white or black or Hispanic or Indian or Asian? Can you tell me their race?"

"At least one of them was black. They were football players."

"Football players? How do you know that?"

"Football player party. The escort service told me. The guy that paid me said he was a captain."

Officer James found it interesting that the young woman was suddenly recalling some details, but nothing that could really help the police find who committed the rape, if a rape had really been committed.

"Who paid you?"

"Some big guy."

"Was he one of the men that raped you?"

"I'm not sure."

"How did he pay you?"

"Cash money."

"Do you have the money?"

"Did you go through my purse?"

"Yes."

"Was it in there?"

"No."

"Then I don't know what happened to it. One of them probably stole it. Maybe I lost it."

"How many people were at this party?"

"I don't know. A bunch, I think."

"How much did you get paid?"

"Three hundred. I split with the escort service, which means I would've made a hundred and fifty. I usually get tips, but not tonight. And the escort service is going to be pissed when I go in there empty handed."

*She's thinking clearly enough to do the math on her money,* Officer James thought. *And now she's worrying about consequences from the escort service.*

"So you got there at midnight?"

"Yeah, I think so."

"Did you dance?"

"I started, but it went wrong somehow. Next thing I know I was in that bathroom and they were raping me."

"Did they beat you? Did they have weapons?"

"They just trained me."

"Trained you?"

"Just one after another. I didn't fight. I was scared. It's like a dream."

"Do you have any serious injuries?" Officer James asked.

"I don't think so. I'm sore down there, but they didn't hurt me bad."

"How did you get out of the house?"

"I think I walked."

"So they just let you go?"

"When they were done."

Officer James didn't quite know what to think. She took out a note pad and jotted several things down while they were fresh in her memory.

"I'm going to have to take you to the hospital, Ms. Self. You're going to need to do a rape kit, talk to the nurse and the doctor, and I'm going to get in touch with a detective and he'll be there to talk to you, too."

"He? Don't you have a woman who can talk to me?"

"Not right now. We had a woman on the detective squad, but she got married and moved away a couple of months ago. Right now, all we have are men. We're not a very big department."

"Don't take me to Woodlawn. I'm not crazy. And I have babies at home."

"Babies? How old are your babies?"

"Two and three. My cousin is keeping them tonight."

"So they'll be all right? Do you want to call your cousin?"

"They're asleep. I'll see her in the morning."

"Have you ever been through a rape examination before, Ms. Self?"

"Yes."

"You have? When?"

"My stepfather raped me when I was young. Then my foster father and brother both raped me. I've been through it twice."

Officer James shook her head, not knowing whether what she was hearing was the truth. If it was, then the person she was carrying in her back seat had to have some serious psychological baggage.

"I'm sorry to hear that," Officer James said. "At least you know what you're about to go through. You know it isn't going to be fun. But it's extremely important. So just be brave and do what the medical people tell you to do, okay?"

"I can handle it."

Officer James turned her blue lights on and did a U-turn in the parking lot. Twenty minutes ago, this woman could barely talk, or at least that's the way she was acting. Now, she seemed far more lucid and was telling a tale, albeit an unusual one, of being gang-raped.

James called her supervisor.

"She claims she was raped," James said. "The plan has changed. I'm going to take her to the medical center."

# SUNDAY, AUGUST 25

Investigator Bo Riddle was dreaming of putting the noose around the neck of a black man named Howard Felts when his cell phone began to buzz on the bedside table. Riddle had been instrumental in convicting Felts of murder a week earlier, and the jury had later come back with a death penalty sentence. A thirty-year-old patrol officer with a wife and two young daughters had responded to a domestic disturbance at Felts' apartment eighteen months earlier, and as soon as the patrolman walked through the door, Felts ambushed him and shot him in the face. Felts had never shown a bit of remorse and had been a terrible disciplinary problem at the jail and in the courtroom for the past year-and-a-half. As soon as the verdict was announced, he'd been shipped off to Death Row at Riverbend in Nashville, which, Riddle believed, was exactly where he belonged. The only problem was that he'd be on Death Row for fifteen years. Riddle believed death penalty sentences should be carried out on a flatbed truck in front of the courthouse in the county where the crime was committed. And forget the appeals process. The man was tried and convicted by a jury and that same jury sentenced him to death. End of story.

It was 6:30 a.m. on Sunday morning, and Riddle would have rolled out of bed in fifteen minutes, so the hour didn't annoy him. But the interruption of the dream did. It was one of the better dreams Riddle had experienced in a while.

He picked up the phone and growled, "What?"

The voice on the other end of the phone was Tonya James, a five-year patrol veteran of the JCPD.

"There's a woman who claims she was gang-raped by at least three ETSU football players at a party last night," James said.

"And?"

"The watch commander wants you to take the interview and get a statement. I took her to the hospital and they did a rape kit. They're just finishing up, but she's a little strange. There were some problems with her story."

"What kind of problems?"

"Details. Important things. Like what time she arrived at the party, what time she was raped, how long she was raped, what time she left, exactly how many attackers there were. She can't describe them. Then there's the fact that she'd been hired to strip at the party."

"Sounds to me like you don't believe her," Riddle said.

"She didn't mention being raped until she figured out I was taking her to Woodlawn for a mental evaluation. I ran her name through a couple of databases and talked to a guy at the Carter County Sheriff's Department because she lives over there. She's had some problems in the past. The guy I talked to in Carter County thinks she's got a screw loose."

"So she has mental issues? Has she been committed?"

"A couple of times, both involuntary and short term. I don't have official confirmation of that, no records. Just going by what my guy in Carter County told me."

"And who is your guy?"

"I talked to the Chief Deputy of the Sheriff's Department. Name's Clinton Drake. Known him a long time. Good guy."

"Yeah, I know Drake," Riddle said. "Does this woman have a criminal record?"

"Minor stuff. Drug and alcohol related. She's on probation for a possession charge right now, plus she has one D.U.I. and two public intoxication charges. Drake said she came up really rough. Sexual abuse by her father. Mother wouldn't intervene. She was removed from her home when she was fourteen and the father went to prison, but then she was raped by a foster father and a foster brother. The foster father went to prison. The brother went to juvy."

"Good God," Riddle said. "She must be the personification of jail bait."

"She's good looking. I spent a couple of hours talking to her. She's been a stripper since she was eighteen and has done some hooking through the escort service. She has two young kids but no man. What's weird is that she managed to earn an associate's degree from a junior college and is enrolled at ETSU part-time."

"What is she majoring in?" Riddle said.

"Psychology. I guess she's trying to figure some things out."

"Who's doing the rape kit?" Riddle asked.

"A nurse named Franklin and a doctor named Bosco. Don't know either one of them, and they don't seem too friendly. So how about getting here as soon as possible and helping me out? I don't want this woman to get away. She might be nuts, but she might have been raped. If she was, I want whoever raped her held accountable."

"I'll call Judge Murphy and go by his house. We need an order for a blood draw that we can send to an independent lab for Drug Facilitated Sexual Assault analysis," Riddle said. "The TBI isn't set up for that kind of test. I'm sure they've done a tox screen, but from what you've told me, that might not be enough. We're going to need to know exactly what was in her system and how much."

"I already did that," James said. "I did it as soon as I brought her in and they started the exam. I didn't go to Murphy, though. I woke up Judge Tinker. He'll sign anything and he's friendlier than Murphy. I figured we'd need the blood before so much time passed they couldn't get a reliable result from the test. They drew the blood about 2:30 a.m., two-and-a-half hours after this alleged party."

"Well, aren't you just an up and comer?" Riddle said. "Nice work. I can be there in about thirty minutes, but don't get too close to me because I'm not gonna take a shower."

Riddle arrived at the emergency room exactly thirty minutes after he hung up the phone.

"Morning," Tonya James said. She introduced Riddle to Sheila Self, who was sitting in a chair wearing a paper gown covered by blankets. Riddle was immediately struck by how pretty she was, although it was a rough kind of pretty. He guessed she was quite a bit younger than she looked. Still, she had long, striking red hair and clear, blue eyes, cream-colored skin and full, sensuous lips.

"I'm going to talk to Officer James out in the hall for a minute, Miss Self," Riddle said. "I'll be right back. Just sit tight."

"What do the nurse and doc say?" Riddle said when he and James were outside.

"The nurse told me the vic had definitely been involved in sexual activity. There was some swelling of the vagina and a couple of bruises, but the bruises were minor. No cuts, no tearing of the vagina or anus. She obviously didn't fight them, or at least she didn't fight them hard, and they didn't beat her. The rape examiners got a bunch of hairs and fibers and she had sperm in her, so there will be DNA."

"What did the nurse say about rape?"

"She said it was possible."

"Possible? Is that a strong possible? A probable? Or anything is possible?"

James shook her head. "I pressed her, but that's as far as she'd go."

"What about the doctor?"

"He left at six. The nurse said he'd tell me the same thing, though. Based on their observations, the swelling, the sperm, the bruising, and the victim's account, it's possible that a rape occurred."

"Talk to the vic any more about descriptions, who the perps might have been?"

"She said somebody gave her a drink when she got there and it must have had something in it. She said she doesn't remember much after the drink. I asked her to sign a consent form so we could get a copy of her tox screen and see what kind of drugs or how much alcohol she had in her when I brought her in, but she wouldn't sign it."

"Doesn't really matter if we got blood for the DFSA," Riddle said, "but I think I can get a look at it anyway."

"How's that?"

"I've been at this a long time, James. I have friends in low places."

James shrugged.

"She's not a suspect in a crime unless maybe it's for filing a false report, so I guess there's no harm in you going around the rules. It isn't like we're going to use the results against her in court."

"Right," Riddle said. "You can take off now. I'll handle it from here."

Riddle walked back into the room where Sheila Self was sitting. She hadn't moved.

"Can I get you anything?" Riddle said.

"A different life," Sheila said.

"I think we all wish for that once in a while," Riddle said. "Yours truly included. But sometimes we're stuck with what we have. We make the best of it, right?"

"I wish I could talk to a woman detective."

"Sorry, we're fresh out. Looks like you'll have to deal with me, but I'm not such a bad guy once you get to know me. I'm sure this has to be difficult, but I need to hear everything you can remember about last night. What you've described to Officer James is aggravated kidnapping and aggravated rape. Those are extremely serious charges. If we can identify the men who did it and they're tried and convicted, they'll go to prison for a long time."

"They should go to prison," Sheila said quietly. "They deserve to go to prison."

"When did you first find out about the party?" Riddle said.

"My escort service called me Friday afternoon around five. Asked if I could dance at this party last night on Elm Street. I said I'd do it and I called my cousin to see if she'd keep my kids. I told her I had a date. She said yes, so I was good to go. She picked my kids up about six."

"She picked your kids up from where?"

"My apartment."

"A man live with you?"

"No. Just the kids. We live in Section 8 housing over by the Tweetsie Trail. I get food stamps, Aid for Dependent Children, all that. I go to school part time and I dance and work for the escort service on the side. It's decent money sometimes."

"But you don't declare any of it, right? Are you a prostitute as well?"

"No. I'm a dancer and an escort. Whose side are you on here?"

"Just doing my job. No offense. And you got to the party when?"

"Around midnight."

"How'd you get there?"

"I already told the other officer. I took a cab from my apartment."

"What did you do between six and midnight?"

"My boyfriend came over and we partied a little."

"What's your boyfriend's name?"

"I'd rather not say."

"I need to know his name."

"Bobby Vines."

"Did you have sex?"

"That's none of your business."

"You're a real peach," Riddle said. "I'm trying to help you and you're jerking me around. The nurse told the officer who brought you in here they found sperm in you. It'd be good to know if this sperm came from your boyfriend."

"It might have."

"Fine. Okay. Did your boyfriend know you were going to strip at a party at midnight, and if so, what did he think about it?"

"He doesn't care. He knows I have to make money to take care of my kids and pay my rent. He doesn't give me money."

"Is he the father of your children?"

"No."

"Who is?"

"I'm not sure."

*That's great. That's just grand,* Riddle thought to himself. *This is getting better by the second. She'll be such a sympathetic victim in front of a jury.*

"I understand you're on probation for a drug possession charge. What was the drug?"

"What difference does it make?"

"You're really starting to piss me off, you know that? I can find out, but that's extra work and you making me do extra work would make me feel not so sympathetic toward you. You want to do it that way?"

"It was heroin."

"So you did some heroin last night before you went to dance?"

"No, no heroin. I did some ecstasy and I drank two beers and did a shot of tequila. After I got to the party, somebody handed me a drink, though, and I think there might have been something in it. I lost it after that. Just really lost it, you know? All I have are flashes of memory. I can see hands on my arm pulling me into the bathroom. I can hear the music playing and people hollering."

"This hand on your arm, was it white or black?"

"It was black."

"So you remember that? Are you sure?"

"Pretty sure."

"On a scale of one to ten, how sure?"

"Seven or eight."

"Was there a light on in the bathroom?"

"I don't think so. Maybe some light filtering through the window from outside, but I can't say for sure."

"Did these guys talk to you? Did they talk at all? Did you hear any names?"

"I think they were talking a little, calling me bitch and slut. Talking dirty."

"Did you see a weapon of any kind?"

"I think I remember one of them had a broom and said he was going to stick the handle in me."

"Did he?"

"I don't know. Maybe."

"Were you in a lot of pain?"

"I don't know. Whatever was in the drink, the molly, the alcohol, all of it combined… I was pretty messed up."

"Are you in a lot of pain now?"

"Not really."

"So you don't know if you cried out for help?"

"I don't know."

"Did anyone try to help you?"

"I don't think so."

"How long were you in the bathroom?"

"Long enough for the three of them to do what they wanted to do, I guess."

"So when the lab analyzes this rape kit, besides your boyfriend, they're going to find sperm or pubic hairs or something else containing DNA from three different males in you or on you, and those males will more than likely be ETSU football players?"

"I guess."

"You guess? That's not very encouraging, Miss Self. And when it was over, what happened?"

"I don't remember. I started coming to after that officer arrested me and put me in the back seat of her car. I think I was at a convenience store, but I don't really know how I got there or what I was doing there."

"Did you ever actually dance?"

"I think I started, but it didn't last long. There might have been some kind of argument. They maybe wanted me to use toys or whatever, but I didn't have anything like that. They started hollering and calling me names and I think I just told them to go screw themselves, I was leaving. That's when I got grabbed up and pulled into the bathroom."

"So you remember that? You remember starting the dance, them calling you names, and you telling them to screw themselves? And then you remember being pulled into the bathroom?"

"I think so. Vaguely."

"And again, you think it was a black hand that pulled your arm?"

Sheila nodded.

"Anything else you can remember about the guy that pulled you in? Long hair or short hair? Anything about his face? How big was he?"

She shook her head. "I'm sorry. Maybe it will come back to me later."

"The others?"

"Not really."

"When did you realize you'd been raped?"

"In the back of the police car, I think."

"So that's why you didn't report it, correct?"

"I was drugged. Somebody had to drug me."

"Ms. Self, it would help me a lot if I could get your consent to look at the toxicology screen." He decided not to tell her that some of the blood they'd drawn from her was already headed for a lab.

She shook her head vigorously.

"You can't. I'm on probation."

"But if you took the drugs involuntarily, your probation—"

"I didn't take the ecstasy involuntarily."

"Your probation officer doesn't know that, and I won't tell him."

"Her."

"Okay. I won't tell her. You can say the ecstasy was in the same drink as the other drug, whatever it turns out to be. Will any heroin show up on the tox screen?"

"No, I've been clean."

"Okay, there you go. I'll back you up on your claim that it's probable that the ecstasy and whatever else they found were mixed in the same drink. No probation violation. You give me consent to look at your tox screen and it ups your credibility as a witness a ton. What do you think?"

Sheila looked at the ground, then up at Riddle. Riddle was again taken aback by her sexuality. To him, she had a strange kind of vibe going, very sexy. The kind of woman you wanted to protect and ravage at the same time. She reminded him of a teenage girl he knew, a close friend of his daughter's. He'd been divorced from his first wife for ten years and didn't see that much of his daughter, but sometimes, when she came over on a weekend, she brought this friend named Lisa with her. Lisa was a sixteen-year-old version of Sheila, although she came from a wealthy family and would be going to college instead of a foster home. But Riddle always found himself wanting to protect Lisa as much as he wanted to protect his own daughter. He'd also fantasized about Lisa, sexual fantasies that had awakened him at night. He knew he shouldn't be fantasizing about this teenaged girl, but Riddle didn't feel guilty. It was what it was. He was old and horny, she was young and sexy, and his daughter kept bringing her around. It wasn't his fault.

Finally, Sheila nodded her head.

"I guess I don't have any choice," she said. "Once this gets out, and I'm sure it'll get out, I guess my probation officer will get the records anyway."

"Don't worry about it," Riddle said. "Investigator Riddle will take care of you."

"Just promise me you'll get the people who raped me," Sheila said.

"I'll do my best, ma'am," Riddle said. "I give you my word. But you need to come to the station and give me a written statement. Can you come after you get out of here?"

"I need to deal with my kids."

"Okay. After lunch, then. Let's exchange numbers, and I'll see you this afternoon."

If you enjoyed the beginning of *Due Process*, you can purchase here via Amazon:

Due Process
Again, thank you for reading!

Scott

Made in the USA
Columbia, SC
14 July 2021

41821959R00174